MW00720103

# MASK OF DECEIT

## A NOVEL

## DAVID A. DAVIES

DAPCON PUBLISHING

Copyright © 2016 Dapcon Publishing
Print Edition
Everett, WA, 98208

All rights reserved. No part of this book may be reproduced, stored in, or introduced into a retrieval system, or transmitted in any form, or by any means (electronic, mechanical, photocopying, recording, or otherwise) without the prior written permission of the publisher except by a reviewer who may quote brief passages in a review.

The scanning, uploading, and distribution of this book via the internet or any other means without the permission of the publisher is illegal and punishable by law. Please purchase only authorized electronic editions and do not participate in or encourage electronic piracy of copy written materials.

This book is a work of fiction. Names, characters, places and incidents are products of the author's imagination. Any resemblance to actual events or locales or persons living or dead is entirely coincidental and beyond the intent of the author.

Warning: This book contains scenes of violence and strong profanity.

10 9 8 7 6 5 4 3 2 1
Printed in the United States of America

LCCN 2016905629
ISBN 978-0-9974727-0-7

For more information on Mask of Deceit, The Potential and the author, visit: www.davidadavies.com
Editor: Julie Scandora
Cover Designer: Martina Dalton
Interior Design: Paul Salvette

HE WHO DECEIVES SHALL BE DECIEVED

WELSH PROVERB

*To Big John*

*Enjoy !*

*David A. Davies*

# DEDICATION

## FOR MY BROTHERS

# ACKNOWLEDGEMENTS

First and foremost I thank my wife Patty for her continuous support, love and understanding, without which, I could never have completed this project. Many thanks go to Lawrence Kane, Mike Howard and John Gargett for their faith, understanding and hands on assistance. Thanks also to Julie Scandora, an artist in more ways than one, and fellow Indie author Martina Dalton for her creativeness and advice. Thank you Stevan Rankic for your continued friendship and help over the years. To Arshia Fathali for his valuable insights and Matt Cail for his expertise. Last but not least, I must thank the real Dana Munson, Insurance Analyst and Jenna Caya, graduate student, for allowing me to use their names in this book.

# CHAPTER ONE

## DAY 30
## March 2000, Potsdamer Platz, Berlin, Germany

*TODAY IS A GOOD DAY TO DIE*, the old woman thought as she plodded along the streets, laden with bags full of groceries. Although puffing, wheezing, and pausing from time to time to catch a breath, she calculated her actions as she expertly watched and listened to everything around her.

Before crossing a busy intersection, she heard a man's English voice behind her—not unusual in this part of Berlin, but the halting, direct, almost aggressive tone gave her concern. She turned to look at the man speaking into a phone, and he returned her stare with deep, steely-hard, suspicious eyes. She knew in an instant he was a threat and placed her bags on the ground in front of her as if to adjust her heavy burden. As she crouched, she fumbled with a ruby ring on her finger, but when she stood straight, the man was gone. *You had less than five seconds, my young English friend, less than five seconds.*

When the old woman finally reached her destination, she looked around for somewhere to sit and took a long, deep breath of fresh air. Although still cold, it was clear and crisp now that the sun that had finally broken free from the fog that had shrouded the city that morning. For too many weeks the residents of the city had suffered from the dreary cycle of wind, rain, sleet, and snow, and now the sun in all its glory was the sign that spring was just around the corner. The old woman found a spot, put down her shopping bags, turned her face towards the warmth of the sun, and closed her eyes.

High above, another was also thankful for the break in the weather.

The unobstructed view of the city below and the lack of environmental factors now made the task at hand that much easier. Although at ground level the temperature was becoming pleasant, here, high up on the sixteenth floor of an office complex construction site, an area without floor-to-ceiling walls or windows, the crow's nest felt frigid and uncomfortable. Standing five feet back from the window ledge, the shooter expertly surveyed the entire area with a Zeiss spotting scope concentrating first on the far distance, then middle distance, and lastly near distance. Satisfied that the old woman was a non-threat, the sniper began emptying the contents of the two shoulder bags, carried up the sixteen floors to the final lie-up position. Although time was of the essence, rushing the process would only lead to failure, greater stress, and increased heart rate. The first device to be erected was a dead shot pod, a tripod-shaped device, similar to one used by a photographer. But rather than topped by a camera, this apparatus would support a rifle, taking the weight and physical stress away from the shooter. Once set in place, a shooter's rifle could be angled up or down in varying degrees to attain a target and lock onto the general vicinity of the area in question. The beauty of such an arrangement was that a shooter could set the up the pod quickly and leave it in place, be it for minutes, hours, or days, until ready to take the shot. Today, however, only a small window of opportunity remained to acquire the target, bring the rifle to bear, and take the kill shot.

The shooter took the time to place and elevate the pod for a standing shot and removed the weapon from its case. After a further two minutes, she had completely assembled the Accuracy International AWM sniper rifle, ready and pointing downwards at an angle of roughly 60 degrees. It was another two hundred meters to where the target should appear. Before loading a .338 Lapua Magnum round into the chamber, she went through the motions of identifying the landmarks, gauging the wind, finalizing the triangulation to the target area, and closing off other areas of concern. This was to be a one-shot deal as no counter-snipers or opposing forces were known to be operating in the area. Satisfied that the fundamentals of the target area were well within the shooter's own operating parameters, she returned to the rifle and loaded a round into the chamber. The sniper waited thirty seconds more before assuming the final firing position, anticipating a noise, a movement, something out of the ordinary that would lead to abort the mission.

Nothing stirred.

After getting comfortable in the standing firing position, the sniper held the weapon firmly and snuggly into the right shoulder. The left eye was closed, the right was positioned perfectly over the scope, and the cheek was married to the stock of the weapon. The left elbow did not need to support the hand under the stock as the tripod did most of the strong-arm work, but out of habit, the shooter placed her hand in its regular shooting position. The fingers of the right hand on the pistol grip were strong but not so much that the knuckles turned white and constricted blood flow. The index finger rested on the trigger guard half an inch away from the trigger. Only two and a half pounds of pressure would be needed to send the round downrange.

The sniper waited patiently and began to take three big breaths and then exhale to let all the air out of the lungs. The ritual of tactical breathing continued with her visualization of the lungs being filled, the finger moving to the trigger, the correct amount of pressure being applied. The breathing and the fitness of the sniper slowed her heart rate down to fifty-five beats per minute, but she continued to visualize the shot, the bullet speed, the bullet drop, and the wind allowance. Continuing to watch and wait and visualize each step, she dropped her heart rate down once more to fifty bpm. The sniper was poised and ready to kill.

"Get in the building now, Chris! The shooter's somewhere between the thirteenth and eighteenth floors."

"Well, that narrows it down for me. Thanks!"

"It's all the intel we have. Get moving. The motorcade's almost there."

Chris Morehouse jogged and dodged through the throng of shoppers entering and exiting the Potsdamer Platz shopping mall as he headed into the tall triangular-shaped building, Debis B1 Building, or Piano Hochaus. He'd been to the mall many times before, but this would be his first into the high-rise office complex above the mall. His exact destination, he didn't know, just up. An assassin was in the building with a rifle. The target was approaching, and Chris had to intercept and, if necessary, take out the assassin by whichever means.

"Chris." The voice on his cell phone was Jenna Caya, the on-duty operator at the CIA's operations desk of the counter-terrorism center, CTC, in Langley, Virginia. "Expect at least another person in the area. The shooter may have a spotter."

"Roger, that," Chris replied.

Frustrated with the lack of information—Jenna could not provide blueprints or other plans for the Debis building—Chris remained focused on the mission. He would be on his own. What he did know was the shopping arcade was two stories above ground and one below. Office spaces started on the third floor, and that's where the labyrinth of corridors and businesses, large and small, would begin. Knowing that he had to get above the thirteenth to begin his detailed search, he headed for the fire escape stairwell, which he hoped ran the entire height of the building. On reaching the stairs, he looked up and, without a second thought, knowing he would be a hot sweaty mess by the time he stopped, he dumped his overcoat and scarf on the floor and began running up.

"Chris, GSG9 are en route. There's no helipad for a touchdown on the roof, so they'll be behind you and on foot. ETA eight minutes. Respond."

"GSG9. Eight minutes." he responded. Knowing that Germany's elite counterterrorist team was minutes behind was reassuring. If he had the heart attack he half-expected from running up hundreds of steps, he would, at least, have someone to rely on to finish the job.

"Chris, *we* are taking the target down. We cannot let GSG9 have this one. Do you understand?" It was Richard Nash, Chris's boss who either had been listening in at CTC or had just entered the room.

Chris took a breath on the ninth floor. "Understood."

Nash continued, "No matter what you find up there, all persons are targets, and they will be eliminated. Respond."

"Eliminate all targets. Copy." This wasn't exactly what Chris had signed up for with the CIA, but he was told from the outset that this mission was of national security importance and all he had to do was follow orders. Chris left the cell phone line open and kept his earpiece plugged firmly into his left ear. He was about to begin his run back up the staircase but paused and said, "There's someone else in the stairwell. Do you have another asset in play?"

Everyone in CTC could hear Chris's heavy breathing. The room was abuzz with hushed voices, monitors and screens humming away diligently providing information to the operators who were deciphering and disseminating bits and bytes to those in the room and to those thousands of miles away. On the large screen in the center of the room were a map of Berlin and a more detailed image of the Potsdamer Platz area. Chris's question silenced everyone. "Negative, Chris. It's not from our end. Repeat negative assets from here," Jenna replied.

"Well, whoever it is, is coming up hard and fast."

Nash jumped in on the call. "Chris, anyone who is there is a target. We will let you know when GSG9 arrive. Consider any others as hostile. Respond."

"All others are hostile. Roger."

"Is your man going to make it?" asked the senior officer from the Canadian Security Intelligence Service, standing in the CTC.

Nash gave him a stern look but did not reply.

Jenna didn't want to rock any diplomatic boats but was concerned with Chris's safety. "You don't have any assets on the ground, do you?" she said directing the question at the Canadian.

Nash put a hand on Jenna's shoulder indicating she should shut up. "You don't have to answer that," Nash said diplomatically. "I'm sure we are all transparent here." Nash wanted to change the subject and get back to the work at hand. "Jenna, where's the motorcade now?" he asked.

"They're about one minute west of the Brandenburg Gate and approaching the right turn onto Ebertstrasse. They should be on site in three to five minutes."

Although the motorcade was coming in from the west, the small convoy crisscrossed its way through the sprawling city of Berlin with a defector sandwiched snugly between two BKA officers in the rear of the first armored Mercedes car. The follow car was close behind and, while equally protected, was weighed down by sheer body mass and the weaponry other members of the BKA team had packed, enough to take on the most determined of opponents.

Nash turned to an agency operator in the CTC and asked about air support, "How are the choppers doing?"

"Sir, we have two up from the German Border Police and a local police chopper to keep the media out if they show. I can hear their chatter. They are all in sight of the convoy."

"Thank you. Keep me apprised if something transpires from their end." Although Nash shouldn't have been quarterbacking the operation, he was in the thick of things and enjoying every minute and was pleased that Chris had cleared the thirteenth, fourteenth, and fifteenth floors so quickly. "Jenna, how many of our team are on the groun—"

"I'm between the sixteenth and seventeenth floors." Chris's voice came over the loudspeaker. "I see a body on the stairway. Stand by."

An awkward silence ensued in the CTC as operators and analysts shot looks of concern at each other.

Chris drew his Sig Sauer 9mm pistol and moved in to investigate. As he advanced, he took in his surroundings. The sound of someone running up the stairs had ceased. He kept his weapon pointed at the body and the face that was turning grey while he examined the area for evidence of what had happened. He noted a blood spatter on the stairs above and on the wall and on the stairway bannister. It seemed the man had been on the stairway going down when he was shot.

"Chris, we need an ID. Give us some basics." Jenna pushed.

"Give him a minute, Jenna," Nash whispered.

Although Chris knew the man was dead, he gave the corpse a kick to the legs and received no response. With the gun in his left hand, he felt the man's wrist for a pulse, but as expected, there was none. The man's head and neck were peppered with bullet entry wounds. *Holy shit! Somebody's got some skills!*

The seconds were ticking by, and Jenna once again prompted, "Chris, respond. We need an ID."

Chris rifled through the man's pockets, "I found a Serbian passport, Marko Jovanovic, Mike-Alfa-Romeo-Kilo-Oscar, break, Juliet-Oscar-Victor-Alfa-November-Oscar-Victor-India-Charlie."

Jenna made a note and passed it over to another CTC operator.

Nash wanted to get things moving, "Chris, get back on mission. That's probably not our target. There's still a shooter in the building. Respond." Jenna and Nash had gotten into the habit of requesting a response from Chris each time they talked. They were communicating over a cell phone, not a two-way radio, and the coverage until this time was good. But nobody knew how long that it would last.

"Roger, moving forward."

All in the CTC were nervously staring at their screens anticipating a warning, a coded message, or unexpected event that would change the game plan. It was tough for the operators to decipher visual and audio signals from electronics and speech, but their job was to observe and report. There was only so much they could do to help someone in the field.

Chris heard the steps in the stairwell again. "I have footsteps again, slower this time."

"Roger that, Chris."

"Sixteenth floor. I'm going in."

Tension in the CTC was rising. Time was running out, the motorcade was fast approaching, and Chris seemed no closer to finding the shooter.

Chris had made his way into the sixteenth-floor office complex. There was nothing more he could do for the dead man in the stairwell.

The floor was still under construction, and building materials were evident everywhere. Dust and debris were spiraling all around the area, which supported his hunch that the shooter must be on this floor as it was void of any solid walls or windows, thus providing a clear shot to the streets below.

"I'm close. Going silent. Will keep the channel open as best I can. Respond."

Chris gingerly made his way through the wooden and aluminum frames and structures that would one day house dozens of office workers. Some of the rooms were near completion with drywall in place, so his line of sight at times was limited. As he slowed his movements in an attempt to control his adrenaline, he realized he was cold. After sprinting up sixteen floors, he had finally stopped sweating, and now his damp clothes were beginning to send a chill through his body. He began fine tuning his senses. Again he checked his phone. "Jenna, respond." Still silence.

Chris looked down at his phone . . . no coverage; he had lost the signal. *Shit, shit, shit,* he thought to himself. *Up shit creek without a paddle again. What's new?*

He contemplated his next actions, trying to reason things out quickly. He didn't know how much time he had left. They only way Chris would know he had failed was if the sniper came out of the hide or if he heard the shot, otherwise it was still game on. He thought about backtracking out to the stairwell to find cell phone coverage to get instructions, but at the same time, he gloomily thought if he went backwards and then heard a shot, all would have been for naught. He ripped his cell phone earbud out of his ear, moved forward, and thought, *Once more unto the breach, Chris . . . once more.*

He was actually happy he didn't have the CTC in his ear, in his brain—*respond this, respond that.* He wanted desperately to say, *Leave me alone. I know what I'm doing.* But he was in the middle of the big game now, right where he wanted to be. Although only a contractor for the CIA, he was still an agency rookie without much of this type of experience under his belt, and for now, he was content with taking orders from his mentor and boss, the deputy director of Operations CIA, Richard Nash. Although Chris was a tactical tool for the CIA, he could not think where else in the world he would rather be.

Chris moved forward with trepidation, concentrating on his every move. He needed to be careful about which way he looked, which way his gun was pointed, which way his body was facing, and how much shadow and silhouette his form was giving. He was sure the shooter was focused on getting the shot off, but the sniper could quite easily have heard him moving through the area already, have called off the shot, and now be in hunter mode with Chris as the target.

He tried his best not to get tunnel vision and to keep his eyes scanning for danger. His senses were telling him that it was cold, cold enough to see his breath, cold enough to dry his sweat. The air was crisp, so he knew the shooter's shot would be true without much heat deflection to push the round off target. It was a dry day without much wind, and the warmth of the sun kept any ice or frost from forming. Although Chris was on a pinpoint edge and ready to pull his trigger, his fingers were reminding him that without many windows, the sixteenth floor was a cold place to be. He regretted not having his coat with his gloves stashed in the pockets. The shooter, Chris assumed, was bundled up in heavy clothing in anticipation of waiting for the target to appear. Being warmly clad would be an advantage for the shooter who did not need to move around too much but had the disadvantage of being restricted needing to move fast.

Once Chris had a better sense of his bearings, he managed to spot an opening at the apex of the triangular building that looked directly over Potsdamer Platz and across the intersection to Leipziger Platz. He spotted the red-and-white maple leaf flag that fell loosely about the pole at the Canadian embassy, and he rightly surmised there was little or no wind to prevent an accurate shot. Chris quickly calculated that the range was about two hundred meters from where he was standing, which in his mind was a perfect spot for a sniper. At first, he thought the intelligence was off, but that didn't explain the body in the stairwell. Just as he was about to move from his position, Chris spotted the motorcade waiting at a traffic light at the busy intersection below. With his back to the point of the triangle, he took a fifty-fifty chance and moved to his left side hoping he would find the shooter somewhere nearby.

Before, his steps had been calculated and choreographed like a dancer's—one foot forward, rear foot brought up to touch the front before taking another step. Now he had to move quickly. His time for remaining covert was over, the motorcade was almost at its destination, and as soon as the defector got out of the car, he would be history. Chris's guess to move to the left of the building was correct, as most parts of this side of the construction zone were just plastic sheeting trying unsuccessfully to keep the elements out. The framed office spaces were bare but from time to time drywall prevented him from seeing into a room completely. Time was running out for Chris who still had not found his quarry. He made it halfway down the side of the building, and when he looked back to see if he could still see the Canadian embassy, he realized he must have missed the shooter because he could not see the maple leaf flag anymore. He began to double back when he sensed something strange and stopped in his tracks. Until now, he was so focused on finding the assassin he forgot about the steps he had heard in the stairwell earlier. Now he could hear someone in the general area, and it sounded as if he—or she—was throwing up. *Can't be in shape*, Chris thought. As the person continued to retch, Chris heard the sound of a foot or object scraping the concrete floor. The shooter had heard the retching too and might be getting ready to investigate. Chris moved toward the scraping sound and came to a room that was enclosed in plastic. He could make out the shape of a person standing with a rifle pointed downwards towards Leipziger Platz.

Chris's orders were clear: intercept and stop the shooting at all costs. But his intuition and need for caution took over, and for a second, he thought he was a cop. "Drop the weapon!" he shouted, not knowing if the shooter could even understand his language.

The shooter did not move.

Chris repeated his order, "Drop the weapon. I am not giving you another warning."

The shooter did not move an inch.

Chris aimed his gun at the head and was about to pull the trigger.

"Chris, this is not the time. Back off."

His blood turned to concrete, and he almost froze in place. "Pam?"

"Chris, this is not the time or place. You don't know what you are getting into."

Chris ran up to the plastic and removed it from its fastenings on the ceiling to reveal his girlfriend clad in a black parka with her right eye placed firmly on the scope of the rifle. Her right finger was poised to pull the trigger. His courage failed him, and he let his gun fall to his side. A tear ran down his cheek. "What the hell are you doing?"

"Keep out of this. Chris."

As they were talking, a helicopter from the Bundesgrenshutz hovered over Potsdamer Platz obscuring the view from the sniper's vantage point.

"Goddammit, Chris!"

With the momentary lapse in Pam's concentration, Chris made a move to kick the rifle away, and Pam backed away.

"Chris, behind you . . .!"

The footsteps were back.

# CHAPTER TWO

## DAY 1

## December 1999, Hyderabad, India

"HOLY SMOKES, GREG, YOU DO NOT LOOK WELL."

"Actually, Chris, I feel worse than I look," replied the officer. "I'm not sure what's going on."

Chris had to push, as there was a schedule to keep. "We haven't got much time left, but if you want to take a break, go throw up or something, go do that."

"Thanks, but no. You're right. Let's move on."

As Chris began the surveillance briefing, he could tell Greg wasn't quite with it. More than once, sentences were repeated, and too often, Greg stared at the map of the city as if nothing was there. Chris was getting worried. The whole operation was going south right in front of his eyes. He'd already lost two members of his surveillance team, and now the technical officer from the CIA's Office of Technical Services was sick and fading fast. Chris leaned back from the hotel room desk. "Greg, this is not going to work. You are in no condition to pull this off. We need to think about calling in for some kind of backup."

"Chris, there is no backup . . . I don't know what to tell you, but I am on my own here. We can't just abort either. This may be a lower priority target, but it's part of the bigger game, and the mission still needs to go ahead."

"What about Delhi station. Don't they have someone to send?"

"Everyone is tasked out. We've got people in Mumbai, Delhi, Bangalore, and even some operations ongoing in Pakistan. We're at the max, Chris. I have to do this. There is no choice."

"Greg, you're as white as a sheet, and you're sweating three buckets a minute. This is not going to happen. What if you collapse while you are at Navistar?"

Greg had to concede to that one. "You're right. Then it's got to be you."

"What? No! Jesus, Greg. I don't want to throw myself under the bus. I have no training for this kind of stuff. I'm going to call it in and recommend we abort. Where's the sat-phone?"

Greg reluctantly passed his backpack over to Chris and mentioned he was going to close his eyes while Chris made the call.

Chris made his way out to the deserted hotel pool and found a remote spot away from potential passers-by. He dialed the CTC at the CIA headquarters in Langley on the encrypted satellite phone.

After two rings, it was picked up. "Identification, please."

"Golf seven zero lead alpha, authentication Dorchester five."

"Standby," the operator dryly responded.

After a brief pause, a man's voice that Chris did not recognize came over the phone. "This is Munson. Why are you calling?"

Chris gave him a rundown of Greg's condition and conveniently left out the part that he had lost contact with two of his team.

There was a slight pause, and then Munson's stern voice commanded, "This mission must be carried out. There are no ifs, ands, or buts. Get a briefing from the OTS guy and get this thing moving. The next thing I want to hear from you is that the mission is complete. Get on with the program."

"Where's Nash—" Chris's words were too late. The line was dead. Chris stared at the ground in front of him. He began to weigh all his options when he spotted a small snake in the grass. It was enough to get him motivated.

When Chris returned to the room, he found Greg throwing up in the bathroom toilet. Chris retrieved a bottle of water from a nearby counter and handed it to the ailing officer. As Greg took a break from shining the porcelain, Chris filled him in on the good news. All Greg could do was nod his head and throw up some more.

It took the officer almost two hours to brief Chris on what he had to do. Greg kept telling him that it takes months if not years of training and experience to get this kind of skill and only hoped the young Brit would understand. Focused, Chris was memorizing every little detail and asking for clarification time and time again. He wasn't comfortable, but he wasn't getting paid to be so; he was a surveillance expert who had just gotten a crash course in uploading computer viruses.

There was a knock on the hotel room door. Chris got up hoping his team had returned. "Are we clean?" Chris said quietly.

"Yeah, no problem, Chris." Satish made his way into the room and took one look at Greg. "Oh my God! Greg, are you okay, man?"

Greg looked up from the coffee table that he was staring at and tried his best to wave his arm. As he did, his eyes closed shut, and he dove head first into the table.

Chris and Satish rushed quickly over to Greg who had by now slumped to the floor. As they both rolled him over, they could tell he was unconscious. Chris felt for the pulse, but it was weak. Greg was soaked with sweat, and his pallor was completely grey.

"Jesus Christ, is he dying?" Chris blurted and cradled Greg's head in his arms. "Greg, Greg, can you hear me?"

There was no response.

Chris looked at Satish and then looked around the room. "Call for an ambulance and get me a cold, wet towel. I'll start picking up the paperwork, but I can't be here when they arrive. I'll take everything with me. . . . Start thinking of a cover for when the medics get here."

Satish sprang up, and within a few seconds, he returned with the towel and helped Chris move the furniture around Greg. Chris removed Greg's shoes and loosened his belt and then elevated his legs onto a chair. Satish got busy on the phone while collecting the paperwork strewn across the desk.

Chris, still kneeling by Greg, looked at Satish. "You've got to look after him. Do you understand? Don't let him out of your sight. I will be in touch as soon as I can. I've got to get out of here before everyone and his brother shows up. Where's Deepak?"

"I don't know," Satish replied. "I thought he'd be here."

Chris gently laid a pillow under Greg's head and grabbed the backpack and sat-phone. "Okay, can't worry about him now. Got to get out of here. I'll be in touch, Satish."

# DAY 2
## Hyderabad, India

Chris had been trolling the dark streets of the primarily Muslim suburb of Charminar in Hyderabad for longer than was safe. His disguise would help him pass casual notice, but in the daylight or intense lighting, it would be easy to tell that it was a westerner dressed in Indian garb. He was operating alone and flying on adrenaline. The plan to brief Greg on the route he needed to get in and out of his target was dead in the water. All his assets were used up, and his mission, in theory, was over. All he was supposed to do with his team was to conduct surveillance of the target and brief the officer on how to get in and out. But now with Greg in the hospital, things had changed in a big way. His first order of business was to secure transportation, and his instincts told him that a motorcycle was the best and only way to navigate through the overpopulated streets of any Indian city. It was up to his teammate, Deepak, to secure transport, but he was nowhere to be found, so Chris would have to improvise.

Stealing a motorcycle was, of course, a crime, but here it was much worse. The two-wheeler, as it was known in that country, was more than a means of basic transportation; to some families, it was sheer existence, so Chris had to choose wisely. He knew that when purchasing a vehicle of any kind in India, the head of the family had to consider that his entire immediate family would have to fit in or on the vehicle. As such, it would not be an uncommon sight in the vast Indian metropolises or secluded rural communities to see five individuals sandwiched on the wheels of a motorcycle dodging traffic and putting their lives on the line each time they traversed the crowded streets. It was usually the father who drove with his firstborn balanced between him and the handlebars. His next-born would be squeezed between father and mother, and then the youngest would be strapped to the mother. In India, if the cow was the first sacred being, then the two-wheeler was the second.

Another challenge of finding the right two-wheeler was to make sure the machine functioned and had enough petrol on board to get Chris where he needed.

Chris picked his way cautiously through the smoldering trash heaps, the cow feces, and the detritus of human castaways that typically peppered the streets and alleyways of Indian cities. He was taking a huge risk with this approach, as he was flying solo with no backup to support him if things went downhill. He carried no ID or cell phone or any "get out of jail free" passes, but it was the way he had to operate to get the job done. His job description had gone out the window as soon as he had ended the phone call with Munson; from here on out, Chris was acting the part of a real CIA officer, and as bad as things were, he loved every minute of it.

As a contract employee of the CIA, Chris belonged to a group known as 8G70, which rolled up into the CIA's Viewpoint surveillance program. The mandate of the program was to send surveillance specialists to all corners of the world to observe and report on individuals, organizations, facilities, military installations, and any other area of interest to the CIA. Getting in and out of countries without being caught or seen while gathering basic human intelligence was their prime objective. The members of the group came from a variety of backgrounds around the world. In most cases, local nationals were used to blend into a community they were operating in; sometimes on larger operations, other nationalities were used. Decisions about which were used usually came down to mission parameters, upper-level tasking, complexity, and risk. The group headed by Richard Nash had only eight full-time CIA officers working for him under Viewpoint, but those officers, in turn, managed the group of seventy operators who plied their trade in all corners of the globe.

Chris finally came across a Honda 175cc two-wheeler leaning against a shack in a dark alley. This moment was crucial for Chris. He had memorized his route into the area, and he formulated a plan if he were to be chased, but it would be a long perilous run back to his hide where he had stashed his western clothes.

As Chris pushed the two-wheeler out of the alleyway and back towards the main streets, he checked to see if there was enough fuel in the machine to get it going. As he did so, he gave the two-wheeler a quick once-over under the dim streetlights to make sure everything was still connected and parts were where they were supposed to be. One surprise that he didn't want was for the motor to be jury-rigged in such a fashion that only the owner knew how to start it in a specific sequence. Satisfied that everything looked in order, he began to look for a quiet spot where he could make his own adjustments to get the bike going. This was another crucial point fraught with danger. He didn't want concerned Indians—known for their hospitality—trying to help him get his two-wheeler going and then realizing he wasn't who he was supposed to be. Disguises apart, if you didn't speak the local dialogue or understand basic commands, you were a fish out of water.

Chris decided to play it safe and propped the two-wheeler against a light pole. He left it there and took a walk around the block from where he had come. The streets were relatively quiet for 4 a.m., but soon the imam at the Makkah Masjid mosque would make his call for morning prayers; a little haste was called for.

Having completed a loop of his immediate surroundings, Chris decided to get down to business. It didn't take long to get the bike running. He depressed the clutch, selected a gear, said a quick mental prayer, and twisted the accelerator slowly. Away he went.

It took Chris almost forty-five minutes to get to his destination, a holding position one and a half miles away from his target. Still too early to conduct his morning surveillance, he found a spot near an intersection and watched as the city around him came to life. The consistent sound of car horns blaring and the screeching of vehicle brakes reminded him that he needed to be on top of his game if he was going to survive driving through the madness of normal Indian traffic. For an hour, he observed how the locals navigated the roads where few rules and even less logic applied. The takeaways from his observations were that you had to be bold when negotiating traffic, not be too courteous, not wave your hands in thanks, and most important, never look back.

When he finally got back on the road, Chris joined a swarm of other two-wheelers heading in his general direction. He tried his best to stay away from prying eyes, but he supposed it could not be helped that someone at some point was going to notice he was not a local.

Chris arrived at the gates of the Navistar Electronics Company just in time to witness rush hour at the sprawling twenty-acre campus. He pulled off the road and watched how people accessed the facility; he'd often seen curious Indians do this at other facilities, and they were never challenged by security, who probably were never trained to look for signs of surveillance. He immediately spotted the fixed CCTV cameras looking down on the entry/exit point into the complex. Although they were probably focused on the driveway, he didn't need to advertise his presence. After only one minute, he relocated ten feet further away from where he initially stopped, and out of the field of view of the cameras. As he expected, to ensure that workers got in to the complex on time, the four security guards at the main gate were frantically waving bodies in through the opening so that they could clear the main road of traffic on the busy main road.

Things continued in the same way for another twenty minutes. Chris had seen enough. He started his two-wheeler again and took a slow ride down the fence line along the road looking for gaps in the CCTV coverage. He was not going to penetrate the facility; he just needed a closer look at the buildings and cameras. Part of the surveillance package from Satish and Deepak gave him a layout of all of the buildings on the campus, but he wanted to see for himself how accurate his information was. He spotted the building that he wanted and found another good vantage point as close to the fence line without being seen and took in all the activities around the building. Again, the lack of good security was apparent as he spotted a security guard at a side door holding it open for anyone who walked up. This was not the main entry into the building, but Chris decided that this was his best way in. He smiled to himself and confirmed his decision as he was about to leave but then spotted two individuals, who from their appearance could have been Europeans, Russians, or North Americans, walk up to the door. The security guard came to attention like a Buckingham Palace Guardsman and saluted the two visitors as if they were royalty. Following his salute, he opened the door to allow access, and from what Chris could tell, no questions were asked.

Chris made it back to his hotel room in the middle of the afternoon. He'd abandoned the two-wheeler and walked back to his stash of clothes where he had left them the night before. Once changed, he'd been able to jump in a rickshaw that dropped him near his hotel; then he completed his journey by foot. Chris was lucky that a busload of American tourists arrived at the hotel at same time, which offered confusion and cover for the last vestige of his disguise. The doorman did his duty and also offered a British-style salute as Chris entered the hotel, but the man gave a second and more inquisitive look at the young visitor with oddly darker skin color than the other arrivals. A bag dropped to the floor, and the doorman's curiosity was redirected. Chris saw the hesitation of the man and had no desire to hang around for a question. Snaking his way in with the other tourists, he made for the stairs. He couldn't take the chance of using an elevator and be stuck in awkward silence with Billy Bob and Mary Sue from Kentucky, so he walked the nine flights to his floor. When he got into his room, he confirmed his suspicions and made a mental note that he had to be more careful with disguises and skin coloring the next time he wanted to remain incognito.

The rest of the day Chris spent in his room mentally rehearsing how he would play out his part in his first solo mission. He had hoped Satish would show up for support, but he and Deepak were nowhere to be found. Chris also faintly hoped the sat-phone would ring with Nash on the other end shouting, "Abort, abort, abort," but that was not to be. It didn't really matter; he had been given an order, and he would do as he was told and go the extra mile to get things done.

In the evening, Chris ordered room service and tried his best to relax by watching a Bollywood movie, which made little sense to him—everyone singing and dancing and then the hero going out and shooting everyone in sight. Indian movies were a mystery to him.

Early the next morning, Chris packed up what little luggage he had, but before leaving, he opened a secret compartment in his backpack and removed Greg's Navistar Electronics ID badge. There was some similarity between the Brit and the American—they both had the same blond hair; both were clean-shaven. But Chris had brown eyes whereas Greg had blue. Greg also had more freckles than Chris and, in his picture, looked like a mid-forties, tired, overworked corporate lackey. Chris, on the other hand, was slightly tanned, confident looking, and fit. He couldn't worry about it now; he was banking on the reluctance of security guards to scrutinize a westerner closely, and he was going to wing it if something went sideways.

Chris checked out of the hotel, and the clerk provided him with a driver to take him the forty or so minutes to the electronics company. On the drive, Chris produced a lanyard and attached the badge in plain sight of the driver. Merely a photo ID, it had no embedded technology for electronic access. If the security guard was not at his post or did not open the door for Chris, he theoretically could not get into the building, as the doors were controlled with an electronic locking-and-card-swipe mechanism. His backup plan would be to tailgate in with another party, smile, and plead ignorance if questioned.

As he expected, the driver flew through the entry gates of Navistar without a second look from the guards. As a precaution, Chris held up his fake ID, obscuring his face slightly just in case someone was bothering to look inside the car. On arrival at the building that Chris wanted, he tipped the driver, grabbed his backpack, and headed straight towards the side entry as if he had a deliberate purpose and belonged. He already had his shades on, but he put on his baseball cap and pulled it down further as another precaution from the prying

CCTV camera above the door. As the driver peeled away, Chris pretended to adjust his shoulder straps of his backpack while waiting for a small group of workers to enter the building so he could fall in behind. As he did so, his cell phone alarm clock sounded off, which was a cue for him to flip open the phone and begin a one-way conversation with himself. He was banking on the fact that the Indian group he was attached to would be too polite to engage him in conversation while he was on his cell phone. He reached the side door to the building still chatting about construction plans and fictitious schedules when Sergeant Singh snapped to attention, saluted, and held the door open for the guest. Chris made a point of sounding important on the phone and pretended to give orders to a subordinate. Chris was in. The guard shut the door behind him and waited patiently for the next entrant.

Chris kept his phone to his ear, but toned down the authoritative manner and began speaking in a much quieter voice and then began to scan his surroundings. The layout was as his surveillance package had described. The plans for the building were inch perfect, even to the point where it described the exact locations of the interior CCTV cameras and other access control doors. The corridor that he was in ran the entire length of the H-shaped building, and to the rear of the reception was a lounge with soft seating and a small break area. Chris planted himself out of eyesight of the reception desk still continuing his hushed one-way conversation on his phone. He eventually hung up but was stalling for time. As he waited, he set his alarm again to ring in five minutes and took out his notebook and began doodling, all the time scanning the area for possible threats and planning what-if scenarios.

The five minutes passed quickly, but he again acted out his one-way conversation while focusing on a door halfway down the corridor that led to the Navistar communications and server room. The server room housed the company's call manager servers, application servers, data storage, routers, and switches. It was his—and had been Greg's—target.

Chris was willing to be patient, but time was slipping away. He played his phone game twice more, pretended to make a few calls, booted up his laptop, and once even compared a spreadsheet to nobody on the phone. The act was tedious, but it was working; nobody approached him, and nobody seemed to care.

But as with all surveillance operations, Chris knew he could not sit in theater for too long. Although he had infiltrated the facility, he still needed to get to his prime target—the main server room, which was locked. If he stayed in the common area any longer, someone would notice sooner than later that he was out of the ordinary, which would force him to move on and come back the following day, thus endangering the operation further. At the outset, based on his plan, Chris had boldly rated his chance of success at 100 percent. However, his continuing failure to secure entry to the main server room was pushing that rating downward—and more with each passing minute. Anticipating an outcome below a 90 percent success rate would call for an aborted mission. All Chris could do was remain patient and wait for the right moment to get into the room without the proper access control badge or key.

Time was perilously slipping away, and he unenthusiastically began thinking about his exit strategy and a backup plan for the following day. He depowered his laptop and reluctantly thought that day one was a bust. As he stood to leave, an opportunity presented itself when a Navistar employee entered the server room with a key for the first time since Chris had been watching the door.

Chris was now in a precarious situation and hoped that the roll of the dice would land in his favor. He could not stand and stare in place, so he made a move to a nearby bathroom where he chose a stall and waited a few minutes. After spending another minute washing up, he headed back into the corridor and walked with purpose towards the server room. His gamble had paid off—the employee had propped the door open with a wedge. Chris didn't hesitate and went straight in and removed the obstruction.

The room was a brightly lit, air-conditioned palace of cleanliness. In the huge room, banks of servers housed in long rows of cabinets spewed red, green, and blue messes of spaghetti data and power cabling that ran up to ceiling-mounted cable trays that eventually ran throughout the building and elsewhere on the campus. It was the central hub for all of Navistar's data and storage capabilities and was critical to the day-to-day running of the company.

Chris's phone rang again, and he began a rehearsed discussion with himself, another risky tactic as he was now in a highly technical environment, and he needed to act and behave like a techie nerd. As he mumbled his way through data encryption, firewalls, IP addresses, firmware updates, and more gibberish, he scoured the server room for other signs of life. He found none; he was on his own. The man that he saw earlier must have left.

He ended his fake conversation and quickly found the cabinet and device he was looking for and booted up his laptop. Chris didn't know where the intelligence came from to get him to this exact point, but he was more than impressed; things were looking up. He removed an RS-232 cable from his backpack and connected it to his device and a Clayman 3590 multi-port switch in the exact cabinet that he was looking for. It took a few seconds for the program on the laptop to run. Once it opened the Clayman switch software, it prompted Chris for a password, which he entered by using the factory-default administrator account. Six months before this operation, members of a CIA Office of Technical Services team had hacked into the Clayman corporate database and retrieved all the proprietary information needed to circumvent the firewalls and create an administrators account. The only challenge to get into the device at Navistar was that it had to be done on site at the machine.

Chris wasted no time. He had memorized the steps Greg had drilled into him and managed to upload a Trojan virus that would corrupt the data on the Clayman device at a later date. The operation took less than ten seconds, which seemed to a sweating and slightly nervous Chris more like ten minutes. He disconnected his cable and moved on to the next cabinet on the list. Again the intelligence was perfect, as he found the cabinet that housed the five digital video recorders used for storing the CCTV footage throughout the facility.

He made his way around to the rear of the cabinet and plugged his cable into one of the DVRs and waited once again for the software program to run. Chris again marveled at the accuracy of the password that he used to get into the DVR as an administrator. Once inside the DVR, he erased all data from the last two days of recordings, which would also cover his entry into the facility. He then uploaded a program from his laptop that would crash the DVRs beyond repair as soon as the first person to access the machine tried to retrieve data. For anyone looking at the cameras live, they would see no difference, but as soon as they tried to access recorded data, the DVRs would die an electronic death.

Chris began packing up his equipment just as he heard voices outside the door. He immediately went back to the dummy phone routine and packed the rest of his gear away. Two Navistar employees entered the server room. They both stopped their conversation and stared at Chris, who just smiled, waved, and carried on his telephone call as if he belonged. One of the two workers shrugged his shoulders and moved on, but the other stopped and stared at Chris for a moment longer. He then noticed the ID badge the visitor was carrying and went about his business. Chris was still talking on his phone as he exited the room.

# CHAPTER THREE

ON EXITING THE SERVER ROOM, Chris automatically switched his one-way conversation to German as he saw before him a group of people heading in his direction. His instincts detected something wrong in the body language of some, and his heart rate jumped up a notch sensing that he could be in trouble. He needed to evaluate his options quickly, as he was past the point of no return; he couldn't simply turn around and head in the other direction as the party was as surprised as he was to see each other in the corridor.

Chris started categorizing and assigning quick-reference names to the opposition who were getting closer by the second—three Indian office types in cheap suits carrying paperwork and talking up a storm and a fourth Indian behind the main group not speaking to anyone but carrying a handheld radio. *Radio guy is the first to go down.* Chris schemed. The group was less than thirty feet in front of him and approaching rapidly. Chris was getting animated in his one-sided conversation and even laughing to keep the pretense up, but he kept his eyes on the group. He checked the remaining three who did not look native, and as he did, he received a curious stare from the tallest of the team that could have stopped a train in its tracks. Chris designated the man as Stretch. *Shit. Executive protection*, he thought. *Grab Radio Guy, push him into Stretch, and then run like hell.* Chris deemed the other two members of the group as no threat. One fit the typical description of a mad scientist, disheveled, bad shoes, papers everywhere, and reading glasses on top of his huge bald head. The last man in the group didn't pay attention to

Chris as he was too focused on trying to listen to the corridor discussion between the mad scientist and the Indians. Chris tried his best to memorize faces and general descriptions of the group. As he was doing so, Stretch made a protective move around the mad scientist to place himself between Chris and his charge. Radio Guy almost bumped into Chris and held back a curse. Chris took a breath realizing his misplaced concern—they were not here for him; the group was simply on the way to a meeting, and he was in the corridor, which Stretch perceived as a threat. *Well, that's what I would have done if I was in that situation too,* Chris reflected.

Stretch was now within five feet of Chris and almost into his personal space. *Is this guy going to kiss me or what?* he thought. Stretch wanted a staring contest, but Chris wasn't about to play. Instead, he focused on the two non-Indians in the party. Chris didn't need to know who the Navistar employees were, but he was interested in the others. As everyone in the corridor finally came together at the same point, Chris nonchalantly smiled and waved and let the party go by. Stretch seemed to ease off slightly and focused on moving forward with the group. Chris decided to test a theory and dropped his backpack just after everyone had passed him. It had the desired effect as Stretch spun around and reached for his right hip. Stretch didn't need to pull his weapon out, but Chris saw the glint of black metal under Stretch's palm, ready to draw if necessary. Chris pretended not to notice and picked up his bag and went on his way. *So, a visitor important enough to have an armed bodyguard here at Navistar. That's a nice tidbit to take to Nash.*

Chris then switched his focus to getting out of the building. He was back on mission track and concentrated on getting away. All he needed now was for the place to stay quiet and not have someone shout at him down the length of the corridor.

He spotted Sergeant Singh at his post, and Chris hoped that the guard still had his finger up his butt and his mind stuck in neutral. Getting into Navistar was one thing, completing the task was another, but getting away with it was completely different. His pulse rate was racing, and he tried to calm his breathing, but he knew he was about to sweat bullets. Although he was confident that he had taken care of the CCTV cameras, there was always a lingering doubt that some eagle eye security guard in the security control room had been watching his every move since he had entered the campus. But he couldn't dwell. He had to get moving; he had to get out.

# DAY 2
## Paralia Vrsana, Greece

Professor Robert Crauford sat on the hood of his car sipping the bottle of water he had just purchased from the Lidl Super Market in the small town patiently waiting for the show that was about to begin. It was just after midday as he stared off into the distant Stefanion forest pondering if the mission was a success and hoping that his team was on the way back down from the mountains when he heard the sirens of police cars, a good sign. It didn't take long for two white and blue Skoda's to come whipping down the road spewing up dust as they sped past his vantage point, but they slowed down enough to take the next right turning from Route 2 and northwest towards the village of Nea Vrsana. Crauford suppressed a smile and continued to wait a little longer before he got into his car to make sure it wasn't obvious that he was about to follow the small convoy up into the hills. He told himself not to rush and to get there safely and in one piece. It didn't take long for Crauford to catch up with the police cars as they both had a hard time navigating their way through the tiny village streets constantly being slowed by a bus or tractor that had nowhere to go to let the two vehicles pass. Crauford was fine with this, as the more delay was more time gained for his team.

The cops finally bust through the village and pushed onward to the next obstacle, Arethousa. Although this was not their final destination, navigating the streets was somewhat easier. Nonetheless, they still had to get through the small winding streets and to the site of the emergency in Stefanina as soon as they could. Crauford continued the same route but knew that he would peel off a few miles up the road onto a track that would lead him further upwards into the mountains and away from the cacophony of sirens.

After finding his exit, he continued to drive roughly four miles up the track where he stopped at a makeshift picnic table, turned off the car, and got out with a map in his hand. To any locals or hikers who would happen by, he would look like someone who took a wrong turn and was lost, but he felt relatively confident that he wouldn't be seeing anything but a goat or two in such a remote spot. After a short while, he went back to the vehicle and retrieved a bottle of water and placed it on the table in front of him.

That was the "clear" sign Pamela Corbin was waiting for, and she emerged from the trees behind Crauford. "Hi," she called out from the tree line.

Momentarily startled, Crauford spun around and then said with a broad grin, "Hi, Pam." Another "all clear" sign. As she approached, he noticed she placed a revolver back in her jacket pocket, and as she got closer, Crauford asked, "Terminal?"

"Yeah, no problem. It was clean. Nobody else around. It was a good one."

Crauford showed no surprise to her deadpan response, but he did notice. It worried him that she showed no emotion. As they loaded Pam's backpack into the car, Crauford asked, "How far up is she?"

"She's two miles up the track. It's a good spot, and she's probably watching us right now."

It didn't make Crauford nervous to know that Rita Dorman, the other third of the Primal Ocean team, was out there watching, as she was not the assassin. But the woman standing in front of him was, and thoughts of her kept him awake at night. One of these days, she was going to come unhinged and he'd lose control of her.

Crauford contemplated making some small talk as they drove up the trail to pick up Rita but let it go, as he could tell that Pam wasn't in the mood. It would be difficult, anyway, as she sat in the back of the car freeing up the front seat for her spotter. The debriefing would come later, but now all they had to do was get out of the mountains.

"Slow down," Pam commanded.

Crauford complied.

"Stop here," she added.

Again, Crauford did as he was told and scanned the tree line for movement. There was none. After a brief pause, he heard the trunk opening, which surprised him for a moment but realized that Rita was loading her pack into the back of the car, along with the rifle that had been used for the attack earlier in the morning. Rita got into the passenger seat next to Crauford and settled in. She didn't speak a word, but Crauford didn't need another command to get moving, and without causing a dust storm, he gently eased the car forward following the preplanned escape route.

It took the trio over three hours to navigate their way through the forest. More than once, they paused to take a break where Rita retrieved a set of binoculars and exited the car to "take in the view." But Crauford knew that she was watching for a tail, watching for a trap, calculating options, and preparing in her mind what to do, what to say if she spotted something out of the ordinary. Both Crauford and Rita had practiced the run on three occasions, and Rita, like a rally car navigator, had plotted on the map each turn, each dip in the road, each obstacle along the way, each incline, each safe zone, and anything else that would help or hinder their escape.

Polite or jovial conversation was out the window as the three rode along, Rita was concentrating on the map to ensure their safe passage, and Crauford could tell that although both girls must have been exhausted they were fully aware of their surroundings and ready to take immediate action if needed. It was only when they crossed under the E90 motorway and into the seaside town of Serraiki Akti that Crauford reached over to Rita and placed his hand on hers as if to say, it's over, we're safe. As he did, he realized that he had made a mistake, as she withdrew her disfigured hand immediately away from his, and her face turned to one of embarrassment. It had been four years since her rape and torture at the hands of Serbian troops in Srebrenica, and although she had come a long way, she still carried the shame and guilt of having survived the massacre that took the lives of so many of her family. Still to this day, she avoided human contact and interaction with men in particular. She trusted Bob Crauford like a father, but she was not sure if she would trust any person completely for the rest of her life. Crauford kicked himself in the head mentally as he knew how stupid his brief act of affection was. He wanted so bad to communicate with her, just to be there for her to show her he cared for her as much as he did for her aunt, but it backfired. He knew that she still needed time, but this mission, this attack was meant to put some of that pain to rest.

As the team made its way to Route 2 and south towards Asprovalta, a small farm on the edge of Stefanina was being crawled over by a dozen police officers and crime-scene investigators. The owner of the farm lay where his wife had found him hours earlier, face down in a pool of blood behind one of the outbuildings with his head split open. She had neither heard nor seen anything, which perplexed some of the local police officers but did not surprise the lead investigator from the city of Vrasna.

The investigator knew that the deceased man would be missed by only a few closest to him; however, as this was a person of interest in the community at large, he didn't think it would take long for the press to get hold of the story and for the conjecture to begin. Everyone in the area had heard that the farmer had recently returned from the International Criminal Court in The Hague and had been acquitted of war crimes committed during the Bosnian War. The dead man was neither Serb, Bosnian, nor Croat but a Greek who was purported to be the leader of the Greek Voluntary Guard who were fighting in support of the Bosnian Serbs and active during the Srebrenica massacre. Rumors abounded that the dead man had hoisted a Greek flag over the town while the murders and rapes were being conducted and some of his troops engaged in the atrocities. But these stories were just hearsay, and nothing ever could be proven. With the lack of interest shown by the Greek government of the time to conduct its own investigation to assist the International Criminal Tribunal for the former Yugoslavia, an acquittal on charges was a forgone conclusion.

As the lead investigator pondered his next move, he decided to send some of his officers into the surrounding mountains and search the area for anyone suspicious. He knew he wouldn't find anything or anyone, but he had to show that he was at least making an attempt to investigate the murder. As he watched the officers take off in different directions, the investigator looked at his watch and realized it was almost time to go and meet the American who had borrowed some firearms from him.

## DAY 2
### Hyderabad, India

Chris made it out of the Navistar building without further incident. On exiting, he looked for a shady spot to conduct one last exercise—counter-measures. He found a tree near the parking lot next to the company cricket pitch where a bench was insightfully placed. The location gave him a good view of the door from where he exited, and he got down to work. He booted up his laptop again. While waiting, Chris took out his cell phone, removed the battery, and stuffed it in one pocket of his trousers and the phone in the other. With the laptop running, he activated a disk wipe program that destroyed all the data on the hard drive. Once done, he removed the battery from the laptop forcing the laptop to shut down. He then used a plastic screwdriver to remove the hard drive from the laptop, which he stuffed into his backpack with his laptop, and then walked briskly over to the entry gate of the campus. Marching past the security guards, Chris made sure he did not engage in any conversation. He needn't have worried, as the guards were too skittish to talk to him anyway. As he walked up the road away from Navistar, he hailed the fourth random empty rickshaw that he saw for a ride back to the city.

As they sped through the suburbs of Hyderabad, Chris took every opportunity he could to discard equipment. The phone went first. He knew it would take less than a minute for it to be driven over. It didn't matter if it wasn't—the phone was a fake with only a circuit board to light up the display and set alarms. He waited for a bus to be directly behind him until he dropped his laptop to the floor. He screamed at the driver to stop to retrieve the device, but it was too late, as the bus had done a great job. He dismissed the driver in a huff and decided to walk the rest of the way back to the hotel. When he walked onto a bridge, he dropped the empty hard drive into the murky water below, and the laptop battery followed shortly thereafter. He then found another rickshaw and directed the driver to take him to the Taj Deccan Hotel in Banjara Hills in the center of Hyderabad. On the way, he removed the plastic film cover from the Navistar ID badge, and within thirty seconds, Greg's image disappeared from the card for good. Chris spotted a storm drain along the way and threw it in.

After being dropped off, Chris went to the gift shop on the ground floor where he perused the trinkets and postcards for ten full minutes. Feeling comfortable that no one had followed him in, he left the hotel and walked up the steep hill to the Taj Krishna Hotel and headed straight for the bar. He ordered a coke, no ice, and patiently waited with his eye on the lobby for thirty minutes. Satisfied again that he had no tail, he headed out once again and walked for fifteen minutes more to his room at the five-star Taj Banjara Hills Hotel, where he finally relaxed and started thinking about his encounter in the corridors of Navistar. He began listing out his thoughts in his mind. If he was going to pass on the information to Nash, he knew he had better get his facts right.

*Armed security for a visitor. Why?*

*Indians were pretty non-descript. Couldn't follow the conversation. Didn't need to know. That's not what I was there for.*

Chris was there only to get in, plant the program, and get out. Anything else was gravy.

*Radio guy was out of his league, didn't see me as a threat. He was there just to open doors, probably a junior security guy or facilities manager.*

*The mad scientist . . . exactly that. He seemed to be the main focus of everyone's attention. His face was different from the rest. Won't forget that in a hurry.*

*Stretch, just a hired gun. But how does he get to carry a weapon in India if he is not Indian? Only governments get away with that. How important was this guy?*

*They were Arab looking but maybe not. Stretch and the mad scientist's assistant were wearing suits with collarless shirts. That's the typical business attire in many countries in the Middle East, but which one?*

*Stretch was tall, good-looking with a full head of hair, well-groomed beard, and tanned. The assistant was equally well groomed and had an air of academia. Or maybe he was even an authoritative figure who preferred not be in the spotlight.*

*Interesting crew, interesting puzzle,* Chris thought. *Interesting puzzle for Nash but then again, maybe not.*

# CHAPTER FOUR

## DAY 4

## SVR Headquarters Yasenevo, Moscow, Russia

GENNADY BIELAWSKI WAS SIFTING THROUGH THE MOUNTAIN OF PAPERWORK THAT HAD FORMED into two crumbling columns of crap on his desk with the enthusiasm of a man approaching the gallows. He was bored, unmotivated, and reluctant to keep to the task at hand when a welcome tap on the door allowed him a reprieve.

"Yes, come" he answered glumly.

His secretary briskly walked in. "Sir, sorry for the disturbance, but Zoya Girbov would like some time to speak with you. She is waiting in my office."

The deputy director for SVR's Directorate S stood up from his desk with a smile and a wave of his hand. "Yes, yes, please bring her in."

As he waited, he brushed his hair back and straightened his tie. When the most highly authoritative, respected, and prolific KGB assassin turned up at your door requesting a meeting, it was generally not to talk of politics, state of the economy, or vacations on the Black Sea. The reason for the visit piqued his interest and gave him a much-needed excuse to move away from his desk, even if for just a few welcome minutes.

"Zoya, it is so good to see you. How are you? Please sit down." Bielawski ushered the seventy-one-year-old woman to a comfortable chair and walked over to a silver samovar at a side table and began to pour two cups of tea. He couldn't help but notice that she seemed distant, a little off. They had not seen each other for months, but they had known each other since the Second World War, and over time, he became her mentor, her boss, and her closest friend.

"Gennady, I need something from you," she said.

Bielawski knew she could be curt with people simply because she didn't have time for niceties. Zoya was a woman of action, not of flowery discussions; she could be all business—and was when she really wanted something. Bielawski placed the two cups of tea on the coffee table that separated them and sat opposite her, his mind moving quickly. She never needed an appointment to see him, and he would even cancel meetings at short notice when she appeared at his door, but he felt that this time something was seriously wrong. . . . She seemed aloof, strained, almost emotional.

His first thoughts were about her job. While many at The Center had called for her to be retired years before while she worked for the Active Measures department, Bielawski had argued that she be maintained as a teacher for the Andropov Institute at SVR headquarters instructing new recruits on the art of assassination, which she excelled at. But now, with young blood circulating the halls of Yasenevo, his sphere of influence had faded, and even he was being ushered out and put to pasture. There wouldn't be much he could do to help her, however; it wouldn't surprise him to learn that some low-ranking nerd had pissed her off and she was on the warpath. It couldn't be anything else. She had no family, only a very small group of friends that she never fully trusted, but there was a long list of enemies, both foreign and domestic. Had she been targeted, she would have taken care of the problem herself. Appearances and age aside, she was still an unyielding foe. Even into her mid-sixties, she was performing kills on behalf of her government, but Bielawski knew she wouldn't come to him with a trivial request to slap a wrist of another officer.

Bielawski decided to be direct. As much as he hated to go back to his desk, he needed to get to the point, and as he began speaking, he thought he saw a small tremble in her hands. His eyes squinted a look of interrogation as he faced her. "Tell me, Zoya, what's going on?"

Zoya took a deep breath.

*Wow, that's new. She normally has ice running through her veins. What the hell is going on with her?* he thought.

"I need your help, Gennady. . . . I need . . .,"

Bielawski was right. The tremble was back and this time with a vengeance. He was now sitting on the edge of his seat. *Holy shit, she's falling apart. After all these years, she's coming apart!*

"I need a mission." She'd regained her composure and gotten back to business. "I need another mission. You need to find me something, Gennady."

"Zoya," he said, taken aback, "I can't simply pull something out of my desk and hand it to you. I have nothing. I have less than three months before they kick me up the ass and throw me out the door. You know that."

"Gennady, you always have something. I need this. I need to do something worthwhile."

Yes, Bielawski thought, she was getting scared by the prospect of retiring—the SVR would push her out eventually, and it was a certainty that without his protection when he was gone she would soon follow. "Things are changing around here," he complained. "It's not the KGB anymore." He waved his arms in the air. "These pencil necks are watching everything now. I can't take a shit without accounting for the amount of paper I used, and besides, not much is coming to my desk these days. The bureaucrats have it all." He didn't want to put her back out in the field again—he didn't want her in danger. Bielawski had become too attached to her over the years. She needed to be looking at retiring, not being active.

"We both know that is not true," she countered quickly. "I know there are operations going on right now that only you could authorize. I see these kids come through the academy, and I know what they're up to. It doesn't take a brain surgeon to figure it out. Things are heating up again, and I want to get involved. Give me a mission!" Zoya delivered with gusto.

"What is wrong with you all of a sudden?" he contended. "I thought you were comfortable as an instructor. Are you not getting paid enough? Don't you have anything you want to do on your time off?" He waved his index finger. "And killing people is not a hobby,

Zoya. You must have interests outside this place other than that."

"Gennady, give me a fucking mission!" she demanded.

Shocked, Bielawski moved back into to the comfort of his chair. Again his brow furrowed, and his interrogative look was back. If anyone else had talked to him like that, she would be on the next slow train to the Kamchatka Peninsula.

"I need this," she pleaded. "I need this more than you know. You have to do this, Gennady. You have to."

An awkward silence ensued as both parties stared at each other. It was Zoya who broke first as a tear and then another rolled down her cheeks as if floodgates had just opened.

Bielawski had never seen her this way. His heart was in his mouth. He felt warm and clammy, feeling her pain, but he still did not know what was making her this way. He remembered her as a teenager, the first woman sniper to enter the Berlin Reichstag in May of 1945, a recipient of the Hero of the Soviet Union medal for her bravery and courage as she killed with impunity during the Battle of Berlin, the KGB master assassin with 121 confirmed kills, not the trembling, weeping shell of a woman who now sat before him. He let the silence continue knowing she had something to share and not wanting to push her away. She looked lonely and abandoned. He felt sadness and unfair guilt.

As if by a flick of a switch, her tears stopped. Zoya stared despondently into his eyes, her voice one of anguish and suffering. "I have stage 4 pancreatic cancer, Gennady. Give me a mission, or I will make my own."

# DAY 5

## Special Operations Command Europe, Patch Barracks Stuttgart, Germany

"Richard, can we talk?"

If Richard Nash was surprised to see Bill Price, the lead in-house CIA investigator in Stuttgart, he didn't show it, but he did wonder why Price was not looking under the floorboards in Langley instead of hanging around here. "I've got a full schedule here, Bill. Shouldn't we be meeting in a more formal setting?"

Price tried to keep his cool and avoid any eye contact with people as other members of the 8G70 debriefing team filtered out of the meeting room, but he was almost skipping as if he had to pee. He waited for the right moment and lightly touched Nash on the elbow ushering him politely away from the door and further down to a less populated corridor.

"I'm sorry to be pushy with you, but the Brits have lost two of their agents in Moscow, and Percolate has missed two of his scheduled drops." Price let the information sink in for a second.

Nash looked on, nodded his head, but knew what was coming.

The investigator continued, "The Brits are looking to confirm it, but it seems there was some kind of purge and maybe a dozen guys were picked up for whatever reason, and they think two of their assets were among them. This has all been happening in the last twenty-four to forty-eight hours, and I think by the time I get back on the phone, the Russians may have interrogated and tried them. It may all be over, and they are already dead. My guess is that Percolate will be next. . . . As for others, I don't know."

"Is it your guess, Bill, or do you know?" Nash didn't give Price a chance to answer and realized he was being rude towards the investigator. "I know your remit from the director with this task force you are heading up, and I am 100 percent behind you." Nash was beginning to grasp the gravity of the situation. Percolate was one of the best Russian Army intelligence officers the CIA had ever recruited, and the quality and accuracy of the material that he provided was outstanding. To lose him now as the Russian military machine was restructuring would be a painful loss. "I will kick this around my team and see if I can get something solid for us to work with. In the meantime, get a cable off to Langley stating everything you just told me; then stand down. I need my guys to run with this." Price was about to protest, but Nash headed him off. "I can't have you dealing with tactical issues like this. Get back to the big picture stuff, and let's meet in the office when I get back for an update."

"Richard, if Percolate is compromised, then this will be the third agent we've lost this year."

"Don't you think I know that?" Nash barked a little too loudly. "Bill, look, you're doing a great job. I know there's a lot at stake here, and I know what you are thinking. If we have a mole, we, meaning you, are the person to find it." Nash calmed and took a breath and then offered an afterthought, "Do I need to call the Brits, stroke them a little bit?"

"Well, you could pay them a quick visit on your way back if you want. Some of their assets are major players as well."

Nash shook his head and reviewed the imaginary calendar in his brain. *Not enough hours in the day,* he thought. "Okay, I will see what I can arrange. Right now I've got to focus on taking a piss. Are we done?"

As Price and Nash went their separate ways, Gene Brooks and Chris Morehouse rounded the corner just in time to see their boss heading for the men's room. Chris gave him a wave but received no acknowledgement in return, excusing it with "bad day at the office, I guess."

"You don't want his workload, believe me. The guy is a machine that never quits, and I'm sure he's got a shitload on his mind," Gene replied. "Besides, the guy's got a bladder just like the rest of us. When you've got to go, you've got to go."

"I know how that is. Remember when I had kidney stones in Fayetteville? Jesus, I was drinking gallons of water for days after that. Did I ever thank you for holding my hand and stroking my hair that day in the hotel?"

"Knock it off, asswipe. I didn't stroke your hair."

"But you did hold my hand, Gene. We bonded that day, you and I. . . . I'll never forget the moment and the look in your eyes."

Gene gave Chris a playful shove. "You can be a dick sometimes."

"Is that what you wanted to do, Gene, grab my dick instead of my hand?"

Gene threw his head back to look at the ceiling. "Lord, give me the strength to do something with this wayward boy."

Chris wanted to agitate him more, but it was time to get back on track as they approached the conference room door.

As soon as they entered the room, Chris could tell where he needed to sit. A desk with a microphone and a single seat were placed in the center of the room and faced a row of other desks and chairs, most occupied by people he did not recognize. As he looked around, he saw the sound recorder technician and a stenographer off to one side, tweaking their devices, comparing notes. Others in the room either sat at their desks and consulted their paperwork or talked in small groups in hushed tones. Some on seeing Chris enter used the universal CIA change-the-subject code of touching an ear or scratching a nose.

Gene whispered in Chris's ear, "If assholes could fly, this would be an airport."

His way of alleviating a stressful situation was not lost on Chris.

"Relax. They're not going to chew your balls off. You've done nothing wrong. Take a seat."

"There you go again with my balls, Gene. I'm beginning to worry about you."

"Asshole." Gene sniggered and sauntered away to talk to one of his colleagues.

Everyone was obviously waiting for Nash to return before the final debriefing of the day commenced. Chris made himself as comfortable as he could and waited patiently alone with his own thoughts as he looked around the room. Eight people there were about to grill him, hopefully in the nicest way possible. As he was taking everything in, Chris suppressed a smile as he began to reflect on how far he had come. Here he was about to give a team of CIA officers a debriefing of a mission that he undertook, and after talking it over with Gene, it was looking to be a success. In just four short years, he had moved from a driver at the US embassy in Germany to bodyguard, to college graduate, to contract employee with the CIA—not to mention saving a few lives along the way and falling in love. He was just one step away from his dream of becoming a full-fledged agency officer, and with just a little more patience and positive results from operations like Hydera-bad, he was on his way to a new career. Chris was chuffed with himself and rightly so.

The room went quiet as Nash entered the room. He strode up to Chris and patted him on the shoulder. "Good to see you, Chris. Heard you had fun in India."

Chris stood up. "Mr. Nash, good to see you too. Yup, had a blast in more ways than one." Chris rubbed his belly.

Nash smiled at the reference to the nasty bowel movements that most westerners get when visiting India. "Take a seat, young man. You can tell us all about it, but spare us the details of the chicken vindaloo please."

Others in the room noted the unusual closeness of the contractor and the senior manager—Nash's subtly announced to everyone that Chris was his boy and nobody had better dick with him. Dana Munson, Nash's deputy, noted the interaction and let out an obnoxious cough. Everyone in the room was startled, and Chris looked his way. *Who's that arsehole?* he thought.

"Okay, everyone, daylight's burning. Let's go," Nash ordered.

After twenty minutes of Chris's debrief, he got to the part where he was called to go above and beyond his mission parameters. "Someone called Munson told me to move ahead. I think his exact words were, 'The mission must be carried out. There are no ifs ands or buts. Get a briefing from the OTS guy, and get this thing moving. The next thing I want to hear from you is that the mission is complete—or words to that effect."

A woman from the panel wanted to know what was said on the phone.

Chris did not know her name or title. He was there to report, and that was it—no invitations to cocktails later or BBQ down by the river, just business. As with many interactions with the CIA, no formal introductions are made, and Chris, still the outsider, did not need to know who was who in the room. He just had to answer questions, no opinions necessary, just tell it as it happened.

Ever the professionals, no one in the room looked at Munson, nor did the agency officer flinch on hearing his name. Everyone already knew of the discussion from the taped conversation they had heard earlier, and they showed no surprise when Chris repeated verbatim the actual words used. Nash, who seemed as if he was taking notes, was nodding and smiling. His protégé was shining, and this was turning out to be the best interview from the 8G70 crew by far.

For a while into the debrief, it looked as if some of the CIA panelists were getting bored, but when Chris started describing his encounter with Stretch and the sunshine band, everyone who had their faces buried in their notes stopped and looked up. Nash stopped writing. Munson, who was slouched in his chair and playing with a rubber band, stopped, straightened up, and stared at Chris. When Chris continued with a description of events, Munson for the first time opened his mouth, "What makes you think that the guy you call Stretch was security?"

*I just found Munson,* Chris thought. "The big ass bulge on his right hip might have been my first clue. His body position, his movements, his eyes, his demeanor—everything about him told me he wasn't a bureaucrat, scientist, bored staffer . . . more likely ex-military, someone who knew how and when to fight."

"So he was with the other two protecting them from . . . ?" Munson let the question trail off.

"Well, it wasn't me, although he lined himself up to be ready to take me down. It's possible, and this is only my opinion."

"We don't need your opinion. We need facts. Get to the point."

Nash jumped in, "Dana, let him finish his thoughts."

"I think he was a minder, keeping an eye on the two other guys with him. They were already in the building, theoretically in a secure environment. They were obviously there for a meeting or presentation of something. The scientists were carrying wads of paper, and so were some of the Indians. So my guess is that there is some collaboration going on between India and . . . whatever country these guys came from."

"Which is where in your opinion, Chris?" Munson asked in a sarcastic tone.

"My guess would be Syria or Iran, but what the hell do I know?"

This last comment made a few of the CIA staffers looked sternly at one another.

Munson knowing Chris's background thought, *A driver with an opinion, just marvelous, that's all I need!*

Nash was taking it all in and still marveled at Chris's attention to detail. This was not the first time that he'd heard Chris in a debriefing session. The first time was just after the young Brit had saved the life of the US ambassador to Germany during a terrorist attack. But Nash began to take a deeper interest in Chris as early as 1994 shortly after a Fourth of July party held at the residence of the US ambassador to Germany. On Independence Day, every US ambassador around the world throws a party for US employees and their families, and if the embassy is large enough, other guests are also invited. The US embassy in Berlin was big enough to throw quite a lavish party. Hundreds were invited, and the draw of free booze, MacDonald's, and Coca-Cola would always be enough to drag out the best of party-poopers. The event was so large that the day was split into two parts. The morning session was for invited guests from the host nation, the military, politicians, and local businessmen and businesswomen. Other members of the diplomatic corps were also invited to the morning festivities, and as such, it would not be uncommon to see a Canadian army major sharing a drink with a naval captain from Indonesia. The afternoon party was strictly for families of US diplomats and local employees of the embassy.

As part of his driving duties that day, Chris pulled the car around when he heard his number being called over the car parking lot loudspeaker to pick up his guests. As he waited his turn to pick up Nash and his wife, he spotted a Russian army officer being supported by two of his compatriots after having one too many drinks at the party. The small group was quite near where the Nashes were waiting to be picked up. As Chris pulled his car to a stop, he got out to open the door for Mrs. Nash. But before she could get to the car, the Russian soldiers began pushing and shoving each other, which inadvertently caught Jill Nash unawares, and all three of the group stumbled into her path knocking her sideways. Chris was quick enough to spot the danger and caught her fall before she hit the ground.

Nash saw a potential trap but reacted calmly to the situation and tried to brush everything off as an accident. He had been a spy too long to simply believe drunken Russian soldiers just happened upon the CIA station chief outside a party. He quickly went to his wife's aid to dust her off, but he saw that Chris had everything under control. The last thing Nash needed was for the Russians to be planting a listening or tracking device on his wife. Once all were in the car, Nash surprised Chris by asking to be taken to the embassy. As they were driving, Nash passed a scribbled note to Chris: *Don't say a word in the car; it's possible we've been tagged.* Chris's face turned white. He began to show a hint of nervousness, but he did not say anything.

It turned out after much electronic searching that the accident with the Russians was exactly that, just three drunken soldiers having too good a time. It was a valuable lesson for Chris who now looked at all things in a different light. The day after the party, Chris took a few minutes to speak with Nash about one of the Russian officers.

"Mr. Nash, I have a feeling that I know what was going on with those three Russians yesterday."

"Well, they were arguing about a woman."

Chris forgot that Nash spoke perfect Russian.

"But what's on your mind, Chris?"

"I saw one of them arrive with his wife, and I saw her leave later with another woman. She was crying her eyes out."

"Well, yes, sadly these domestic arguments follow people everywhere."

"The thing is, Mr. Nash, I saw the same guy about two weeks ago with another woman, and they were kind of . . . more than friendly if you know what I mean."

Nash looked at Chris for a long time and thought, *Is he trying to tell me there's a recruitment opportunity there? I'd be impressed if he were.* Nash let his thoughts wander a little more before he said anything.

Chris continued, "There may be some leverage there, Mr. Nash."

"What did you just say?" Nash responded harshly.

"Sorry, I didn't mean to speak my mind, Mr. Nash." Chris felt as though he had just dropped himself in the shit. Who was he to tell a chief of spies who he should go after? *Shit, I am going to lose my job over this. That was way out of line, dummy.*

Although Nash wanted to praise him, he decided to play hardball. He didn't want Chris going off on a tangent and getting involved with things he didn't understand. "You need to be careful of what you are implying there, young man. If there are problems between a husband and wife, it is of no concern to you. Do you understand?"

"Yes, Mr. Nash, it won't happen again."

Nash could tell that his driver felt admonished and looked totally dejected, "Chris, look . . . I appreciate what you said. Thank you. But I trust that you are not discussing this with anyone else, correct?"

"I am very discreet, Mr. Nash. As I said, this won't happen again."

After a few seconds' pause, Nash gave him a pat on the back. "Chris, keep up the good work. Let me know if you see something like it again. Okay?"

Chris let it go and thought no more about the incident.

But Nash didn't.

Now five years after the incident, Nash was sitting listening to Chris who, although acting on orders, had showed great initiative and drive to get the mission accomplished. Nash knew that Munson was way out of line by ordering Chris to carry out the Navistar operation. It should have been aborted, but Chris stood up and played out the role as a true professional. Operation Springfold had yet to be completed, but the added intelligence Chris had brought to the table put a new spin on things. The operation, designed by Nash, was years in the making, but now a new player had joined the game, and the US effort to prevent another India/Pakistan war required another push to ensure that bloodshed would not be the order of the day. They were still a few days away from getting any results from the planned cyber-attack, and now with new information on the plate, someone needed to take a close look and find out who the visitors were in Hyderabad.

Munson and Chris were still going at it as Nash was grinding through his thoughts. They'd already discussed Chris's exit from

Navistar and his countermeasures, but now they were back on the encounter with the group inside the building.

"For some reason, I don't think your opinion matters a shit! You think you saw something that wasn't there, and my guess is that you didn't plant the virus as instructed and now you are trying to deflect your mistakes by creating characters that sound as if they came from a comic book. Mad scientists, radio guy ... Stretch? Please, I mean c'mon. Would you believe me if I was sitting there on your side of the table telling this story?"

*Jesus Christ, this guy is giving my arse a headache,* Chris thought but responded as calmly as he could. "Mr. Munson, I am not in the habit of making comic-book storylines. Let's not forget who put me there in the first place. You wanted facts, and I am giving them to you as I saw them, as I heard them. I was there. You can take my opinions, or shit as you called it, and shove it. . . ."

"Okay, I think we have heard enough for one day," Nash interjected. "Chris this is a great report. We will need to go back and chew on some of this stuff. Don't forget you weren't the only one out there on this project, but it looks as if you went well beyond the call. No matter what the outcome, we owe you a debt of gratitude. Thank you for all your hard work. Gene will be in touch with you for your next mission, but for the meantime, go get some rest. We'll catch up soon."

As Chris got up to leave, some of the staffers starting packing up as well.

"I don't recall telling anyone else that they were done," Nash stated curtly. "We've still got a lot of work to do. Someone go find some food. We're going to have a long night. And Dana, let's you and I have a chat."

Munson was brooding. *A fucking driver, really, seriously?*

# CHAPTER FIVE

## DAY 5
## Gare du Nord Train Station, Paris, France

AS PAM WAS SEARCHING THE READER BOARD FOR THE PLATFORM SHE NEEDED FOR HER TRAIN TO THE HAGUE, she spotted out of the corner of her eye a man approach her obviously in need of something. In halting French he asked her the time. Pam didn't want to get into a conversation with the guy and, although she understood what he needed, simply pointed behind him to his left where a large clock hung from the cathedral ceiling. As the man turned to look, she slipped by to his right and took off at a quick pace. Although she had almost an hour to wait for her train, she did not want to get social with anyone on this part of her journey. As she walked away, she didn't look back and didn't see that the man, although dejected by the encounter, was not about to give up.

Pam found a small café inside the station near her platform and decided on a coffee and croissant and hoped the time would speed by. She was getting impatient, and all she wanted was to get home. It should not have been a long trip back from Greece, but the Primal Ocean team always took precautions when travelling and never took direct routes home. As such, Pam flew from Thessaloniki to Athens, then on to Paris where she stayed the night previously, and then would take the train on her final leg to The Hague. Rita flew from Thessaloniki twelve hours later to Istanbul and then on to Frankfurt where she would board a train to her hometown of Strasbourg. Crauford, on the other hand, flew from the same Greek airport to Rome, to Barcelona, and then on to Paris. None of them was entirely sure when and where they would meet up next, but they did know that their next mission would be in Norway.

As Pam picked up a discarded British newspaper left on a nearby table, she heard a voice behind her.

"Ah, you understand English. I hope you don't mind if I join you," said her time-conscious traveler.

Pam kept her mouth shut. She gave him a deep stare as if to say, *What the fuck, asshole? Get lost!* She wanted to get up and move on but determined that the guy was probably not with the police or authorities, and so she became slightly intrigued. She measured the man up looking for a weakness, a sleight of hand, a quick movement, a weapon, or some correlating act that would throw her into the flight-or-fight mode. After spending so much time with Chris, she picked up on his habits and played the what-if game with him, often times when riding public transportation or walking in busy streets or shopping arcades. He—and now she—was always looking for tangoes, as he liked to call suspicious characters, or looking for opportunities to get off the X in a hot situation and finding the best route out of Dodge.

The man in front of her was also sizing Pam up. *A silent pretty one, but those are the best, the dirtiest bitches. Hmm, this could be interesting. I deserve something like this.* He held out his hand for a shake. "My name is Alihasan. I am but a weary traveler like yourself, and all I am looking for is a little company while I wait to take my journey." This last statement usually initiated a question from the victim as to where he was going, what journey.

But Pam wasn't biting. She stared impassively at him not blinking or giving away an ounce of recognition or emotion, just letting things play out.

"You see, I travel the world looking for my true companion, and when I first saw you, I was mesmerized by your sheer beauty, and I knew I had to do all I could just to spend a few minutes with you."

Pam almost gagged. *Jesus Christ, a pervert.* She sat back in her chair and crossed her arms hoping he would get the message, *conversation over, dude!* She checked her watch and waited to see what else the creep had to say. She still had time before she departed and although she was disgusted by his implications, she let things go.

"I am from the Kingdom of Jordan, and since the death of my wife a few years ago, I have been a lonely wreck of a man. I have tried and tried to find the perfect match, and I realize there is nobody who can equal the beauty and wisdom of my late wife. All I want is a companion to help me, to be with me as I grow old. Nothing more, just friendship, you understand?"

Pam gave a slight nod and lowered her arms, a sign of opening. She studied the man closer. He was short, fat, and balding. He wore an expensive gold necklace, had gold rings on both hands, and sported a Rolex, although Pam could not determine its authenticity. He wore a business suit, which was of probable moderate expense, and his shoes looked relatively new. He obviously cared about his appearance, but Pam was revolted by the amount of chest hair that curled up to his throat and, from further inspection, from the amount of hair that was creeping up from his back to his neckline. She liked men with ordinate amounts of chest hair, but the beast in front of her could have filled a mattress full of chest and back hair and still had enough to spare for a pillow. The thought made her stomach tie a knot.

Still, Pam had to give the man credit—he spoke pretty good English, and it was quite possible that he had money. Nevertheless, he came across as a creep with an air of entitlement, and while it seemed that Alihasan had a captive audience, she was more aware than he could have imagined.

"I hope I am not boring you . . ."

"Susan," she reluctantly replied.

"Ah, Susan, a good British name. You know I spent many years in Cambridge as a student of economics. I long to go back there. Maybe we can get to know each other and spend some time together. Are you from London?"

*That will do,* Pam thought. Keeping her sentences short to hide her American accent, she said merely, "Yes, Chelsea."

"Oh I love Chelsea, and the shopping is simply marvelous, don't you think?"

Pam nodded.

"Are you taking a train somewhere, or waiting for someone?"

"Waiting"

"I have an idea. Let me take you to lunch. I am staying at a hotel nearby. They have excellent room service." Pam leaned forward, placed both elbows on the table that separated them, and placed her fingers into a pyramid.

"Sounds interesting," she whispered with a slight smile.

Alihasan's mouth began to water with expectancy.

"But what's in it for me?" she added.

"Oh my goodness, I will pay dearly for you, my love. I will give you one thousand pounds if you spend the day and evening with me."

Pam got to the point and in a hushed tone said, "What do you want me to do to you for that kind of money? Shall I tie you up? Shall I play with you? Shall I whip you?"

"No, no, it is I that shall pleasure you, my love. I will take you like no other man has before. You will be begging for mercy before I finish with you. I am going to . . . ."

Pam's mind went into shutdown mode as he spoke. It looked as if she was paying attention, but her mind was going in another direction. The guy was a pervert, and it was probable that neither she nor any other woman would get even one pound from the guy, let alone one thousand pounds. She feigned interest from time to time as he spoke, and as he bragged about his sexual prowess, she formulated an exit strategy.

"And when we have finished, we can take my private jet to Amman, and you will stay with me at the hotel that I own, and I will bestow on you only the greatest of riches, my love." As he delivered this last statement, he leaned forward to touch her knee. As they came in close contact with one another, Pam leaned back from the table and put her arms behind her and placed her hands behind her neck thrusting her breasts forward. It looked as if the Arab was about to salivate. They both looked each other. He thought he had made a connection and remained deep in thought; she thought about severing his head from his neck.

"Two thousand pounds," she countered.

Pam took advantage of the momentary relapse in negotiations and scoured her surroundings. She was looking for witnesses. In normal situations, she wanted someone to be in shouting or seeing distance if she found herself in a compromising situation. In many circumstances, she broke the law; she could be and was extremely violent when she wanted to be. But this was not the time or place to rip a man's head off, at least not completely. She was still on a mission, and only when she reached the safety of her home in The Netherlands could she really switch off. Until that time, everyone was an enemy until proven otherwise, but she had to play by the rules until absolutely necessary. But the more she thought about the man and the possible parallels to her late father, the more anger boiled inside.

She'd often wondered how her father had wooed the many women he was rumored to have bedded. Was he so powerful that women ran to be with him, or was he like the Jordanian in front of her, a sexual predator waiting for the right prey? After her father's demise, more than one woman showed up at her mother's home with a child in tow demanding some kind of repatriation for her father's indiscretions. More than once was the late senator's name dragged through the media by a scorned woman accusing him of assault and even rape.

If her father had not been killed by terrorists at his home in Alexandria, Pam might have killed him herself. She loved her mother dearly, and after all the support and sacrifices the woman had made to ensure her husband's political ascent, she had been cheated and dumped in favor of whores and mistresses. Pam also felt embarrassed, violated, and betrayed and up to a point blamed herself for not doing something about her father's affairs when she had a chance. She'd given up confronting him over all the women in his life, and he had distanced her in return, and as such a virtual compromise had existed. In the resulting concession, Pam became introverted, lonely, but very, very angry. Killing her father would have been the last resort, but he had deserved it. She had wanted it not only for her mother but also for all those other women who he had treated with disdain and subservience.

Pam's frustrations were temporarily relieved when she killed a man for the first time. In her early twenties, she dated a Michigan State police officer who worked on her father's security detail while he was governor of that state. The relationship at first was platonic, but from time to time, Pam became uncomfortable with his violent outbursts and his attempts to rough her up, which only solidified her thoughts that all men were pigs. Although she wanted desperately to believe that any relationship with a man could be amicable, loving, and long-lasting, her experiences were proving to be the exact opposite. She naively thought that with a little more compassion and understanding, she could turn her boyfriend around and that things would work out, and as such she agreed to a hiking trip to the Porcupine Mountain Wilderness in Michigan's Upper Peninsula. During the trip, they camped in the Cuyahoga Creek, and their intent was to trek up to the Escarpment rock formation as their final destination. Unbeknownst to Pam, her boyfriend brought beer and booze—more than she thought was necessary. She didn't mind a few drinks, but getting drunk on a camping trip was not part of her idea of a good time. As they settled down for an evening around a small campfire, trouble soon began as the police officer pulled out his handcuffs and declared they were going to have a good time. Pam balked at the idea, but as one thing led to another and alcohol took charge over any rationality, she found herself handcuffed and hogtied within minutes. Despite her protestations and screaming for him to release her, he sodomized her repeatedly while she passed out. At some point during the night, she woke and found herself free of her bonds. Her first thought was to flee, but her second and more resolute thought was of vengeance.

Pam remained awake for the rest of the night contemplating what she could do. She focused on not allowing her emotions get the better of her, and she willed herself not to whimper, tremble, or cry. She knew she had to stay strong; she had to be above this man; she had to bring closure. Pam knew he had to die.

The next morning, the man acted as if nothing had happened, and he went about the business of clearing camp and making plans to ascend the 1,571 foot climb up to Cuyahoga ridge. Pam talked little and without appearing to brood, all the while planning his demise. She feigned her enthusiasm but was disgusted with his laissez-faire attitude and got on with the program. Fortunately for Pam, her rapist's bravado seemed to make him invincible to the elements and their surroundings. A few times he even voiced his wish a bear would show up so he could show her how to take one down with a few well-placed shots of his oversized magnum. Obviously, the man felt no remorse for the previous night's activities, which spurred Pam on even more to fulfill her need for retribution. As they climbed higher towards the peak, a light snowfall arrived, which set Pam's mood into backward motion. She thought he would reconsider moving onward and head back down, negating her chance to take care of him, but fortunately "Mr. Happy Pants" pushed on. As they reached the top, the snow began to fall harder, but the view from the ridge was spectacular. Pam removed her backpack and found a rock to sit on to rest. Happy Pants wandered around a little and then found a ledge that he inched closer to leaning precariously over the edge.

Pam didn't hesitate. She got up from her perch and sprinted towards the monster. The sudden movement from behind Happy Pants startled him and caused him to spin around and lose his balance. His right foot went over first. As he reached out with flailing hands for a savior, his look was one of astonishment; hers, a look of stone. She didn't need to do too much to topple him over the edge. It was only a nudge, a light baby push, but he was gone. He didn't make a sound as he went over, and she wasn't sure if she would hear his body hit the bottom of the cliff. She was disappointed. She had wanted him to scream until his last living second.

Pam was brought back to the present as the Arab rapped a nervous finger on the table in front of them. She stared directly into his eyes and tried to anticipate the man's next move, all the while planning hers.

Alihasan recoiled at the thought of spending more money than he needed to. He wasn't about to pay the bitch a single penny, but he had to come across as sincere but not too giving. As he leaned back in his chair to contemplate the delights that awaited him, he became oblivious to his surroundings as he slowly undressed her with his mind.

"Susan" saw an opening and leaned forward in her chair and changed her placid expression to one of surprise. She looked over the Arab's left shoulder beyond him, and her look changed once more to one of happiness as if she saw some long-lost friend. Alihasan thought that the person she had been waiting for had shown up and turned around to see him. Seeing nothing out of the ordinary or anyone approach their table, he turned back and suddenly felt a crushing blow of an object being forced into his greasy moustache and his nose. He had been so mesmerized by her act and supposed willingness that he didn't see her pick up the coffee tray on the table with her left hand or the right-hand palm hammering down on the edge of the tray boring a ridge into his upper lip. But he did hear his nose breaking under the pressure as she pummeled the tray into his face three times. BAM! BAM! BAM!

Pam dropped the tray and screamed in French so that anyone who had seen or heard the commotion knew what was going on. "You pig, you disgusting pig! I don't want your money! Leave me alone. Don't ever touch me again!" She dropped the tray and made for her train almost smiling as she went. *Fucking slime ball, won't be doing that again in a hurry.*

The streets were relatively bare and quiet when Rita finally made it back to Strasbourg. Although it was still over a mile to her apartment, she exited the tram at the University of Strasbourg and made her way past the small water fountains at the campus entry and into the dense concrete jungle that lay before her. Time and again she would check her surroundings and take unexpected quick turns often circling back on her route. After almost an hour of dry cleaning to establish if she was being followed, she finally made it to the fourth floor No.7 Rue de Lausanne without incident. As she approached her door, she knelt down to the base to retrieve the clear plastic tape that she had placed in the right corner connecting the door to the ground. It was still intact. She reached over to the left corner of the door jamb and retrieved the other piece of tape that was taped only to the door and left hanging almost in mid-air near the floor. If someone had found the first telltale sign, it could have easily been replaced, but the second. . . . If someone had been in her apartment, then the tape would have been folded backwards under the door after he had entered as the door closed behind him. Rita breathed a small sigh of relief; both telltales were as she had left them.

As she entered the corridor to her home, Rita left the light switch off and allowed her night vision to catch up and focus on the items in the small corridor and in the living room in front of her. There were no sounds, save some music coming from a neighbor across the hall. The darkness of her apartment enveloped her like fog shrouding a lonely ship. She neither feared the dark nor enjoyed it, but the unknown of the shadows played tricks and forced sad memories to the forefront of her mind.

After a few minutes of remaining completely still and silent, she was satisfied that it was safe and turned on the lights to search the remainder of the apartment and investigate the other telltales that she had constructed before her trip.

The watcher from across the street sprang out of his chair as soon as the lights came on. He kicked his sleeping partner in the chair next to him and said, "Drago, wake up, you bum. She's home!"

Rita caught the half-bottle of milk as she opened the fridge door. She took one sniff and reeled backwards realizing how rancid it was, just as she had intended. If someone had been in there and opened the refrigerator, the bottle would have dropped and broken, and he would have replaced it with a fresh one. She moved to the living room where she removed a small bag of talcum powder from in between the black seat cushions on her sofa, which was still intact. She inspected the clear tape on the bedroom wall where she lined up her dresser. Everything was intact, parts one and two of her ritual were complete, and she began to relax. She moved to her bedroom, took off her coat and threw her backpack next to her bed and reached over to her family portrait.

It was the only piece of family history that she still retained; every-thing else was gone, destroyed by the Serbs during the war in Yugoslavia. She studied the picture of her family. Jana Imamovic, as she was then known, stood next to her brother, Hasan, and her sister, Edina, while her parents, Adnan and Munira, sat in comfortable chairs in front of the children. The picture was taken just after she participat-ed in the Sarajevo Winter Olympics in 1984 where she competed in the women's twenty kilometer cross-country ski race. She did not place high at the event, but she became a local hero, nonetheless. As she removed the back of the picture frame, a piece of card fell out with three penciled-in hash marks. Rita removed a pencil from a bedside table and etched another mark on the card and whispered, "For you Mama, for you Papa, for you Edina, and for you Hasan." It was the same ritual she practiced each time she returned from a completed mission. She had promised her family that one day she would find those responsible for their deaths and those responsible for ordering the genocide of Bosnian Muslims by the Serbs, and now after kills in Indonesia, Argentina, Peru, and Greece, she was well on the way to fulfilling her promise.

Rita retrieved an apple and some peanut butter from the kitchen and planted herself in front of the TV. Knife in hand, she sliced and dipped to her heart's content. It was a tasty habit that she had picked up while living in the United States only a few years earlier. After the Bosnian War, Jana became a US citizen based on refugee status and changed her name to Rita Dorman to protect her identity, as she knew that one day she would be called to the International Criminal Court in The Hague as a witness for the prosecution at the International Criminal Tribune for the former Yugoslavia (ICTY). When she finally appeared as Jana Imamovic at the courts, she provided a first-hand account of what it was like during the month of July in 1995 in Srebrenica. She explained to the court what happened to her family and how her father and brother were both made to watch as first her sister, then her mother, and finally she were raped by ten Serbian soldiers. She gave vivid details of how her father and brother were shot and killed in front of her in her home, and when the soldiers had finished, they set their house on fire.

As the house burned, a fight broke out between the Serbs, and in the confusion, her mother and sister were both shot and left for dead. Jana knew that she would be next and did the thing that was least expected. She ran into the burning house to escape being killed. During her testimony at the courts, you could have heard a pin drop in the corridor outside the chambers as she held up her disfigured burnt hands and showed the scars on her face and neck as she described running through the inferno of her home to get away from the murderers. Jana described how she ran for miles and miles while crying, not from the pain of her injuries but from the pain of loss. She described how she hid in the woods for days and how she went without food or treatment for her wounds. It was only when she couldn't take the pain of her physical wounds anymore that she summoned the courage to seek help and found it when she stumbled into a village where she staggered into an aid station belonging to Doctors Without Borders.

As much as the doctors in the village tried to save what was left of her hands, there was only so much they could do, so Jana was eventually evacuated to France to receive specialist care, and her dreams of ever competing again in the Olympics were gone forever. In the hospital, after enduring multiple surgeries to repair her damaged hands and weeks after the atrocities in Srebrenica, she learned she was pregnant. It took her a split-second to make a hard choice for some but an easy decision for her—she had an abortion.

When she was finally released from the hospital, she was spirited away from France by her aunt who lived in New York with a promise of a better, quieter, and more prosperous life. Although Jana showed great enthusiasm and gratitude for the chance to escape, she knew that no matter how well she was treated in the United States or how caring and helpful her aunt and cousins were, somehow, someway she would revenge the deaths of her family and the others that perished under the Serbs. It was only when she met Robert Crauford, her aunt's special friend, that she realized her dreams of vengeance could truly be achieved.

"Well, what did they say?"

"They want positive ID," Drago replied.

"Then what?"

"I don't know. They said to call when we have a 100 percent positive identification and wait for further orders."

"So do we kill her then?" Marko, the team leader, pushed.

"Are you fucking deaf or just plain stupid? I just told you what they said—make an ID, then call back. It's not rocket science. Be patient!"

"Kiss my arse already, why don't you? And show some respect to your senior."

"I will when my senior stops being such a dumb fuck."

The two watchers, although long-time friends, continued to hurl abuse at each other while Rita settled in for the rest of the evening.

# CHAPTER SIX

## DAY 6

## De Sillestraat, The Hague, Netherlands

PAM PICKED UP THE PHONE ON THE THIRD RING JUST AS SHE OPENED THE DOOR TO HER APARTMENT. She cradled the handset between her neck and right ear all the while dealing with juggling her bag, the mail, and her keys. The apartment was in darkness. Chris was obviously not home. "Hello," she answered.

"You get back okay then?" Crauford asked.

"Yep, just give me a second to put my stuff down and take my coat off."

Crauford could hear the rustling and bumping around over the phone but waited patiently.

"I'm here, what's up?"

"I've been chatting with a few people from my end, and they are really happy with the outcome." They were talking over an unsecured line and they both knew how to talk in generalities.

"Good to hear. Are we still on for the next trip?" she asked.

"Yes, as we discussed, but I don't have a date for you yet. I just wanted you to know that the result we got was very positive and it looks as if we have a lot more coming our way."

"Hang on a second," Pam said almost too angrily. "I'm happy for us to do the work, but as for the background stuff, it's getting dicey. There is only so much I can do for what we need. We have to have someone else play along."

"I know. I get it, believe me," he conceded. "I've had this conversation with them more than once. They are aware, and they are working on that. They've been doing some work along those lines already, and my guess is they will have something in place at the beginning of the year."

Pam wondered for a second what that meant for her and for her future with Primal Ocean. "That's all well and good, but where does that leave us?"

"We need to be face to face for that conversation, but don't worry. We're all going to be looked after." Crauford didn't intend to have this part of the conversation go on for this long and changed the subject. "How is our close friend? She okay?"

"She'll check in with me tomorrow." Pam checked the clock on the wall as it just passed midnight. "Make that later today."

"Good, good," Crauford replied. "She did a great job. She has come a long way."

Pam softened. "She's really done well, but there's one thing that kinda concerns me, but, on the other hand, it's kinda good."

"Okay, what's up?"

"During our down time, she got to playing with a knife. I have no idea where it came from, but she was getting quite handy with it."

"How the hell does she do that?"

"I have no idea. As I said, it's good that she is learning to use her hands again, but I'm worried that she's training herself to use the knife . . .," Pam forced a pause, "to get up close and personal."

Crauford stared blankly at the wall in front of him in his apartment. He was shocked. Rita was a first-class spotter. She couldn't hold or fire a rifle, as she was missing two and a half fingers of her right hand and two on her left, but she had the keen eye of a sniper, and that was why she was on board. It wasn't that long ago that Rita, due to her handicap, kept dropping her cell phone. Crauford understood her predicament and always procured a new phone for her. She was never meant to be the assassin of the group. That was Pam's remit. Rita was supposed to be the eyes and ears.

"We can't let that happen," He stated forcefully.

"I know."

"She's been through too much in her life. It's not going to happen, and you've got to help me with this. We will stop this before it gets out of hand."

"I know, I know. It's not going to be an issue. I'll keep an eye on her, don't worry." Pam began to regret telling him. She knew that he valued Rita as an important asset, a tool to complete missions, but it was more than that to him; it was also very personal.

Crauford needed to end the conversation. It was supposed to be a brief call. "Listen, I have to go. I will have to think about this more, but we need to get together again soon."

"But it's almost Christmas, and we may need to fit that trip in as well," Pam countered.

"I know. As I said, we don't have a date yet. Maybe I can push it out some. Go get some sleep. I'll be in touch, okay?"

"I've got to admit I'm dragging a bit, and my better half may be home soon. Don't be a stranger." Pam also felt a close bond with Crauford, almost like niece and uncle. Without saying goodbye, he hung up the phone. Pam felt spent. It was time to get back into home mode and forget about operational issues.

Unlike Rita, Pam did not take any security precautions when leaving home. She never knew when Chris would be home, although he tried his best to let her know. She was used to him being away for extended periods and also being home for long periods. It was the nature of his job, and she understood it completely and did not have a problem with what he did for the CIA. She played dutiful girlfriend when she could, but working for the International Criminal Court in The Hague, she would also be away from home as part of an ongoing case or follow-up with other courts and tribunals.

Chris, on the other hand, had no idea that her activities were often illegitimate. He thought, rightly so, that she worked at the court chambers as an assistant in the office of the prosecution and was privy to a whole host of sensitive information for crimes of genocide, crimes against humanity, and war crimes, so he never asked for or talked about details. He respected her need for secrecy and moments of quietness but hoped that one day she would find some other work and be taken away from what he thought were the horrors of her job.

After her phone call with Crauford, it didn't take long for Pam to unpack her clothes, dump them in the laundry basket, and jump in the shower. Although it was late, she needed to wash away the grime and filth that she'd picked up on her travels. The only dirt that she could not wash away was the memory of the perverted Arab, but a long hot shower would, at least, take away an imaginary smell that she thought that lingered in the air, in her nostrils, on her hands, on her skin. The thoughts of the fresh kill in Greece did not affect her in this way, but the smell of a human pig disgusted her. Letting the hot water stream over her hair, her face, her body, she finally began to feel the release, and she felt herself relax and give in to the warm homely feeling. She had no idea, nor did she care, how long she had been in there, but she was able to tune out her surroundings and finally switch off to the safety of her home. Pam faced away from the bathroom door and did not hear it open. There was no shower curtain or glass door on the shower, so the normally super-precautious Pam almost jumped out of her skin when she felt the strong arms of her boyfriend wrap around her waist. She smiled—another reason to relax. He was home.

"Hi," Chris said.

"Hi," she replied.

They didn't need to say any more; they were so comfortable with one another that words weren't needed. They both loved each other so much and were so attuned to each other that sometimes they knew what the other wanted before being asked or prompted. A look, a touch, even a small change in body language was enough.

The made love in the shower, and afterwards, they washed each other and dried each other off. Chris wrapped Pam in her dressing gown and carried her to their bed. He laid her down gently, wrapped her in a blanket, and then turned out the light. Chris left the bedroom to make sure the doors and windows were locked and the lights in the rest of the apartment were out. When he returned to the bedroom, all he could hear was the sound of Pam lightly snoring. He smiled and watched her as she slept. *I'm home*, he thought.

## DAY 6
## Selfridges, Oxford Street, London, United Kingdom

Bill Price was trolling along Oxford Street searching for a gift for his wife with a million other shoppers going through the exact same exercise at the exact same time of year. Christmas was nearing, and the need for getting the perfect gift for a loved one obviated economic sense and good judgement. Speed was the order of the day—get in, get out, and don't get injured in the mad rush. Price was no different from the other men bumbling along as if in a trance not knowing what to get—something expensive, something plain, something exotic, what he just didn't know. He naively thought that being in London would ease the burden as shopping opportunities in the great city were abundant and plentiful, but the place had the opposite effect on him, as it just made for more choices and more ground to cover.

As Price stood outside the famous Selfridges department store, he contemplated his next move. He needed to get back to the US embassy to finish up some work, but he wasn't sure if he wanted to go there first or continue to shop. Although it was less than a mile away, his feet were aching, and he needed a rest. As fatigue grew, he was distracted and drawn to one of the window displays that the department store prided itself upon. He took in the marvelous winter scene and saw his own image in the reflection. Bill Price cared less about his appearance than most; however, he thought that he looked quite dapper in his Harris tweed walking hat and London Fog trench coat. Aside from his grey moustache and beard, the fifty-eight-year-old behavioral scientist and lead CIA investigator looked like an older Inspector Clouseau; however, clumsy and incompetent he was not.

As he was letting his mind wander, he caught another reflection in the window as a familiar face went hastily by. Price turned around in time to see the back of Dana Munson's head as he entered the store.

*Ah, someone else on a mission,* he thought. *Perhaps we can be allies and fight this battle together.*

Price scooted off after Munson in the hope that he had some insider information on Christmas shopping in London. For all his academic prowess in understanding human behavior, Price could not wrap his head around the Christmas spirit and all that it entailed. It was his wife who took care of his domestic life when he was home, but he utilized his sister-in-law's creativity to make decisions for him for birthday and holiday presents for his spouse. It was way too far out of his comfort zone to purchase something meaningful or thoughtful for someone else, even his wife.

As Price entered the store, he searched in vain for Munson and was soon accosted by the perfume snipers that lay in wait at the main entry points. Within minutes, he was interrogated by a host of young pretty females all trying to make a sale for this fragrance or that scent. To avoid any discussion about his wife's preferences, he switched languages to Russian and politely told them that he did not understand. With the first barricade overcome, he decided on a roundabout approach in his search for his colleague. He took the aisle to his left, which directed him away from the main thoroughfare in the store, and easily dodged and wove his way through the other manic shoppers zeroing in on potential treasures. Once in a while, he would stop and scan his surroundings hoping to see his ally, but it was to no avail. As his head swiveled from left to right and back again, he caught a glimpse of the sign that read "Harry Gordon's Bar." *Hmm, that looks interesting, rest and replenishment. I think a good glass of Merlot is in order.*

As he neared the warmly lit establishment, he once again spotted the back of Dana Munson's head sitting at the bar, and Price smiled. *Ah, someone else has the same idea. Good. It's never wise to drink fine wine alone.* But as he approached, he noticed his colleague bent slightly over and whispering into another man's ear. Price checked his pace and furrowed his brow. *Damn, I didn't think that he would be on a mission. I shouldn't be here.*

As Price thought about leaving, he saw Munson hand over a Harrods plastic shopping bag to the man with whom he was in deep discussion. He could not get a good look at the other man, but his instincts told him something was off, something was deeply wrong. Just before Price turned to leave, Munson's "date" looked up and stared directly into his eyes. Price shuddered, and for some reason, he had an urge, a need to get away. As he turned to go, he came face to face with a brute of a man dressed in black clothing. His bald head shined under the lights of the bar, and it looked as if his neck muscles could only be held in by nuts and bolts. The man must have been at least six and a half feet tall and towered above Price's wimpy frame. In his best upper-class British accent, Price commanded, "Excuse me, old chap. Must dash. The missus is waiting."

"Vasili, what the hell is so important that you needed to meet and here in London of all places?" Munson was flustered. After receiving a coded message through an answering service, he had made his way to his meeting at Selfridges. Munson wasn't done bitching his Russian handler out. "Do you know how dangerous it is for us to meet here? I could spit in any direction and hit an American in the face." He paused for a brief second but continued his tirade. "I don't give a shit how good you think your security is, but MI5 and MI6 are probably jerking themselves off and high-fiving each other right now knowing that we are sitting here. You're putting me in a really shitty situation." Munson was starting to raise his voice but checked himself. "So what the hell do you want that's so urgent?" he questioned.

Vasili Timoshev wasn't in the slight bit perturbed by his agent's outburst. He had to concede that the idea of meeting in London was absurd, but his seniors at The Center needed answers. "Dana, please, I understand completely. Nobody is watching us. This is a chance encounter. Don't worry. I have taken precautions." The Russian reached over and briefly touched the American's arm to reassure the nervous spy. Vasili wanted to calm things down and switched topics.

"Have you been shopping, Dana? Something for your wife or your mistress?"

They were talking in hushed tones, but Munson was getting impatient. Normally Russians didn't put much into small talk. "Don't be a dick. You know quite well I don't do that. What the fuck do you want?"

"Would you like a drink? Coffee, tea?"

"I haven't got time for this bullshit. I hope that this wasn't some social, 'how are you doing' type of get together. I don't need pats on the arm and a warm smile. Just keep my bank account healthy was all I asked of you." Munson complimented himself in keeping his composure and not shouting at his partner's face and continued to keep his voice on an even keel. "The product I am giving you should be worth more than cigars and caviar and an occasional promotion from your overlords, so let's stop dancing and get to the point."

"Your team was quite successful in Greece," Vasili responded. "We need to know their next move."

"This was not part of our agreement," Munson countered. "Those are direct ongoing operations that have many moving parts. It's not as simple as you think."

"Then help us think it through. Help us understand the team's objectives and motives. How do they get the intelligence on their targets? Give us something, Dana."

"Why? Why now? This team has been around for some time. Why do you need to know?"

"Dana, I don't want to get into a deep discussion about this now, not here."

*You chose the place, asshole,* Munson thought smugly.

"But our Serbian friends are very restless, and they have asked for our assistance. We need you to put us in the same place as your team the next time that they are active. We will take care of the rest."

Munson wanted to think. He needed to decipher the request. An analyst by trade, he needed to see the big picture before he answered.

The Russian could see that Munson was struggling with his decision and said matter-of-factly, "What's in the bag anyway, Dana?"

As Munson handed over the bag, he looked away to his right and caught a glimpse of something familiar in a mirror. He answered, "Your Christmas present, Vasili," but he could feel something change in the air and noticed that Vasili became as tense as a steel rod. Still, he let the words out: "Norway."

By the time Munson comprehended what he had seen in the mirror, Vasili was already nodding an order to his minder. As their eyes locked, Munson let out a distressing "no, no, don't." But it was too late. Vasili broke contact and headed for the exit before Munson could get out of his chair.

After receiving the silent order from his boss, Baldy stepped to one side to let the "Englishman" pass but spun around to follow his target.

Price slipped around the giant and threw himself back into the throng of attack shoppers in the store. As he scurried through the aisles, his mind began to race. He searched his own vast database of faces and names as he went and narrowed his search to Slavic features only. The man he saw had a very serious, worn face, light skin, was balding, and his forehead was broad with a nose that was almost as flat as a boxer's. His hair was salt and pepper, short, almost militaristic. The man had an air of authority about him, and it looked as if he was in charge of the conversation he was having with Munson.

*Munson, oh my God, Munson!* The thought chilled him enough that he did not feel the bitter cold as he exited the department store. His mind was working in overdrive trying to figure out what his colleague was doing, and he felt as if his senses were exploding. He could feel a rush of adrenaline sprinting through his veins, and he knew that he had to get away. As he turned right out of the store and walked quickly, he glanced backward in time to see Baldy on the street looking in the opposite direction. Price's heart dropped as fast as a heavy boat's anchor. Any thoughts of misinterpretation of his encounter were gone. Baldy was searching for him.

Bill Price was not a physical man; he never played sports. He wasn't overweight, but he couldn't or wouldn't move fast, even if his house were on fire. After moving as quickly as he could along Oxford Street dodging shoppers, pushchairs and crying children, his muscles were complaining after only a few feet. He looked back hoping to see he was wrong about Baldy, but he wasn't. He knew he had to escape; he had to get back to the American embassy, which was still over a mile away. Price steeled himself for the challenge and pushed on, but his mind was still embroiled in trying to make sense of Munson. He had his suspicions about a number of people who were thought to be a CIA mole, and Munson was on the list. But the investigation was focusing on low-level field officers and not senior staff at headquarters.

As Price realized that he was not getting anywhere fast with the crowds around him, he decided to cut across the street in the hope of losing his hunter. As he did, he squeezed himself between two tightly parked double-decker buses. As he came out of the jam, he instinctively looked left before he crossed the street, and as he took his next step forward, he was hit by another bus from the right. The city of London went to great lengths to educate visitors to its traffic being on the opposite side of the road, even painting "Look Right" on pavements to avoid such accidents. But Price was not the first nor would he be the last American to lose his life by looking the wrong way on busy London streets.

# CHAPTER SEVEN

## DAY 7

## US Embassy, Grosvenor Square, London, United Kingdom

"I'M HEADING OVER TO THE CONNAUGHT," Munson announced. "Someone needs to go through Bill's stuff."

"Can't you leave that to station security?" Nash responded.

Munson shook his head. "I don't think we should. I know this is out there, but don't you think, given what Bill was working on, he might have had some notes on what he was doing or whom he was seeing? I don't think we need someone unfamiliar with his work stumbling upon something in his hotel room that could open up a can of worms and jeopardize his investigation."

"Good point, Dana. I find it highly unlikely that he wrote anything down. He had a steel-trap memory, but we don't know if he came from a meeting with the Brits or someone else. He could have easily scribbled some notes somewhere." Nash pondered the situation some more. "But if you are going to volunteer, then I think you should also head over to the morgue to go through his clothes. See if he had a diary or notebook."

Munson tried his best to look sullen in his delight with the outcome. He didn't know if he had been a person of interest to Price or his team, but he needed to be careful. Even if there was a scintilla of a link to his illicit Russian activities, Munson needed to find out and be proactive for his own preservation. Although slightly saddened at the death of a colleague he knew relatively well, it came at a very opportune moment when he was meeting his Russian handler. Munson's first gut reaction at the bar in Selfridges was to stop the Russians from following and taking Price out, but in retrospect, the accident alleviated the need for a more complicated and time-consuming elimination if some kind of implication ever came to light.

Dana Munson had been spying for the other side since 1985 when his attempt to recruit Soviet nuclear scientists at the Twenty-Ninth IAEA General Conference in Vienna backfired as members of the Soviet delegation were pre-empted by the KGB from launching an official complaint due to overt and aggressive recruitment tactics used by the CIA. Munson, who headed Operation Caravan Road, was identified by the KGB as the instigator of those efforts, and the Soviet intelligence agency took matters into its own hands by proposing that Munson be turned and used as an asset for the Motherland.

However long the KGB was prepared to wait, it was surprisingly Munson who started the ball rolling not long after he was passed over for promotion by Richard Nash because of the Caravan Road debacle. The career intelligence officer was destined to climb the ladder quickly within the Operations Division and actually head the Counterintelligence wing, but his brash tactics and disparagement for political correctness stymied his rise, and when his brainchild operation in Vienna flopped, his downward spiral began. It was during a bout of severe depression, not long after the Vienna conference and unbeknownst to the CIA, that Munson sent a letter of apology to the head of the Soviet delegation in Moscow as a means of appeasement for his handling of the hostile operation. As such, he became a person of interest, and Vasili Timoshev from the First Main Directorate KGB was dispatched to Washington, DC, to recruit the disillusioned agency officer. After many months of correspondence through a number of post office boxes in the DC area, their first and only meeting on US soil occurred at the Foxstone Park in Vienna, Virginia. There, the two opposing agents established the ground rules of the engagement, and when the Russian realized that all Munson wanted was money, the KGB pounced on the idea. Munson's stipulations were that he have only one handler and that he call the meetings, whether they be in Europe or elsewhere in the world. In Munson's twist of logic, he made it clear to Timoshev that he would never spy on his country while he was in the United States and that any tangible information he had to offer would be provided at a time and place of his choosing.

Over the years, both Munson and Vasili communicated through numerous post boxes and dead drop sites in dozens of cities around the world, which became a logistical and security nightmare for the KGB. Munson argued that since he travelled a great deal, this tactic would keep himself out of any obvious routine and thus provide a level of security to his alternate activity. At first, the KGB was reluctant to play ball with his outlandish requests, but as soon as Munson identified Dimitri Polyakov, a general in the Soviet Army, code name Top Hat, as an informant for the CIA for over twenty years, they took him as a serious player and thus acquiesced to his demands. For that one action alone, he netted fifty-five thousand dollars, and then his payments began to flow like water on a regular basis.

"So why were you at Selfridges, Dana?" Nash asked. "I didn't think you were an avid shopper."

"I'm not. It was Bill who wanted to meet." Munson was winging it. He knew Price had a reputation for being as dumb as a donkey when it came to shopping, and he wasn't alive to contradict Munson's story. "He told me he wanted to shop for his wife while he was in London, so I kind of volunteered. I guess I have a habit of volunteering these days." Munson decided to throw in another sympathy-gathering act. "I forgot to tell you that I've arranged to fly back on the plane with his body. I thought someone from the office needed to do it. . . . I felt so bad being the last person to see him alive." His last statement was true. He did feel genuine sympathy for the passing of an American, but he was hopeful that there was no evidence to bring him down.

"You're a good man, Dana. I know we've had our differences in the past, and business is business and all that, but I am sure his family and the director will appreciate the gesture. Just let me know if you need some help with the arrangements, but work with the local chief to get the Brits moving in the right direction." Nash began firing off trivial tasks to his deputy. "We don't need some numbskull dropping his casket off a forklift or some shit, and don't forget to get a cable off to the office. I'm not sure what's going to happen when you land. You don't want to walk in unprepared if there is some welcoming ceremony or something. Call Carla at the office; perhaps she knows what's going on. Oh, and don't forget if you find something of Bill's to drop it in the next available diplomatic pouch. Mark it for my eyes only if there's something we'll need PDQ!"

Munson stared blankly at Nash. He wanted to roll his eyes but remained passive. He was sick to death of the simple orders he was receiving from his boss, and it wasn't the first time he was given menial tasks. *Why do you continue to treat me like a child? Do this, do that, call this guy, call that guy. I can think for myself, you grumpy old fuck!* Munson had no intention of dropping anything into the pouch. If there was something worth reading, he would find the appropriate home for it. *Fuck you, asshole.* His contempt was growing once again for Richard Nash.

Munson reluctantly sucked up. "Yeah, sure, good idea. I'll give her a call. If anyone has the inside scoop, it will be Carla. She's always the first to know what's going on at home." He hated his boss's secretary almost as much as he hated Nash. *I'm not sure who should go under the next bus first, you or your bitch. But if you continue this shit while we're here, I'll happily give you a size nine up your ass the next time I see a double-decker.* Munson wanted to change the subject before he'd have to go get some coffee and threw some spaghetti at the wall to see if it would stick. "Isn't she retiring soon? She'll be sorely missed if she goes." Munson was starting a rumor. He knew the old bat wouldn't be giving it up anytime soon.

Nash was incredulous. "What? What . . .? Who the hell told you that?"

"Oh, maybe I misunderstood. I thought that, well . . . ," and just let it hang there. Munson had achieved his aim in diverting the conversation from the present, as he let Nash throw a mini-tantrum about what his secretary of fourteen years was about to do. Nothing could have been further from the truth, but Munson let Nash continue to spin in his thoughts.

# DAY 7

## Leeuwardervaart, Bolsward, Netherlands

Chris was sitting on the ice again. It was the third time he'd fallen over in the last five minutes, and Pam, who'd initially thought it was funny watching him slip and slide everywhere, got the message from his dour expression that he was not in the mood to be made fun of. As he was struggling to get up from his latest fall, Pam rushed over to help him one more time. Chris began to wave her off. "No, no bugger off. I can do this. You go do your speed-skaty thing and just leave me to plod along like an old granny."

Pam smiled and backed off slightly as he tried to get to his feet.

"Sorry, honey, but there are some days when even the best men can't perform," he said trying to make light of his ineptitude.

Pam could tell he was a little embarrassed by the whole thing, and since it was usually Chris who excelled at sports, it was a pitiful sight to see her partner struggle with such an enjoyable activity. "Okay, okay, I get it. You hate me. You don't want to be with me. I understand all too well. No worries, Christopher," she jibed, as she dutifully followed his orders and skated away from him smiling like a Cheshire cat as she went. Pam saw the split in the frozen waterway ahead, which led north to Burwerd. She called back to him, "I'm going straight ahead, okay?"

"It's okay. Leave me here to die. Go on without me. Save yourself!" he croaked and replied as if he was in dire straits.

Pam loved Chris more than she had ever loved anyone in her life. She was totally happy with the way things were, but today she did feel a sense of pride and accomplishment over him because of his inability to skate. But instead of making her feel superior, it made her heart warm, her smile broaden, and her desire for him burn stronger.

Chris finally managed to stand up straight and began shifting his feet slowly forward, and his momentum began to gain traction, although he still felt he was moving at the speed of a sloth on the frozen canal. As his confidence grew and his speed increased like a toddler sprinting, he began to take his focus away from his feet, and he raised his head to take in the surroundings and appreciate the crisp clear day and the beautiful setting that he found himself in. The trees were bare, but a thick frost camouflaged the green and brown colors of nature and offered a picturesque winter landscape.

Although Pam had gone on by herself, Chris was not alone. There were dozens of people out on the ice, and he was ashamed to think that next to all the kids that whizzed past him, he looked the most infantile. Now and again a group of skaters whisked by, each wearing one-piece suits complete with hoods, skating in unison low to the ground and swinging their arms to and fro as if they were scything hay. Their speed and control were awesome. Chris thought those skaters must have been getting ready for the Elfstedentocht speed skating contest that was held in this northwestern part of the country. Due to the ever-changing climate, the annual race over canals and waterways was not regularly run, as the ice cover over the two hundred kilometer Eleven-City competition was not solid enough or safe enough for the more than three hundred serious speed skating contestants and the sixteen thousand leisure skaters to participate. However, the whole country was hoping for a complete freeze so that everyone could enjoy the spectacle, and although there were still several weeks to go before the official announcement that the ice would be suitable for competition, everyone was out practicing. Chris hoped there was a two-kilometer classification for dumb-ass foreigners and a two-day limit for completion of the course. Right now, he had two things on his mind—first, staying upright and moving forward for the next time he saw Pam, and second, a small bulge in his inside jacket pocket.

As Chris was finally trundling along at a safe and steady pace, he spotted Pam coming from the opposite direction. He smiled—he was still upright and still moving. "Yabba dabba doo!" he said announced to himself. His girlfriend was still some distance off, so Chris began to put a plan into action. His heart began to beat faster, he was getting warm, and he felt a small trickle of sweat down his back. As he scanned the area in front of him for the perfect spot, a bunch of kids, probably not more than ten or twelve years old, came hurtling towards him. One of the boys in the group was tethered by a rope and pulled along by his friends at great speed. Now and again, the group would come to a complete stop and let the boy at the end of the rope go speeding by sometimes completely out of control. Chris tried to ignore them as he looked again for the perfect spot, and he found it—some large bushes that formed a border between the ice and the canal embankment. Now time was of the essence. There was still some ground to cover between him and Pam, but the out-of-control kids were covering his line of sight. He stuck up his right arm to wave to her and, in doing so, slipped and started to fall over. Chris's action couldn't have been timed better. He began to lose control, but he willed himself to head for the bushes he had just spotted.

As Pam got closer, she saw Chris fall to his knees and headlong into the bushes. She wanted to scream, but she began to laugh at the comical sight. She wanted to sprint to his aid but held back and casually ambled towards him. "Chris, are you okay?"

Chris was on his knees, almost in the bushes, when she heard him scream, "Pam, Pam, come and look at what I found!"

As she picked up speed, she heard another scream that took her look away from Chris.

"Help! Help!" It was coming from the group of kids with the rope, from the boy attached to the end. He was in the water and floundering.

Pam was the first to respond and sprinted towards the group. As she got to the screaming kids, she realized the rope they had been playing with had snapped and the boy on the end of it had gotten too close to the thin ice and was now in a deep section of water. She stripped off her jacket, gloves and hat, snatched the remainder of the rope from the kids, and went down flat on her belly onto the ice.

Meanwhile with his face in the bushes, Chris did not know what was happening and was concentrating on his mission. He began to talk as if Pam was still there, just behind his shoulder. "Check this out!" he said to a missing audience. Chris extracted himself from the bush and came up on one knee, holding a ring box he had retrieved from inside his jacket. To his astonishment, Pam was not there. He looked around with sad puppy-dog eyes and caught sight of his girlfriend going into the water head first. "Holy shit!"

Chris made it to his feet and began to scramble towards the now growing crowd of onlookers and rescuers, but his inexperience as a skater slowed him down immensely.

As he stumbled forward, he began to frame a picture of what had happened and what was going on. While he was trying to get to the scene, he cursed to himself that he should have been more prepared. It was his job—not Pam's—to look after others. He should be the one saving the kid, he should have been more adept at skating, and he should never have left her side. Now she was the one in trouble, and he couldn't help her. If she didn't get out of this, it would be his fault. By the time Chris got to the group, the boy was out of the water and being cared for by some adults. Pam was eventually dragged out with the remainder of the rope by two hefty men. Chris tried to get to the rope as well but slipped and fell on his arse leaving the two unknowns to save her. He was totally embarrassed.

As quickly as the incident began, it was over. Chris found Pam's jacket and hat and moved as fast as he could to wrap her up. He wanted to admonish her but couldn't. He felt so proud, so honored, and so lucky that he had her. She had saved the boy's life without a moment's indecision or care for her own well-being. Things could have easily gone the other way—he could have lost her, and there was no way of knowing what obstacles were under the ice. But she didn't care. She went in head first. A tear of relief, pride, and happiness welled in his left eye; he was so happy she was okay. The thought of losing her was too much for him. Chris had to put the feeling aside and get back to the situation in front of him—he had to get her warm and dry and out of the elements before hypothermia set in.

Word spread amongst the crowd that an ambulance was on its way. The group began to swell with onlookers, and Chris decided this was the time for him to do something. "We need to move. Everyone off the ice. Let's away from here. We're too heavy. Move, move!" he shouted. He wrapped his arms about Pam, and they shuffled awkward-ly to the bank together. By the time the group of kids and Pam and

Chris made it to the safety of solid ground, a wail of sirens could be heard in the near distance; help was on its way. As they held each other to keep warm before they were to be rescued, Pam shivered and asked, "What did you find, Chris?"

"What?" Chris looked at her with a confused face and tried to backpedal and think of something witty, but this time, he couldn't. He mentally checked his pocket; yes, he had placed the ring back. Another tear welled up, as he realized again that he could have easily lost his to-be wife. "It was nothing, I thought it was some money, but it was only rubbish." *Now is not the time. Let it go*, he thought, but his sad expression gave him away.

Without understanding all behind it, Pam picked up on his miserable concerned look. "It's okay, Chris. I'm fine. I just need to warm up."

"Don't do that shit again, okay? I love you too much, and it took me forever to find you, so don't put yourself in situations like that. Okay?" He didn't know whether to be upset or proud of her, but there wasn't any place or time he wanted to be, except right here and right now.

Pam nodded and knew that he was lying about what was in the bushes. She didn't know what he had found, but she let it slide. She was just happy he was here by her side, keeping her warm and now safe. She thought of Primal Ocean. *If only he could be with me more.* "Jesus it's cold," she said.

"For once, I have to agree with you," he sincerely replied.

## DAY 8
### Strasbourg, France

It was three full days since Rita had returned home from Greece, and although she was quite content sitting in her apartment alone, it was time for her to check on the mail drop for new instructions. As she exited her building at the ground-level front door, she turned left and left again straight into the bakery, which was directly four floors directly below her apartment. The last three days had been almost a form of torture as the everyday smells of bakery products wafted and snuck their way into her living room and bedroom. She could have easily run down to grab a few rolls or a baguette, but she usually refrained from tasting the delicacies as her paranoid sense of security had forced her to remain in a low profile and keep away from regularity. Today, however, hunger prevailed, and she decided to grab a bite before she embarked to the mail drop.

Sticking to a pre-arranged schedule concocted by Crauford, she needed to get out of her apartment and make her way to the post office on Rue d'Obernai where she would use her mailbox key to retrieve an envelope, which contained a numbered key to another mailbox in the city. Rita had memorized the key numbers for each of the five other mailboxes in Strasbourg that she would use, and each one would contain packages with some of the information for the next mission— tickets for the next trip, details of the next target, where and when to pick up the logistics for the operation, maps, or other details. It was her job to gather all the information from the mailboxes over the course of the next two or three days and depart on her outbound three-leg journey when she deemed fit.

But first the bakery called. As Rita waited in line in the shop, she turned her back to the counter and pretended to peruse the wares in the front window all the while scrutinizing her view of the street outside. She saw nothing untoward but kept an air of expectancy about her, silently praying that the police or other foes were not waiting to pick her up. She let down her guard for just a few seconds and ordered two chocolate croissants as the baker asked for her order. The man who had seen her on several occasions gave her a warm smile, but she gave only a ho-hum upward turn of the mouth in return. She was not there to make friends; she was there to work. As she exited the bakery, she took a left turn again and began to walk quickly away from her building and into the throng of pedestrian and vehicle traffic.

As Rita strode away from the bakery, out of her earshot, a Serbian voice crackled over a radio. "Here we go. She's on the move. She's coming your way!"

Drago was already on the ground level sipping coffee at a café nearby waiting patiently for this very moment. "Why the hell didn't they give us more men for this shit?" Drago asked.

"Shut up and get after her. I'll be right behind you," Marko replied.

But his partner kept complaining. "Two men to make an ID is pretty stupid if you ask me. She'll spot us within five minutes."

"Well, it's lucky nobody asked you. Just go, and stop your complaining, or we will lose her. Five minutes is all we need. Keep your eye on the rabbit. I will keep an eye on you and we will rotate when the time is right. Understood?"

"I say we kill the bitch the first chance we get. Screw this surveillance shit."

"Drago, stick with the plan! You should see her by now, and cut the chatter."

"Okay, okay, I have her."

Rita was moving briskly along, and as she crossed a road, she made a beeline for the Simply Market store and dove in. Drago spotted the move but did not fall into the trap. Within a few seconds, Rita emerged chewing down on her croissant and headed back in his direction.

Drago turned his back to her and whispered into his radio mike, "She's on the way back."

Marko froze in the stairway that he was traversing down. He had to make a choice—should he go back up to the observation point to watch her re-enter the apartment or should he get out on the street and make the ID? He remained in place for a few seconds more and thought about what he had just heard. He came to a quick conclusion: she was practicing surveillance detection. Now he knew he had his target, but to get a facial view or even a photograph would be the ultimate proof.

Drago squawked again, "I have her. She's gone past her apartment. Looks like she is heading for the university."

Marko continued his descent, and as he exited the building, he caught sight of Drago's head in the distance. "I have you," Marko remarked.

Drago was wrong in his initial assessment of being spotted by Rita within the first five minutes. The eye-and-rabbit game continued for almost ten minutes before both Serbs stopped to observe her waiting to get on a tram. Both operatives had cameras, but neither was sure who was going to get the better shot.

Drago had his hand on a pistol inside his jacket. "I'm telling you, I could pop this bitch right now and save us a whole bunch of time."

"Don't be an idiot. We have our orders. Once we get the ID, then maybe they'll let us loose, but, for now, cool your shit." Marko was in a good spot away from the tram stop and out of Rita's line of sight.

Minutes were ticking by, and Drago was getting more impatient and made a move.

"Back off. You're getting too close," Marko screamed into the radio. The noise of the street traffic and trams drowned out any shouting. "Drago, back off!"

But Drago would not listen; he kept moving toward Rita. As he moved to pull his weapon out of his jacket, a tram stopped, and a uniformed police officer got off in front of him. As Drago tried to dodge the officer, Rita stared directly into his eyes. Drago knew the element of surprise he thought he'd made was gone, and he dug the weapon deeper back into his pocket.

With the cover of the tram obstructing his view, Marko did not see the police officer or what Drago was doing. In a moment of panic, he sprinted across the street and spotted Rita taking a seat on the tram facing away from him, she raised her deformed hand to brush away some hair. In an instant, he drew his camera and shot twenty frames in her general direction. He had no idea if he would get a clear picture, but he knew then that Drago was right—this was not a two-man job. This was the best outcome they could expect. As he continued to shoot with his camera, traffic around him screeched and honked its way around him. Rita spun around in her seat, with a mouthful of her second croissant. All she could see was the back of a man dodging traffic, and she thought nothing of it.

When Marko eventually made it to the safety of the sidewalk, the policeman stood there looking at him as if he had two heads. The officer motioned for him to come his way and in doing so pulled out his notebook and pen, about to arrest him or fine him for jay-walking. If Marko had to produce an ID, he could be in deep shit, and as soon as the policemen saw his covert earpiece and the two-way radio, a thousand questions would arise. As Marko drew closer, he saw Drago who was peddling full speed on a bicycle towards the policeman. The cop had no idea of what was about to happen, but Marko was ready to sprint off. Drago connected with the officer and knocked him completely off his feet, which almost caused him to fly into a bus shelter on the street. Drago maintained control of the bike and sped safely away. By the time the police officer had gotten back to his feet, his jaywalker had gone, the mysterious biker had gone, and all he had left was a bump on the back of his head.

# CHAPTER EIGHT

## DAY 8
## Rue de Lausanne, Strasbourg, France

IT WAS LATE IN THE AFTERNOON WHEN MARKO RETURNED FROM THE FEDEX OFFICE WITH JUST A BAG OF CHINESE FOOD. Working on a shoestring budget with no official backup, the two former members of the Serb Volunteer Guard improvised their mission at every turn. After taking the hasty pictures of Rita, Marko had to find a photo shop that could process the images within a few hours and, once done, sort them and send them overnight to Belgrade.

Drago snatched the bag away from his partner. "I say that we should have killed her when we had the chance. The boss would have wanted it that way."

Marko wanted to change the subject. "Eat your food. You've done enough damage today. Once you're done, get rid of the bike."

"We should go over there and rape the shit out of her and then kill her," Drago responded.

"Will you just shut up? I've had enough of you for one day. If you wanted her dead, you should have killed her the first time when you so bravely killed her family. We wouldn't be here in this shit hole if you had followed orders in the first place. That family was not to be touched, and you knew it. Eat your fucking food. I don't want to hear about it again. We are not going anywhere. Drop it!"

Drago felt chided but did as he was told, and stuck his nose into the fried rice like a horse eating from a nosebag.

After a few minutes of chomping at the rice and noodles, the phone rang. Marko picked up. As he recognized the voice on the other line, he stood up to attention. "Yes, Arkan, I can confirm that we have spotted the target in question, and I can confirm the identity."

Drago stopped what he was doing, but rice dropped from his agape mouth. He could not believe that Arkan Raznatovic, leader of the Serb Volunteer Guards, was in a conversation with Marko.

"Yes, sir. I have sent a package to you today, and it will arrive sometime in your office around midday tomorrow. How shall we proceed?"

Drago tried to do his best to listen in, but he couldn't hear a word from the other side of the phone. After a few more "yes sirs" and "no sirs," Marko finally hung up. He looked over to his partner in crime. I'm leaving for Norway tonight. You are staying here." He pointed across the street to Rita's apartment. "Arkan thinks she is heading for him with a team of assassins. If you ask me, he's bat-shit crazy, but what the hell do I know? He wants me there to ID her if she shows up."

"What the hell am I supposed to do?"

"Go get drunk, sleep, pick up a whore. I don't give a shit. Just keep an eye on the place until I get back."

# DAY 9
## Heathrow Airport, London, United Kingdom

Chris tried his best to be as nonchalant as possible as he waited his turn in the immigration line at Heathrow Airport. He could have easily taken a separate line for European passport holders, but he thought it would be nicer for Pam to have some company, as being an American she had to present a form and answer a few questions from the immigration officer before she was allowed passage into the UK. As Chris looked around, he tried to avoid looking directly at the overt CCTV cameras, but he knew that it would be an exercise in futility as there were as many covert cameras dotted around the arrivals hall. He also surmised that there were probably stacks of hidden microphones scattered amongst the ceiling tiles and support structures in the huge space, all devices monitored by numerous watchers and listeners diligently waiting for a misspoken word or phrase or for a familiar pattern or face that would be profiled, analyzed, scanned, and filed for future or direct use.

Immediately to the front of the line of visitors and placed behind the row of immigration officers was an elevated room in plain sight with one-way mirrors that looked over the huddled mass before it like a sentinel guarding a portal. Chris wondered how many eyes behind those mirrors were looking directly at him.

"Are you together?" the immigration officer asked.

"Yes," Chris answered. He was determined to keep his responses short and sweet. Years of experience had taught him when travelling to give only yes or no answers and not to get trapped into a discussion that could be manipulated into something else. He had briefed Pam on this before, and she always took his lead.

The immigration officer made a cursory scan of Chris's UK passport and handed it back to him. "Thank you."

He then took Pam's US passport and entry form, and as he began his scan, the officer surreptitiously placed his right foot on a pedal hidden on the floor under the desk. The signal alerted the watchers in the booth behind the mirrored glass.

"And what is the purpose of your visit, Ms. Corbin?"

"I am visiting my boyfriend's family for Christmas," she replied.

He continued looking at his computer screen while pressing the mouse button, "And where will you be staying while you are here?"

"With his family in Marlborough."

"And how long will that be?"

"Five days." True to Chris's instructions, Pam was blunt and to the point. But she was uncomfortable being there and wanted to get moving.

The officer offered a thin smile. "Well, I'm sorry we don't have any snow for you, Ms. Corbin, but please enjoy your stay."

Pam picked up her passport and smiled back. "Thank you. Happy Christmas."

"Yes, thank you and happy Christmas." He raised his hand, the transaction was over, and he barked, "Next!" while turning his attention on the next set of unwashed visitors.

As Pam began stashing both passports into her handbag, Chris spotted a door opening and a tall lanky man exit from the mirrored guard post. Chris noted that the man, although not in uniform, carried an ID badge around his neck on a lanyard. Chris gently grabbed Pam's hand and made to walk away, but he had the distinct feeling the badge guy was heading in his direction. Chris turned his back on him.

"Mr. Morehouse?"

Chris turned to face the man but did not say a word.

"Inspector Smith, UK Immigration Service." He held up his badge to prove his credentials. "May we have a word?"

"What's this about?"

"Just a little chat. If you please, sir, just this way." Smith was officious but polite and gestured back to the door that he previously appeared from. "You too, Ms. Corbin, if you don't mind?"

If Chris was worried, he did not show it. However, as the trio entered through the door, they were met by a uniformed member of the service who tagged along behind the group, which put Chris on alert. Something was wrong.

"I hope that we don't lose our bags while we are in here," he exclaimed to no-one in particular.

Smith answered, "It's fine. No need to worry; we are taking care of it. You'll have them waiting for you when we're done. You'll be on the way home soon enough."

*Fricking ambush!* Chris thought, *They knew we were coming, knew where we were going. This wasn't random. This shit stinks.*

As they navigated their way through the labyrinth of corridors and doors, they were finally shepherded into a small interview room where they were told by Smith to make themselves comfortable and relax. Pam took a seat, but Chris paced the room. When they made eye contact with each other, they knew instinctively that the best course of action was to remain silent.

After a few minutes of going around in circles in the room, Pam gestured for him to sit. She could tell he was getting wound up and probably cooking up a thousand what-if scenarios. Chris grudgingly complied, and as he sat next to her, he placed his hand on hers.

"Are we having fun yet?" Pam asked.

Chris smirked, "Yes. I hate to tell you this, but this is going to be the highlight of our trip."

"Is there something I should know?" she continued.

"No, I have no idea of what is going on. Let's just be patient." He willed her to stop asking any more. It was quite likely the room was bugged and they were probably being watched. He had nothing to hide, but he wasn't one for talking openly about his work, especially to immigration officials.

Although Pam was reassured by his words, deep down she had a fear that he was not the subject of the pending chat and she was. This was not the way she wanted him finding out about Primal Ocean; actually, she didn't want him finding out at all. After a few minutes of silence, she leaned over to him and rested her head on his shoulder. "I love you." She meant what she said, but it was also an act of insecurity. She wanted to maintain the pretense that he was the one in danger and she was just along for the ride.

"I love you too, honey," he responded genuinely. "Don't worry. We'll be out of here soon enough."

After another ten minutes of sweating it out, the only door to the room opened, and in walked the uniform followed by another man with Smith trailing behind. Chris's instinct took over immediately. He knew straightaway this was a person of authority, and it was confirmed when the man sat opposite Chris across the table from him while Smith and the uniform stood close behind.

"Mr. Morehouse . . . may I call you Chris?"

Chris wanted to take the upper hand. He didn't appreciate being cornered like this He knew what type of person this was just from his upper-class snobbish aristocratic tone. "I hate to be a bother old chap, but I really need to go to the toilet. I do hope this won't take long," he said imitating a Hugh Grant character, mimicking his opponent.

"No not at all, old boy," replied the snob. "We'll get you out of here in a jiffy."

"You see, it's my time of the month, and well, it's kind of embarrassing, but I don't have anything to stick up my crotch right now, so if we can speed things up, I won't bleed all over your nice floor."

The uniform coughed and smiled. Smith turned to him and gave him the evil eye and motioned for him to get out.

Pam wanted to crawl under the table. She smiled but looked like a TV comedian trying to keep composure after a funny joke or act that was out of sequence.

The man opposite Chris did not look happy. He had a face of stone and didn't appreciate being embarrassed in front of underlings, and he certainly didn't appreciate Chris's pub humor. When the door finally closed behind the uniform, a stalemate silence ensued as both Chris and the aristocrat stared each other down.

Chris knew he shouldn't do it, but he couldn't resist; he wanted the guy to crack and to de-escalate the unknown situation he was in. He turned to Pam. "Do you have a tampon? I'll give it back to you when I'm done, honestly."

Pam put her hand to her mouth to hide her laugh but thought, *Shut up, Chris. You're making this worse than it is.*

"Interesting. So you are the flippant one." The aristocrat emphasized *you are* as if to drive home a point as he stared impassively across the table. "Unlike your brother, though, but he's more the physical type, isn't he?"

Chris quickly shutdown his comedic act at the mention of his only brother.

"I'm sure there is more than one police officer in Marlborough who has received a broken bone or bruise from him. He does like to swing his fists after a few drinks, doesn't he, Chris?"

Chris paused and let silence rule for a few seconds as he quizzed the eyes of the furtive man in front of him but then countered, "So which type are you, one of the Eaton boys that shoved broomsticks up each other's arses? Or were you one of those that was rogered by his daddy and all his pals after a good game of polo while mummy sipped tea in the flower garden?"

Although relieved to find that Chris was the target, Pam was beginning to bore daggers into the man's skull for attacking her man as the
pissing contest continued. She had no idea that Smith was watching her
every move, every motion, or lack thereof. He stood there in the
background, hands deep into his pockets not saying a word.

"You have no idea of whom you are talking to, do you?"

"I don't give a flying fuck if you are the Lord of Fartbottom Manor
or the stable boy that cleans donkey dicks. What do you want from
me?"

Without a word, the upperclassman pushed his chair slightly away
from the table, reached into his suit breast pocket, and retrieved a silver
cigarette case. He then pulled out an expensive lighter from another
pocket and lit his cigarette.

"Sir, I'm afraid there's no smoking in here," Smith stated sheepish-
ly.

The aristocrat ignored him, remained silent, and crossed one leg
over a knee. He drew in a sharp pull from the cigarette, obviously in
deep thought. "I am here to give you some advice, no, let's call it what
it is. I am here to tell you something, and you need to listen to what I
have to say. Let's cut the child's play, shall we?"

Chris conceded, sat back in his chair, and folded his arms in front
of him. Time to switch on. "Who are you?"

"My name is George St. Clair, Her Majesty's Security Service."

*Ah, that explains some things. MI5. Okay, interesting. Where is this going?*
Chris thought.

"We know who you work for and," he briefly glanced towards Pam,
"of course, you Ms. Corbin; however, your friend here is my concern."

Pam stared back at the man without saying a word. Her eyes were
giving nothing away, but the hate and disgust were building inside. He
reminded her of a smooth-talking 1920s gangster with his slick back
hair and expensive clothes. His watch and a gold ring were probably
genuine, and he had the air and attitude of expecting and always
getting everything he wanted. She could tell that Smith was scared of
him, and she bet he was a viper, a predator, an enemy.

St. Clair continued to stare at Chris. "The CIA has no business conducting surveillance operations in this country, and that means you, Morehouse. I am here to tell you, to warn you that you are not to undertake any covert operations on behalf of the Americans while you are here. You are a British citizen and a former soldier. As such, you are a subject of the Crown, and may I remind you, in case your judgement is a little clouded right now, you are still bound by the Official Secrets Act. You are not an American, and you will not be protected by them. Do you understand what I am saying?"

Chris didn't appreciate the condescending tone. "Last time I checked, the British government does not pay my checks. So you can get off your high horse and stop ordering me what to do. I have no intention of doing any kind of work while I am here and nor will I ever." He didn't need to explain himself, and he should have kept his mouth shut, but when Chris was riled up, he usually let rip. "It was one of the stipulations that I set out when I went under contract with them. So I suggest if you want to make this more formal, I'll give you the number for the American embassy, and you can take it up with them because this is way too much drama for me. This sounds like some petty bullshit someone's having a wet dream over, and if there's some kind of political or intelligence agenda or it's all part of The Game, as you wankers like to call it, that I am unaware of, keep me the fuck out of it!"

"Well, we are concerned as to where your loyalties lie. . . ."

Chris almost burst a blood vein in his head and screamed at St. Clair, "Loyalty? You're fucking kidding me, right? What the fuck do you know about that? Where were you when I was pulling my mate's dead body out of a tree in Northern Ireland? Where were you when the acid and petrol bombs were maiming us on the streets of Belfast? What were you doing while we were dying and getting the shit kicked out of us, sucking your mum's little tits or hiding under the stairs with Winnie the Pooh? You fucking cunt, don't ever talk to me about loyalty."

Pam reached over and touched his forearm in an effort to calm him down. She didn't often see this side of him, and she preferred not to when he was in a rage, but she could understand where he was coming from.

"Nobody is questioning your actions in Northern Ireland, Chris, and I apologize for angering you. I meant no disrespect. But you have to understand where I am coming from. You are not an American, and the way you are going, if you were to undertake activities while you were here, it would result in grave consequences for you and your family." St. Clair could tell that Chris wanted to scream some more but never gave him the chance; he continued, "Mark my words, Chris, one day the Americans will turn their back on you, they will not come to your rescue, and if you pursue any type of activity here, neither will we. You are jeopardizing your status as a citizen of this country."

"Are you deaf? I said I wasn't going to do any work while I was here." The thought of abandonment by the Americans had crossed his mind more than once in the past while working on the Viewpoint program. He was super sensitive to his own security; he never took risks that could land him in jail, and he depended on Nash to bail him out if he ever got caught. But what St. Clair was saying was worrisome, and in the back of his mind, Chris thought there was some truth to it. "This has nothing to do with my family, so you can stop that shit right now!"

"On the contrary, it has everything to do with them." St. Clair said with a smirk. "Terry, for example, has such a violent temper it would not take too much for him to wind up in prison for the rest of his life, or if he met his match one day. . . ."

Chris thought that everyone in the room could hear his heart stop. He blinked twice; three times he looked for salvation from Smith. *What did he just say? He can't say that, can he?* He felt his mouth slowly opening but fought back his physical motions. Again a pause, but the MI5 man dug the blade deeper. "Did you know your father made a lot of enemies before he passed away?"

Chris had no wit left. Almost exhausted, he asked, "What, what are you talking about?"

"Well, while he was a prison officer, he was often accused of mistreating prisoners, and a rumor went around that during one riot he was actually responsible for a few deaths. In actual fact, some of those who survived are still serving terms. Now I wouldn't want you or Terry to wind up in the wrong place at the wrong time, and I would hate for some kind of happenstance to occur where you would come across such individuals such as those who cherished your father?" St. Clair jabbed.

The blade was hurting. Chris sat dumbstruck. Pam was in shock. Smith was pretending he hadn't heard what he had and prayed the recording device in the room was switched off.

"Which reminds me, I understand your mother is living comfortably with the remains of your father's pension. I would hate for that to somehow disappear, you know, with all the bureaucratic nonsense, cutbacks, and all that rubbish. I'm almost positive that there is a good solid, reliable Eaton chap in charge that would make sure something untoward would not happen to your mother's finances. But let's not dwell on that, shall we?"

Chris was beaten, spent. St. Clair had pushed his buttons and won wholeheartedly. The threats were real, and there was no way to combat the power and authority this man obviously had. It seemed he had the ways and means to make anything happen. But what Chris couldn't figure out was why St. Clair delivered this warning. There were no Viewpoint activities in the UK that Chris was aware of, but if there were, he wouldn't be involved; Nash had promised.

St. Clair wasn't done, and his arrogance and air of an untouchable surfaced again as he turned his attention to Pam. "Ms. Corbin, I do hope you enjoy your stay while you are here, but the warning goes for you also. Please do not conduct any extracurricular activities for the ICC while you are in our country. You do not have a work visa, and I would hate for you to be red-flagged for some misunderstanding at an airport for not having the correct documentation. . . ." He let the sentence hang but continued. "When one airline gets a sniff or a red flag warning for a passenger, the information spreads like wildfire. The next thing you know, you can't get on a plane in Greece or some other godforsaken country. You understand how that goes, I think?"

Pam shuddered. *Holy shit, that cunning bastard. This was about me. He knows of Primal Ocean. What the hell just happened?*

Chris saw that Pam was jolted by the remark, which surprised him. He could tell that she wasn't expecting to be a target, but he was nonetheless curious since he was the one under fire and scrutiny. He didn't have time to dwell, as Pam calmly responded in a professional and diplomatic manner.

"Thank you, Mr. St. Clair. I was never intending to work here in the UK, but you never know. Scotland Yard is extremely helpful in our investigations, and from time to time, they ask me to visit, but I have never had the chance. I was not aware of the requirements for a work visa so thank you for bringing that to my attention. I don't want to break any rules or regulations, especially with all the travel I do. You never know where I will be sent next, and no offence, the last place I want to end up is an interview room like this. I think you need some decorations in here or something to liven it up, just a picture or two, you know."

"I quite agree with you, Ms. Corbin. It does need freshening up, such a dreary place. But I am sure we won't be seeing you in here again. . . . Now, I think we are done here, and we can all go about our business of enjoying the holidays."

Chris was mute and just stared blankly at St. Clair.

"If you're still looking for feminine products, Chris, I am sure Smith here will oblige."

Smith stared silently at the back of the MI5 officer's head in contempt wanting only to shout out "prick" to the man.

Chris still did not say a word.

"I didn't think so. . . . Well, happy holidays, old chap. Say hello to mummy for me, won't you?"

As St. Clair got up to leave, he brushed away the remnants of ash from two cigarettes, sure that Smith would find someone to clean up his mess. As he approached the door to leave, he turned back to Chris and said, "Oh, and one last thing, Chris, from time to time clerical mistakes happen all the time. It was fine when we had a typing pool and lots of girls to type everything up that was said, etc. You could really rely on them to get things right the first time. But now with these new computers, things seem always to get missed, sometimes even on army records, you know, when it says honorable discharge instead of dishonorable or vice versa. And those men that were killed in Northern Ireland by the armed forces, the families are still looking for the soldiers that did it. . . ." He let the words hang like a straining guillotine. "I'm not saying anything, in particular; you've just got to be careful nowadays is all I am trying to say. Well, that's all. Must run. Have a merry, merry Christmas, won't you?"

Chris jumped up from his chair. "You fucking twat."

But it was too late. St. Clair was out the door, and Smith was blocking his way. "Okay, mate, take it easy. It's no good; he's gone."

Chris turned back to Pam and kicked over the chair he'd been sitting in. "Have you ever met such an arsehole in all your life?" he asked Smith.

"Chris, calm down," Pam said. "He's gone. Let it go. We can talk about this later."

But Chris was livid. He wanted to rip St. Clair's head off and shit down his neck. "Jesus Christ, what a prick."

Pam grabbed his hand. "Okay, okay, I get it. Let's get out of here. Let's go."

Smith chimed in miserably, "I'm sorry, mate. I had no idea. I've never met the guy before. I just had to follow his lead. I didn't know anything about this, really."

Chris understood. He knew Smith was there just because he was on duty that day. If it hadn't been him, it would have been another inspector doing the same thing. It was just a job.

His head throbbing and blood pressure off the charts, Chris stormed off. He was brooding to himself, but he wanted blood. *This is not the way to start a holiday. I was supposed to be engaged by now. I fucked that up, and now my girlfriend thinks I'll end up in jail and she'll be deported. What a wanker! I am a complete wanker! I am so fucking useless!*

Pam held Chris's hand but remained silent as Smith led them out. Now was not the time to console or question him. She was dealing with her own issues and beginning to question how the Brits knew about Primal Ocean. She needed desperately to speak to Crauford, but that was not going to happen anytime soon. *How did the Brits know? Did Crauford tell them? Is it common knowledge within MI5 or MI6?* She had no answers, but she was more concerned with Chris right now, as she could tell he was slipping.

The problem for Chris was that he believed in the rule of law. Those he met in law enforcement were like a brotherhood and there to uphold the law, and he felt a part of that in some distant equation. He didn't care much for politics and didn't identify with any party. He had never voted in his life, and he wasn't about to. He didn't care who a country's ruler was—black or white, gay or straight—as long as the law was upheld and corruption and intimidation were quashed. Chris realized too late that St. Clair was a shadow in MI5 that allowed him to interpret the rule of law when it came to the security of the state but obviously operated in areas that were unconventional and probably garnered big results. Those in the power seats of government knew that men like St. Clair existed but never crossed them for fear of retribution, retaliation, or a stab in the back at an inopportune time. Chris knew that people like the slime he had just encountered resided in dark, dingy basements and were dragged into service with a bag of dirty tricks to get things done, no matter what the consequences and no matter who the victim. The young Brit was not naïve, and he thought it was probable the Americans had teams of schemers too lying in wait in dungeons far below the CIA and FBI. But Chris thought St. Clair was like J. Edgar Hoover, a man who loved to bring the fear and the power of the government to the table without question, without recourse at any time and at any place. For a second, he wondered where Nash figured into the same equation. How much did he deceive and plot?

# CHAPTER NINE

## DAY 10

## Reading Moto Services, M4, United Kingdom

CHRIS SAT OPPOSITE PAM AT A TABLE IN THE COSTA COFFEE SHOP AT THE READING M4 MOTORWAY SERVICES. He supported his heavy head in the palm of his right hand, which was fixed in place by his elbow at the edge of the table. He looked despairingly in front of him as he thought about his encounter at Heathrow the day before. Sometimes he felt sorry for himself; other times he wanted to smash his head into a wall. Sometimes he thought he could hear the nails in his own coffin; other times he had a brilliant plan to get himself out of his melancholy mood. He was on a roller coaster that was on fire, and he didn't really care if anyone took notice or not.

To Pam, it looked as if Chris's hand would swallow his face whole. His features contorted as if he was trying to dive into a deep hole. *If he keeps his face in his hand much longer, he is going to need surgery to pull them apart,* she mused. Her hope was he wouldn't find his way to a bar, a beer, a fight.

They sat there for another ten minutes in silence as Chris contemplated going all football hooligan and Pam deliberating on how to rescue him before it was too late. She continued to stare into his distant brown eyes when she saw a moment of spark, a recognition of something in him that made him perk up.

Chris kept his face jammed into his hand but made eye contact with Pam. With a quick fleeting glance across her right shoulder, she knew the person they had come to meet had arrived. As planned, Chris extricated himself from the uncomfortable plastic chair and walked away from the table and headed for the door. He hated exposing Pam while he practiced his trade, but this was an exceptional circumstance, and they were on relatively safe ground. When first Chris proposed his plan to her the night before, she played the part of skeptic well, disguising her vengeful mood all the while milking a passive, gushing "you're my hero" act. While Chris talked, the gears in her head clunked forwards and backwards contriving a plan of her own.

Pam sat alone at the coffee shop table for what she estimated was ten minutes when Chris reappeared in front of her soaking wet from yet another British downpour. He did not say a word as he took off his jacket. When he finally settled back down into the uncomfortable plastic chair, the man whom they came to meet placed a tray with a cup of black coffee on the table next to them, smiled, and said, "Chris, I know when we first met I was a rookie and I didn't know my ass from my elbow, but don't you think I would have learned to spot a tail by now?"

"I know, I know. I'm a little jumpy after yesterday's mess. Just being cautious." He awkwardly replied.

"Hi, Pam. How you holding up?"

"I'm good, Nick." She smiled back at the young, confident, good-looking man.

Nick Seymour tried to engage Chris, but he was busy scanning the horde of travelers who used the motorway service station and were dashing to and fro to get out of the rain. The last thing he wanted was for St. Clair to walk in flanked by another Smith, but he had to face the fact that the likelihood of that happening was improbable.

Pam reached across the table and held his hand, which broke Chris of his robotic moves. "Holy shit, Chris, this guy's has you really spooked."

"What do you have for me, Nick?"

"What, no pleasantries?" he snorted. "No 'Hi, Nick. How are you? Thanks for doing this, Nick. I really appreciate the FBI helping me out here'?" Or even, "'I owe you one, Nick. By the way, how're the wife and kids, Nick?'" The snotty but justified response hung in the air. Seymour continued and scowled at Chris, "I don't hear from you in months, and you call me up asking—no, wait a minute—demanding information on an MI5 officer? You know, like what the hell, Chris? But you're probably right." Nick threw his hands up in exasperation. "I am bored with my job, my career, my reputation. And you are right about another thing—I do want to push a broom in Leavenworth with my ass for the rest of my miserable life when I get caught giving you information on a career intelligence officer. How stupid of me to think I know what I am doing!"

Nick Seymour had come a long way in the FBI. The first time he and Chris met was in Cyprus at the US consulate where they talked about football and Twinkies but were later involved in a shootout at the hotel that they were staying in. Nick openly admitted that he shit his pants that day all the while Chris looked and acted the part of Steve McQueen. Over the years after Cyprus, they became good friends as Nick climbed the ranks of the FBI and eventually became the legal attaché at the US embassy in London.

"I'm sorry, Nick," Chris croaked. "It's been a day, you know. A factory full of aspirin won't cure this headache I've got. I really do appreciate you helping me out here, but this is personal. This guy has crossed the line, and I suppose that I am not on my best behavior."

Pam squeezed his hand and beamed him a warm smile. She was happy that he realized he was being abrasive. She had more than once been on the receiving end of an outburst in the hours after Heathrow.

"Okay, okay, let's not turn this into a Jerry Springer show and we all end up needing counselling or going on a retreat to find ourselves or some shit," Nick declared. "But here's a warning, Chris. Don't piss this guy off too much. He's connected all the way up the Yazoo! He's got some interesting history, but I am not going to go into that. You need to be very careful what you say and do with him." Seymour understood the question behind Chris's quizzical look. "No, don't ask me for details, Chris. It's more than my job's worth. I'll give you the basics with a small bonus and that's it."

Chris nodded in respect and pondered what a small bonus was, but he first admitted to himself that, yes, he was lucky to have Nick as an ally and he had to be careful not to burn a bridge. He remained quiet.

Seymour wanted to help his friend, but he was restricted in what he could do. After the phone call at the office the day before and the quick impromptu meeting an hour later, he scrambled to find out as much as possible about St. Clair without raising flags all over town. He read more than he thought was prudent and scribbled a note down and that was it. He was taking a liberty with his position and possibly damaging the hospitality that the British so keenly bestowed to their American cousins.

After gauging Chris's poor, gloomy demeanor, Seymour thought it was time to leave. There wasn't going to be any group hugs, which was fine with him. "As you Brits say, I'm going to bugger off now. Try to have a happy Christmas, but take my last piece of advice with you. Leave this prick alone." He stared directly into Chris's eyes and hoped that he got the message. "Don't be a stranger, Chris, and Pam, you have my permission to slap him upside the head if he gets out of hand." Seymour got up to leave. "You can take care of my tray for me, right?"

Chris ran a hand over a tired face and contemplated what Nick had said. He wanted to get up but felt too tired to move. He blurted out a weak "thanks, Nick" at Seymour's back. Nick was headed for the door and raised his hand in a wave without turning around. Pam reached across to the tray that was left behind, and as she slid it toward her, an envelope appeared from underneath.

## DAY 10
### InterContinental Hotel Lobby, Frankfurt, Germany

"Excuse me sir, but do you know what a vacation is?"

Gene carried on reading the newspaper not needing to look up to see who asked the question; he recognized Robert Crauford's voice immediately. "Like the ones you take all the time, you mean?" he countered.

"Seriously, Gene, when was the last time you took time off? You look like shit."

Gene stopped reading, folded the newspaper, and dropped it onto the coffee table in front of him. "I appreciate the compliment, but take a seat, Bob."

As Crauford placed himself in a comfy lounge chair opposite Gene, he continued the harmless chatter while taking in his surroundings. "Where you headed anyway?"

"Believe it or not, I am meeting my kids in Switzerland. I'm going skiing for Christmas."

That brought a smile to Crauford's face. He was relieved to hear that Gene was, at last, taking a break. "That's great, Gene. I think you deserve to spend some time with them. You need to take advantage of that, go break a leg or something, milk the system a bit. Why not?"

"Yeah, I know, I know. They are growing up too quick. I wish I could see them more often."

The two old friends continued to chat about each other's personal lives for a while longer as the hotel waiter hovered nearby picking up empty coffee cups and small plates.

Just before Gene got down to business, a flight crew from Singapore Airlines entered the lobby followed by another crew from Emirates Airlines. It was what Gene had hoped for, a natural-looking meeting at a busy traveler's hotel. The sound of multiple roller bags and a disharmony of different languages in the large hotel atrium drowned out any possible means of sound recording or even close surveillance. Crauford was the first to nod recognizing that this was Gene's plan. He moved seats to sit next to Gene.

"Norway is off," Gene said. "It seems the target has gotten nervous. My team"—Gene didn't need to mention Viewpoint; Crauford knew—"has noticed increased security activity at his location, and it looks as if they are there to stay for a while."

Crauford nodded, but he was disappointed, as he knew that Arkan Raznatovic was considered a high-value target and more than one nation was waiting on the man's impending demise. Despite the news, Crauford wanted to appease his paymaster. "How many have shown up? We can take a few on, you know."

"It's too risky." Gene furrowed his brow and narrowed his eyes.

"The reports I have seen say at least eight guys have shown up in the last twenty-four hours, and who knows how many more will end up being there. I know you want to fulfill the mission, but we are going to have to shelve this one for now."

Crauford sat with both elbows on the armchair with his fingers forming a bridge under his chin as he listened, but he wanted to know more. "How soon, Gene? Everyone has been waiting for this one for a while."

"Bob, I know, but it's not up to me. Something got the guy spooked, and he's battening down the hatches. The chief says no go, so it's a no go!"

Crauford persisted, "But why now? What the hell happened that made him upgrade his security?"

Gene stared at his friend and colleague for a moment. He knew Crauford was smart, could come up with a hundred permutations and what-if scenarios, and wouldn't let it go. Gene didn't want to say any more, but he didn't have to.

"Did they somehow find out about Primal Ocean?"

Gene remained silent, a sign to Crauford that was a yes.

"Who the hell leaked?"

"I don't know, Bob, but it's possible we need to suspend operations for a while," he confessed. "There's a lot of shit happening that I don't know about, and we've got some nervous people on our end too." As the sounds of the hotel lobby started to quieten down a little, Gene leaned over to Bob and whispered. "There's a fear that a high-placed mole is active in Langley. I don't know what this means for you and the team, or even Viewpoint." Gene let things sink in. "Go take some time off yourself. Go home, go eat your baguettes, drink your French wine, and take a walk or two around Paris. For now, stand down."

## DAY 11
### Sunninghill and Ascot, United Kingdom

Chris and Pam finally found a vantage point at the edge of a tree line looking east towards the stately home of George St. Clair. The property was set back from the A329 Cascade Bridge Road and, as such, was inaccessible for first-line surveillance methods. Instead, Chris circled around the area until he found a parking spot at the nearby St. Michael and All Angels Church and a bridle path that led through a tree line and within yards of the MI5 man's house.

They both stood in silence as they watched from the safety of the trees looking for signs of security or anything that would either help or hinder with their undertaking. Pam could tell that Chris was lost in his own thoughts and probably thinking of ways in and around the home, judging best avenues of approach and exits, looking for cameras, alarms, and lighting, contemplating what he was going to say and what he was going to do.

While Pam was right about the functional part of Chris's survey, she had no idea of where his soul was taking him—his thoughts inevitably led back to what Pam was thinking of the mess that he had created. He thought she was probably second-guessing being there, wishing that she had never hooked up with him in the first place, wishing that she had stayed at home with his mother to watch the telly instead of being outside in the frigid cold.

Chris continued to examine the grounds of the property looking for opportunities while berating himself, *What arsehole brings his girlfriend on a job? I am such a fucking idiot. She probably hates me right now—it's fucking cold, and we're standing here like two fucking lemons.*

He turned around briefly to take in their immediate surroundings, but his act was to check on her body language. *What the hell is she thinking?* As he returned his gaze back to the house, he wanted her out of there. *She should go back to the car.* But instead of saying something, he concentrated on the target once again and tried to find the words to tell her to go.

Chris's perceived notions of what Pam was thinking was farther from the truth than he could have realized. She was also in mission mode. While Chris looked at the big picture of how to get in and get out, she was visualizing angles and distances. She had already found a solid lay-up in the trees for a crouched supported shot. Pam already knew what the wind indicators would be and her general landmarks. She would not need nor have a spotter, so she would formulate her own range card. She would probably use the ambush method of engagement instead of track and put her crosshairs out to where the target would cross while traversing an area of the front of the house. Gauging the short distance to the house and the lack of wind in the closed wooded environment, she would not need to compensate for wind drop or spin drift as the bullet left the muzzle. It could be an easy shot, but it would be much easier if she had a rifle.

Pam unnecessarily chided herself for wasting time on her favored method of assassination. She hoped that Chris didn't turn around too often to look at her, as she was loving being out there almost salivating over another potential kill. It was unfortunate that Rita was not available for the mission, which left Pam with two problems. The first, she needed to spend more time on the target's house to get an understanding of his behavior and daily routine, which was her friend's specialty. Besides the obvious lack of any armament, the second problem was time. She racked her brain to try to find a solution for the challenges she faced, but she wasn't getting anywhere, and to top things off, she realized she had another issue to deal with: how could she get away from Chris?

Chris was becoming uncomfortable. They had been in the same spot for too long. Although they were in a relatively concealed position from the house, he was more worried about horse riders and dog walkers appearing on the well-beaten bridle path. It was one thing to pretend to be out for a country stroll, but to remain in place staring at someone's property was out of the ordinary and out of place. He was also very much aware that he didn't have a team of Viewpoint operators watching his back or monitoring the surrounding area. He had nobody to communicate with or ask for help. If he didn't make a move soon, either to back off or move forward, he risked being compromised and thus failing his mission.

"Do you want to go back to the car?"

Pam felt disappointed by the question and didn't know if he was giving up. "Do you?"

"No." He paused for a second. "You don't need to be here for this. I can take care of it."

Although he didn't say very much Pam noticed that his tone was solemn but concerning. She could tell he was at odds with himself. "Don't underestimate me, Chris. I'm a big girl. I know what I am doing."

Chris nodded slowly but didn't say a word. He should have shown some gratification, but he was feeling tired, worn, fatigued. His shoulders began to slump as he questioned his motives once again. He was appreciative beyond words that he was getting support from Pam, but he didn't want to put her in danger. There was still time to turn back.

They stood in silence for a few moments more, staring at the house in front of them. Now and again, a slight wind blew through the bare high canopy of trees. Leaves rustled on the ground below; it was the sound of nature killing the ultimate silence that should have been a perfect winter's day. From time to time, a small murder of crows circled above the couple and landed on the safe territory of the branches to caw in solo and in chorus that strangers were in the woods.

When the crows finally silenced their noisy racket, a peaceful quiet developed where nothing stirred, save the distant sound of traffic from the roads around the area. Patient as statues, Pam and Chris stood in silence, each contemplating his or her roles and actions to come. They both spotted a movement to the left of them in the open space between the tree line and the house. The shape was low to the ground and trotting like a small dog. The red and white tail gave away the mystery.

*Shit, a fox*, Chris thought. *Someone may be chasing it. We may need to bag this and get out of here.*

*That's all the incentive I need!* Pam thought.

"Nobody fucks with my man!" she blurted and stormed off in the direction of George St. Clair's house.

# CHAPTER TEN

## DAY 11

## Sunninghill and Ascot, United Kingdom

THE VERY MOMENT THEY BROKE THE PROTECTION OF THE TREE LINE, a vehicle approached the house on the driveway coming off the main road. Chris didn't know if they had been spotted by a very covert security team or this was St. Clair coming home from an outing. Pam was two strides in front of him marching across the sodden grass as if she owned the land. He upped his pace and caught up with her quickly.

"Thanks for the push."

"Don't mention it, but get your shit together. You know you need to be on your game with this guy."

As Chris walked beside Pam, he looked over in admiration. It was the first time she had taken the initiative and the first time she had told him what to do. It was the confidence boost that he needed.

As they came within a few yards of the tan colored driveway, Chris realized the vehicle approaching was the quintessential country carriage of the gentry in this part of England, a Range Rover. The slightly tinted windows of the Rover gave Chris an uneasy feeling that this was a security vehicle and the cops were about to arrest them for trespass, but as they came within feet of each other, he recognized St. Clair at the steering wheel and a woman, presumably his wife, sitting in the passenger seat. Chris's initial plan of grabbing St. Clair by the balls and kicking his head in changed when he saw the woman speaking to the man in a "who the hell is this" type of discussion.

The Range Rover slowed to a halt, and the driver's window silently dropped down. "Christopher, this is a surprise. What brings you to these parts?" The wily fox showed no fear or shock by the unexpected encounter. Either St. Clair was a professional in hiding from his female companion that he and Chris were colleagues or friends, or there was no need to be worried, or he had something else up his sleeve and was waiting to pounce at the right opportunity. Chris knew whatever he said or did, he could not let his guard down or put any trust in the man.

"Pam has some long-forgotten roots in the area, and we thought that since it goes way back in time that her great-great-grandfather may be buried at St. Michaels we'd pay a visit."

"Oh my goodness, how delightful," the woman in the car claimed.

"Yes, quite," St. Clair added but thought, *What a bunch of horseshit.*

"I'd love to hear more about it, darling. Wouldn't you like to introduce me?"

"Oh how rude of me, of course." *Fuck!*

"Christopher Morehouse, may I have the pleasure of introducing my wife, Penelope St. Clair," he piped. "And that young lady is Ms. Pamela Corbin. Her father is the late Senator Robert Corbin of Michigan."

"It's a pleasure to meet you both. Why not come up to the house? We can chat some more."

"Yes, let me park the car, and we can chat if you have time, that is," added St. Clair. *Or fuck off would be nicer.*

"Yeah, I'd love to chat actually. Go ahead. We'll be right behind," Chris stated almost too enthusiastically.

As they reached the parked Range Rover, Penelope was opening the trunk to reveal a dozen bags of groceries and Christmas decorations, of which she was grabbing a few handfuls. Chris and St. Clair were staring each other down like two cowboys at high noon.

Pam once again took the initiative. "Oh, let me help you there."

"Why thank you, dear. I think the boys need to chat, so let's leave them in peace, and you come and tell me about your ancestors. I find that sort of thing simply fascinating. You Americans do love tracing your heritage, don't you?"

George St. Clair glared at Chris and waited until the women had walked into the house. "Follow me!" he hissed. St. Clair turned away and punched his hands deep into his pockets and bowed his head as if in deep thought. Chris obeyed and marched two steps behind the MI5 officer.

Penelope St. Clair was placing as many bags as possible on the kitchen table as Pam took in her new surroundings. "This is a beautiful kitchen, Mrs. St. Clair."

"Thank you, Pamela, but please call me Penny. I do hate being so formal. George, on the other hand, well, he is a little more of a traditionalist with those sorts of things."

Pam nodded all the while scoping out her immediate area for possible advantages and angles for attack. "Pam, most people call me Pam."

"How dare you! How dare you come to my home! What the hell do you think you are doing?" St. Clair led Chris to the back of the two-car garage, and as he turned the corner, he got right up into Chris's face. A shovel was leaning against the garage within St. Clair's reach. Chris dropped his knees slightly and shifted his right foot back a few inches anticipating a strike. "I just wanted to talk. I need to clear the air with you."

"Talk about what? You have nothing worthwhile to say to me, nothing I want to hear." St. Clair was agitated, his eyes were straining to stay in their sockets, and the skin on his neck was flushing red.

Chris surmised that St. Clair was not one for physical confrontations, easy to overcome if it came to it.

St. Clair continued his barrage. "I thought I made my stance pretty clear with you. You are standing on dangerous ground with me. You do NOT—I repeat, DO NOT!—want to fuck with me. Do you understand, or are you so stupid that I totally misunderstood you?"

After finally retrieving the remainder of the shopping from the Range Rover, Pam followed Penny into the dining room to place the Christmas decorations on the dinner table. Again, she looked for opportunities, possible entry and exit points.

"So tell me about your great-great-grandfather. You believe he was buried here?"

"Yes, it is possible," Pam lied. "He came over during the First World War and never returned. He died of a heart attack apparently, and his wife decided to bury him in England. So here we are, doing a bit of digging, if you excuse the pun." She knew it was flimsy, but she was working on the fly. Pam wanted to change the subject and strolled around the room as Penny was sorting through her bags.

Chris tried to dial back the confrontation with St. Clair and spoke with an even, controlled voice, "Listen, I don't know why you have a grudge against me. I've done nothing wrong, and I have no intention of working while I am here." Chris wanted to avoid being too guttural and drag the conversation into another pissing match. "If you've got some evidence suggesting that there's some kind of operation that's going on that involved my line of work, then you are mistaken. I am on holiday, and I am trying to switch off for a change. I'm sure I can find someone at the US embassy to confirm that for you."

St. Clair was still on his high horse. "I can't believe that you came here of all places. You've crossed a line. How the hell did you find me anyway?" St. Clair paused and realized what he just asked, but he was still perturbed. "Hmph. Forget I asked that." In the back of his mind he knew he would have to have a serious conversation with his department about this. He shook his head. "I gave you fair warning."

"Fair warning of what? You gave me shit!"

"Believe it or not, Chris, I am actually trying to help you."

"Are you taking the piss? Help me with what?"

As the conversation in the dining room moved to talk of Christmas and holiday plans, something caught Pam's eye in a display case lying on a side table near a window.

Penny caught Pam's glance and could tell she was intrigued. "Do you want to take a look?"

"May I? It looks remarkable."

Penny joined Pam at the small table, "It belongs to my niece Fiona. It's the Sword of Honour. She was presented it at Sandhurst when she graduated as a top officer cadet. She is only the second female officer to be awarded the title."

"Oh my gosh, that's amazing." Pam was genuinely impressed. "She's not here?"

"No she's overseas serving with the army. She is in the Royal Signals. We are just keeping it safe for her until she comes back. Her parents, my sister and her husband, passed away not so long ago."

"I'm sorry to hear that," Pam offered.

Penny opened the glass case. "Would you like to pick it up?"

St. Clair didn't care for Chris one bit. The MI5 officer had come across this type on more than one occasion, and he utilized men like Chris when the dogs of war needed to be unleashed. St. Clair looked at Chris with derision, with contempt, with loathing. *Why did I have to stoop so low to talk with this minion in the first place?* "You have no idea of what is going on, do you? You are so naïve, so blunt, so pathetic."

Chris's violent fantasies were about to boil over, but he kept himself in check.

"There is so much for you to learn, to understand, but I don't think a rabid dog like yourself can be trained. You are no more use than a muzzled hound. You can bark, but you can't bite."

Chris couldn't believe his ears. *Is this arsehole looking to get his head kicked in or what?*

"I suggest that you go back home, Chris, and reflect on your occupation of choice. You are playing with some influential people, and you don't even know the name of the game."

"You and you're fucking game. That's all I keep hearing. I'm not sure if you got the memo, asswipe, but the Cold War is over."

"Chris, you need to know that the game never stops. It never will, and the question you need to ask yourself is whose side are you really on?"

"Side? Jesus, I feel like we are back in school trying to decide whose team to be on for a football match. What are you talking about?"

"One day, Chris, mark my words, it may not be today or tomorrow, but the Americans will abandon you. You are a contractor, a nobody, nothing, just an expenditure on a bottom line, easily deniable, easily discarded."

Chris remained silent. He didn't know what to say.

"Wow, it's not as heavy as I expected."

"Well, it is, after all, a ceremonial sword."

"Yes, but it's exquisite." Pam held the sword in both her hands admiring the craftsmanship of the weapon. "You must be very proud of your niece?"

"Yes, we are simply over the moon with her. Not only is she very smart, but she is also just a beautiful girl. I just wish her mother could have been here to see her exceed and blossom the way that she has."

As Pam placed the sword back in the case, she could tell that Penelope St. Clair was so different from her husband and wondered what the attraction was between them.

"Hopefully, George will mount it above the fireplace for me during the holidays, but knowing him, he will be too busy with this or that."

"He's a busy man then?"

"Yes, quite. . . . We don't often get visitors from work out here. Did George invite you?"

Penny was fishing, and Pam knew to be careful. Penny was not the enemy. "Oh, I don't know what Chris is up to half the time myself. But I guess it was coincidental that we were looking for a graveyard and your house was so nearby."

Penelope St. Clair had learned a few things from her husband over the years. *Oh bullshit, my dear!*

"Look, I will be going back to Europe in a few days. I don't know what to say to you to convince you that I am not doing anything while I am here, but I'm not. I'm tired, pissed off, and I need a few beers at home with my family. Is that too much to ask for?"

"I'd much prefer it if you got the fuck off my property and took the next flight out with that whore of yours."

"What!"

"You heard me. You aren't the only one we consider as undesirable. Just piss off and don't come back."

Chris was beside himself. His knuckles were turning white, and his pulse was raised. *What the hell has Pam got to do with this?* He went into pre-attack mode and gauged the distance to the shovel and the body language of St. Clair for signs of weakness, but he held back; he maintained his composure. "You need to leave her out of this. . . . She has nothing to do with what's going on here. It's between you and me."

*Interesting, he really doesn't know, does he?* St. Clair stewed. "On the contrary old chap, I believe that she may have a secret or two herself."

Chris stored that little nugget of information to himself. "Oh, speaking of which," Chris saw an opening, "who is Henry Rawlings?"

St. Clair's face turned ashen grey. He looked like death warmed up and staggered back a few feet as if he'd been punched in the gut. "What?" he replied feebly.

"Henry Rawlings, Derrick Carver . . . Paul Bletchley?"

St. Clair was shocked, stunned, and for once, silenced.

"Oh, there you boys are. I hope that you are not up to no good. What are you chatting about?" Penny rounded the corner and saw the two men in deep conversation, but her husband looked fragile and sheepish. She needed to rescue him.

"Just gossiping about some old friends," Chris answered. "Perhaps you know a few of them?"

St. Clair's world was crashing in. *No, no, no, please no,* his mind begged.

Chris looked deep into the eyes of St. Clair. *Gotcha!* Chris realized that his revelation of George St. Clair's gay indiscretions could wait for another day, for another battle. "Ah, we can save that for another time. I'd love to fill you in on all the scandals from London, but I think it's time that we made our way."

"Yes, we must run as well. We are due at the country club shortly for lunch. I'd hate to be late. George? Are you okay? You look a little pale."

"I'm fine, dear, he mumbled, but his face told a lie.

"Well, perhaps a good gin and tonic will wake you up."

Chris saw the break that he was looking for. "Well, we'll love you and leave you. It was nice meeting you, Mrs. St. Clair. I hope to meet you again one day."

After both parties traded pleasant, if skeptical, goodbyes, Chris bounced off in the direction of the bridle path. This time, it was Pam who had to jog to catch up. When she did, she looked over at Chris. He was beaming.

"Well, he's not dead or on the way to the hospital. You managed to keep your cool after all."

"Yup, you'd be proud, and I think we can thank Nick Seymour for that."

# DAY 12 CHRISTMAS DAY
## Rue de Rome, Strasbourg, France

It was well after midnight when Rita exited the tram at the Palerme stop on the Rue de Rome. A heavy fog had descended on the city, which gave her surroundings an eerie feel, further haunted by the street lamps that gave off high cones of orange luminescent lights and dangerous overlapping shadows. A few cars traversed the streets as the mist that held the city captive drowned out the sounds of anything mechanical, but the sounds of her footsteps rang out like a shire horse with metal shoes on cobblestones.

Rita was finally heading home after a long day, which started by chasing mailboxes around the city. When she finally came up empty on her last two locations, she found a pay phone and dialed a messaging service. On finding nothing to listen to, she realized that the mission to Norway was no more. As time was now on her side, she decided to travel across the border to Germany and to the Black Forest to pick up an order from a shop that specialized in custom hunting knives.

While waiting at the Offenburg train station, curiosity got the better of her, and she dialed the messaging service again. Once more there was nothing to listen to, and after a brief pause, she called Pam for final confirmation. Disappointed that she heard only a beep and an order to leave a message, Rita hung up and finally resigned herself to the fact that it was going to be a lonely Christmas without much to do. She wondered what could have cancelled the mission, but as she was not part of the strategic planning of operations, she could find no viable resolution but racked her brain nonetheless. She felt a little sad because she wanted to be back in the field and part of the killing machine that Primal Ocean had become. She hoped that one day that she could be behind the scope and take the pleasure of executing a man in cold blood and get the revenge that she so richly deserved.

As she navigated her way past the Ressucitie Catholic Church, she shifted into high gear and became more attuned to her surroundings. She saw a few pedestrians and a cyclist in the vicinity but was not too worried. She knew that within the next twelve minutes she would be turning the key to her apartment door or, alternatively, fleeing down one of four pre-planned escape routes. Pam knew that Rita took her own security seriously, but now and again, she thought the young Bosnian was getting a little paranoid, a belief that she shared with Crauford. The discussion of Rita's security came up often in mission planning, and Crauford more than once considered relocating her closer to Pam or even moving her to Paris to live with him. As mission priorities were above personal issues, security of operatives was put on the backburner to be discussed another day. Rita was on her own.

Rita's suspicions became aroused as she passed through the parking lot of the high-rise block of apartments. As the fog thickened and magnified each and every sound, she thought she could hear someone in the distance singing. When she passed between a tennis court and a playfield, she realized with horror that she was right—someone was belting out a tune, but it wasn't the off-key sound that bothered her; it was the fact that a man was singing in Serbian.

Rita halted her stride. As her breathing and heartbeat thundered from her body, she thought she would wake up every resident in a five-mile radius. She spun in every direction trying to pinpoint from where the sounds were coming from to no avail. Beginning to hyperventilate, she thought she must have fallen asleep on the train coming back from Germany and this was a nightmare as the song kept tormenting her. Memories came flooding back of her home, her family, the fire. She fought back a tear and tried to bring herself under control. The shadows and the lack of proper light thwarted thoughts of plausible reasoning. She did not know what to do, but she grudgingly took a baby step forward towards the unknown.

Drago had done what he had been told, mostly. Although he did not get rid of the bike, he had found find a whore, and he had gotten drunk. In fact, he was drunk now cycling around Strasbourg singing his ass off, and he didn't care if the French liked it or not. When residents of one neighborhood shouted and screamed at him to shut up, he threw copious streams of verbal abuse back at them and rode on to another area with a bottle of rum to cause mayhem elsewhere. He finally found some playfields near a church and began having fun sprinting around the pathways on the bike, only to fall off in a heap and then laugh at himself and get back up to do it all again. He wasn't bored, but he needed to up his fun level, as the effect of his encounter with the sex worker was wearing off, and he still had boundless energy. When he stopped to take another swig of rum, he spotted a figure passing through the shadows. He cleared his throat and belted out his rendition of the Serbian national anthem and headed for the person of interest.

Rita finally got some response from her lead-weight thighs. She started moving and followed the map that she had ingrained in her mind. As she heard the racket behind in the distance, she knew she could not go back, but to reach safety, she had to cross a multipurpose sports field and crawl through a gap in the fence. She knew that once she was through, she had multiple avenues of escape to choose from. As she entered the playing field, she started to make a beeline towards the southwest corner and towards safety. She could not hear the singing anymore, and for a second, she thought she was overreacting and she was safe. But when her mind almost slipped back into neutral, a man on a bike came whizzing by almost hitting her from behind.

Drago had seen his prey enter the field and rushed to catch up. When he did, he childishly brushed past the figure and almost knocked the person over. It was only when he came to a halt in front of the person that he realized it was a woman. *Oh, yeah. Party time!* he thought. As he got off his bike, he attempted a conversation in very poor French. "Hey, baby, want to party? Where are you going so late?"

The woman remained mute.

The alcohol in his system was sloshing around so much that he wasn't completely in control of his faculties, and he stumbled a little as he made a move towards her. "What's wrong? You don't like me?"

Still no reply.

*What's wrong with this bitch?*

Rita took a small step backwards and slipped her right hand behind her back. She retrieved the single-edged knife from the leather case at the base of her spine. As she pulled the weapon out and upwards and away from her back, she transferred her grip to placing her thumb over the butt of the knife and at the same time twisting it so the spine of the knife was parallel to her wrist. She applied enough pressure with her deformed fingers that she could feel the point of the knife almost digging into her wrist, thus knowing it was firmly in place and ready for use. Her prayers had been answered. She'd practiced with kitchen knives and smaller tools for this very moment, and while she had fumbled and fumbled time and time again, she had trained her hands to the point that it became second nature, and today of all days, she now had a custom-made knife to defend herself.

Drago was extremely frustrated. He wasn't getting any response, and the woman was standing her ground. He slipped into Serbian. "Playing hardball, bitch? No problem. I like it rough, and don't worry; you'll like it too!" As he spoke, he saw the woman's eyes light up. It was as if she understood what he was saying. "Holy shit!" He dropped the bottle of rum. "It's you!"

Rita shook with revulsion. She had heard the voice before; she recognized the man.

After the few seconds of pause when Drago realized who was standing in front of him, he lost control and lunged forward with both hands. Rita let him grab her by the scruff as he moved in. When he made contact, she brought her left arm over his right arm and pushed his hands down to his left exposing his neck. With one swift movement of her right hand, she swept the blade from behind her back and slashed upwards towards his carotid artery.

Drago let go of Rita and slumped to his knees. Rita moved around to his left to get away from the arterial spray that launched three feet into the night air and then moved away quickly and silently for the gap in the fence. When she made it through, she was once again surrounded by the mist and silence of the sleeping city.

# CHAPTER ELEVEN

## DAY 14
## Marlborough, United Kingdom

CHRIS SAT ON HIS MOTHER'S COUCH WATCHING CHARTON HESTON and Yul Brynner going at it in *The Ten Commandments*. He'd seen the movie many times, but it seemed not enough according to the BBC. In its infinite wisdom, it had rolled out yet another biblical mega-movie to ensure British citizens could relieve the boredom and overindulgence of food by understanding how all things came to be. Chris was just about to hit the three-hour mark and was looking for something in the living room to poke in his eyes when his brother mercifully walked in.

"What the hell are you watching?"

"It's either this, reruns of *Doctor Who*, or "Come Dancing Christmas Special," and since I am not twinkle toes like you, this is the best option."

Terry planted himself next to his brother on the couch, "Where's Pam?"

"Upstairs with Mum. I think they want to go out somewhere. They're getting ready."

"You going to stay in, or you want to go for a pint?"

"Let's see what they're up to. Where do you want to go anyway?"

"Castle and Ball. There's a new girl behind the bar." Terry held his hands in front of his chest. "She's got the biggest pair of—"

"What are you two boys talking about now?"

"Nothing, Mom," they replied in unison.

Pam trailed close behind their mother and smiled at Chris knowing all too well they were up to no good.

"Pamela and I are going out to the Rugby Club for a game of bingo. Christopher, you can drop us off. You don't need to pick us up. We'll catch a taxi home."

"Yes, Mother. When do you want to go?"

"Now, Christopher, if you please."

"But *The Ten Commandments* are on. Terry wants to watch."

"Don't be flippant with me, young man. I'm not afraid to give a good clip around the earhole, no matter how tough Pamela thinks you are. On your feet. I want to get there before Mrs. Postlethwaite. That's another one who deserves a good lesson in manners, one of these days I will be forced. . . . "

Chris had no idea who Mrs. Postlethwaite was or what the beef was between them, but when it came to bingo etiquette at the Rugby Club, any deviations from propriety were a serious matter. He found the TV remote and killed Moses before his mother could explain why the lady deserved the death penalty. "Okay, okay, let's go, but I can tell Terry is disappointed with you, Mum."

"You'll both be disappointed when I knock both of your heads together. Terrance, get my coat, will you, dear?"

As the family walked out to the car, Chris grabbed Pam and held her a step back. "You okay with going to bingo with mum?"

"I'm excited. This is going to be fun."

Chris frowned. "Seriously?"

"Yes, I love bingo. I used to play with my aunts, but it's been years."

"We're going down to the Castle and Ball. It's a pub on the High Street. Call me if you need something." He gave her a peck on the cheek; it was the closest thing to a personal display of affection he would show with his mother nearby.

"Christopher, the car won't start by itself," she moaned.

"Yes, Mother."

Pam had the biggest grin in the world. It was fun to see Chris follow orders from his mother as they all got into the car.

"And the heater won't work by itself either."

"Yes, Mother."

"Don't forget to turn on your lights."

"Yes, Mother."

Terry in the backseat with Pam was rolling his eyes and smiling at her. He too was enjoying himself.

Chris was standing with his back to the bar looking across the room into a pool of unfamiliar but friendly faces. His brother was looking in the opposite direction at the girl with the large assets he had mentioned earlier who was working behind the bar. For the most part, Terry tried his best to avoid talking about his recent run-ins with the local police, and Chris tried his best to stay away from his line of work. As far as Terry was concerned, Chris was an international security consultant who was always either on the way to an airport or just sitting down on a plane and didn't have much time to talk when either one called the other. Chris sipped slowly on a pint of lager, and Terry drank the same, but he was drinking two for every one that his older brother downed. From time to time, one of Terry's friends or erstwhile acquaintances showed up and chatted for a few minutes, but most disappeared because Chris looked so stern and too much like a policeman on duty.

When Terry did engage in conversation with others, Chris would once again scan the room to ensure there were no threats lurking. He should have been comfortable in his hometown and in one of his favorite pubs, but he couldn't switch completely off. He was paying attention to an unfamiliar sound, a tone of voice, the scraping of chairs on the hardwood floor, a squeaking door swing, a look, a vibe, a sign, or some kind of danger signal to be on guard. He knew he should be more laid-back, but his intuition told him something was wrong, and he couldn't quite put his finger on it. He'd been on edge ever since he had left St. Clair's house, and he couldn't back down; there were too many what-if scenarios on his mind. If Pam had been with him, she would have called him paranoid, a term he hated, which usually did the trick and put him into a less defensive mode.

When Terry got up enough gumption to start chatting to the barmaid, two fit, tough-looking men entered the bar from the High Street. One who looked like Phil Collins walked up to the bar and ordered half a pint of Guinness and half a lager; the other took a table near the large wood-burning fire. Chris gave him the once over and processed a mental image into his memory bank. He then looked at the fellow's partner and did the same. Once Phil Collins got his drinks and moved to the table to join his friend, Chris became distracted by Terry when he started laughing with the girl behind the bar. It looked as if he was making progress. Chris so wanted to ask Terry if he knew the guys near the fire but refrained and once again tried to find the off switch.

"I'm going to take a leak," Chris told his brother.

Terry nodded his response; he was too engrossed to care.

When Chris crossed the threshold from the bar to the hotel part of the Castle and Ball, he checked a mirror that was located behind the check-in desk to see if Phil Collins was following. He was not. Chris made his way down through a narrow corridor to the men's toilet expecting to have company any second, but after relieving himself, he realized he was getting too wound up. He wasn't followed, and he was just putting himself into a situation that did not exist when he should be enjoying himself with his sibling.

When he headed back down the corridor towards the bar, a small crowd of visitors with luggage barred his way. For once, he thought it was nice that so many people wanted to stay in the old coach inn that dated back to the mid-eighteenth century. It really helped the ambience and stir up curiosity in the place when the staff of the establishment talked of ghosts and mysterious happenings during the long history of the old coach house. As he navigated around the luggage on the ground and bewildered Japanese tourists, he thought he saw Collins half in his chair and half out, looking as if he was trying to make a decision. Chris's antennas went up again. When he sidled up to Terry at the bar, Collins was making a move. Chris kept him in his peripheral vision but did not look at him. It mattered not; it looked as if he too was off to shake the snake.

There was a lull in the action with Terry.

"You getting anywhere?"

"Yep, got a number, but her manager is giving me the eyeball."

"You hungry?"

"Feeling a little peckish, now that you mention it."

"Indian or Chinese?"

"Chinese."

"Finish your drink; then we'll bugger off."

As Terry downed the remainder of his glass, Phil Collins returned. Chris managed to glance over at their table before he sat down and noticed that their drinks had hardly been touched.

When Terry had finished his drink and placed the empty glass on the bar, he asked his brother, "You want to drive over there?"

"There's nowhere to park. Besides, I'm a little tipsy."

"Wanker! Since when can't you hold your beer? There used to be a time when you could drink me under the table."

"Still can, but not today. We'll pick up the car in the morning. I just need to get my jacket. You ready?"

Terry said his goodbyes to his potential new conquest, and the brothers headed towards the check-in desk so they could exit through the side door to the car park at the rear of the hotel to retrieve Chris's jacket. As they were walking, Terry began to tell his brother about the girl that he had just met. When the cold winter air of the evening hit him, he complained a little too loudly, "Shit, it's cold."

"Wanker," Chris replied with a smile as he exited through the door. When the door finally closed behind him, he instinctively looked left and then right. A shadow of a man on his left gave him pause. He looked right again, and an abrupt movement caused him to curse inwardly. *Shit!*

Chris thought they were now in no man's land—stuck between the safety of the pub and the car. Terry was totally oblivious to what Chris was feeling, seeing, and hearing, and just as Chris went to shield his brother from two potential attackers from the left and right, the door behind them opened, and out walked Phil Collins and his buddy. Phil

Collins called out to Terry, "Oy, mate, you forgot your wallet."

"What?" Terry reached into his back pocket, and in the time it took from looking down to facing Phil again, the wallet that was being presented in an offering manner was spun around in the man's hand and being used as a weapon. It was too quick for both Chris and Terry to do anything about, but the wallet was hammered into Terry's neck causing him to grasp manically at his throat.

Chris started to move forward, but the figure in the shadow was on him at exactly the same time as Phil Collins's buddy. Two more figures ran to the scene from the short alleyway that connected the pub's parking lot to the High Street. Terry was still standing but bending over struggling and gasping for air when Phil Collins put his two hands behind his neck and pulled him further down. As Terry was about to fall to the ground, Phil brought his right knee violently up and made contact with Terry's balls. Terry fell to the ground in agony. Chris was being restrained but swung out a kick to Phil that completely missed its mark. To control the situation, his two adversaries put Chris in a double arm lock and lifted him so high that he was on his tiptoes and irrelevant to the fight in front of him.

Phil Collins kicked Terry while he was down but stepped back to let his two comrades take over and got in Chris's face. "Call yourself a soldier?" Phil hissed.

Chris got a whiff of bad breath but didn't say a word. He stared back in defiance.

"If I'd served with you, I would have thrown you to the fucking IRA in Belfast, you piece of shit!"

Chris remained silent. He knew where this was going, where it was coming from. Terry was groaning but still gasping for air as the kicks to his body continued.

Phil was getting perturbed that Chris wasn't mouthing off or struggling more to help his brother, but Chris was dangling almost in mid-air; he was not a threat. "I don't know who the fuck you think you are, but I've had better shits today than you and your pisshead brother. Fucking traitor!" With the last insult, he spat in Chris's face.

"You need to fuck off back to wherever you came from, but if I ever see you again, I will skin you alive. I don't care who you think you are or who your American buddies are, but I will feed you to the fucking pigs with your dick in your mouth." Phil turned to his men. "Enough. Let the fucker crawl home."

He focused his attention on Chris again and gave him a hard uppercut to the solar plexus. If Chris hadn't been suspended, he would have collapsed to his knees. "You had better stay away from Ascot, mate, and keep your nose out of places where it doesn't belong. Next time I won't be so polite."

The two men holding Chris let him drop to the ground where he immediately grabbed his stomach. He was on his hands and knees trying his best to not throw up when Phil Collins returned. "By the way, mate, your mum won fifty pounds at bingo tonight. Don't spend it all in one place, maybe some aspirin for Terry? Poor sod."

Pam and Chris were both sitting on the edge of the bed waiting for peace and quiet to surround them from the bustle and noise that had accompanied them on returning from the hospital.

When Terry had first entered the house, his mother had taken one look at him and shamefully cried, "Again, Terry, again?" She had stormed off to her bedroom without waiting for an explanation; she'd seen it once too often—Terry coming home from a night out, either beaten, drunk, or having spent time in the local police station. She was sick of it but vowed not to cry anymore and just to accept it for what it was.

"So you want to explain to me what happened?" Pam asked in a hushed tone.

"I should've seen it. The signals were all there, and I did nothing about it. It was completely my fault," he whispered. Chris went on to give Pam a play-by-play account of the beating and added, "These guys were good, really professional."

"But they beat the crap out of Terry."

"He's got two broken ribs, a couple of scuff marks on his hands from when he hit the ground, and a small bump on his cheekbone. There was no blood, Pam. They knew exactly how far to take it; they didn't touch his face once. They took me out of the picture before I could do anything."

"St. Clair sending a message?"

"Yes, and what's scary is they had eyes on you and Mum. They knew she won money tonight."

Pam was startled by his last comment. "Shit, I didn't see anybody."

"Why would you?"

"No, I mean. . . ."

"It's okay; don't worry. As I said, these guys were good, and my guess is they have been on to us for a while."

"What are you going to do?"

They were interrupted by a phone ringing in the house and paused to see if they could catch a conversation. A few seconds later, there was a knock on the bedroom door. "Christopher, there's a call for you. Please tell your friend that I don't appreciate calls at this time of night. Let's not make this a habit while you are in my house."

"Who is it?" he asked.

"Someone called Gene. Goodnight Pamela."

Pam and Chris looked at each other, relieved that St. Clair was not hounding them at home.

Chris got up to leave. "I'll be right back."

After a few moments, Chris returned to the bedroom where he found Pam lying on the bed with her eyes closed. "Do you want me to leave you to sleep?"

"No, I'm okay, just thinking. What's up?"

"I've got to go to London tomorrow for a briefing. Looks as if I have to go back to India."

"Now? Why so soon?"

"I don't know. I'll find out more tomorrow."

"Well, if you've got to go, you've got to go."

Chris was expecting her to be more upset that he was cutting their holiday short, but she seemed okay with it.

"What are you going to do about St. Clair?" Pam questioned.

"Nothing. . . . There's really nothing I can do." He let the statement hang for a second longer and then said, "I suppose I had better let the office know about the shit I've created. I almost told Gene just now, but it's good timing that I can do that face to face in London if he shows up.

Pam nodded and agreed with him without saying a word.

"When I leave in the morning, I expect they'll be following me, and I'll just let it play out. If I do have to get on a plane, then that will be the end of that, and St. Clair can go back to his boyfriends."

"So you're going to let them run you out of town just like that?" Pam asked a little too quickly. *Shit, I shouldn't have said that!*

"I don't have a choice, Pam. I've got work to do, and I am out of my element here. When I tell the office what I've been up to, they could kick me to the curb for being a complete muppet. I have to go in, and I may need to take this new mission so that things die down for a while."

"I'm sorry. I didn't mean to jump on your case, and I'm not trying to say you're scared or anything like that. It's just frustrating as hell that we can't do anything about this guy."

"I know, I know, believe me, but it's okay. What goes around comes around. He'll get his dues one day." Chris lay on the bed next to her and took her hand.

They both lay there for a few minutes in silence not knowing what to say. Pam eventually rolled over and placed her head on his chest. "I've had a thought. . . . Do you mind if I stay here a little longer? I don't have to be back to work for a few more days, and I can make my own way back. But I'd really like to spend more time with your mum, and Terry looks as if he could use a sympathetic ear."

Chris was taken aback, but he smiled and stroked her hair and responded with sincerity, "Really? I think that's a great idea. I think she could use someone to talk to right now. . . . Thank you, thank you."

# CHAPTER TWELVE

## DAY 19
## CIA Headquarters, Langley, Virginia

SVR AGENT P PLACED HIS COFFEE CUP ON THE CONFERENCE ROOM TABLE, took his place, and opened up the "TOP SECRET" folder in front of him. As if he needed reminding, the words were repeated in all caps on the top of the first page, followed by the title of the document: Operation Springfold. Identical folders were at every place around the large conference table in secure briefing room #1 in the basement of CIA headquarters. As he buzzed through the document, he watched as other officers drifted into the room, and they too silently caught up on the latest information presented in the folder.

He'd been sitting there for a few minutes when he was joined by his boss, Richard Nash, who sat directly next to him. Only a nod from each indicated a notion of familiarity. Nash got down to reading without engaging in any conversation. The room was filling up, but it was still relatively quiet, which was quite the opposite from a larger room down the hall that was turned into the Y2K War Room. In normal circumstances, the secret intelligence agency would close its doors for business over the Christmas and New Year's holidays, and only limited crews of watchers and duty officers were on the clock to monitor activities around the world; this year, however, was different.

Although it was 1300 hours New Year's Eve in Langley, the Y2K clock was racing towards them at what seemed a breakneck speed for the agency. The various brain trusts within the organization played down the media's promises of global meltdowns and anarchy and firmly stated the event would be a non-event. When various CIA stations around the world, also on duty for Y2K, starting reporting that everything was normal and nobody's computers were mysteriously melting away, Langley began to breathe normally. Only when Auckland, Sydney, Beijing, and Singapore checked in and confirmed status quo, did the architects of Operation Springfold begin to realize the plan could be pulled off.

At 1305 hours, the director of the CIA entered the secure briefing room, and everyone present stood up. He motioned for everyone to return sitting as he walked to his seat at the head of the table, but each and all ignored his orders and sat only when he made himself comfortable. The director picked up the folder in front of him and read in silence for a few minutes. As he was reading, Richard Nash took his place on a dais at the opposite end of the room and nearest the giant screen, which took up almost the entire space on the wall. The CIA logo was emblazoned on the screen, and with only a small shift of a mouse, the image changed to show the details of Operation Springfold. At the very top of the screen were two time zones, Washington, DC, and New Delhi. The rest of the screen was made up of maps of the world, which showed the progression of darkness, accompanied by clocks from each of the major cities along its route. A more detailed map of India and other pertinent information for the operation was also featured in the center of the display.

Nash glanced quickly at the clock that read 13:30:00 local time and began his briefing. "Good afternoon, Director, ladies and gentlemen. Under the cover of Y2K, Operation Springfold will go into effect at midnight in India. At 12:00:01, Fabian will be activated, which will set off a chain of events, culminating in the dissolution of the Indian company Navistar while hindering other like companies to function comprehensively, some in the short term but others in the longer term. Although we will see first-hand in this briefing today the first-line effects of Fabian, we will see other more permanent results only in the coming days and weeks." He paused to take a sip of his drink and then calmly continued to the background of the operation.

"The purpose of Operation Springfold is to thwart the proliferation of nuclear conflict between the countries of India and Pakistan. The operation created by this agency is now moving forward towards active measures as a result of nuclear testing by both countries in 1998 and the escalation of tensions in Jammu and Kashmir that led to the Kargil War that took place between May and July this year. It is believed that, although neither country was prepared to use the nuclear option during this short war, there remains skepticism with regards for future confrontations. The director of the CIA has been tasked by the president of the United States to prevent any such undertaking by either government and force the entire region to destabilize and preclude US involvement in de-escalation efforts. Operation Springfold is to be undertaken, as diplomatic missions by the State Department, the White House, and other countries have not been fruitful to date. Operation Springfold is not designed to dismantle either country's defense mechanisms. It is, however, designed to delay each country's capabilities with its research and development advancements and its supply of nuclear technologies from manufacture to field units of the military.

"Before I get into the nuts and bolts of Fabian, are there any questions?"

Nash looked around the room first at the director and then to the deputy directors for Intelligence, Administration, Science and Technology, ignoring each of the deputy's assistants. Everyone in the room had already been "read-in" on the operation, so as expected, no one stirred but the director who silently nodded, and Nash confidently continued.

"At 12:00:01, the Fabian virus will activate itself at the Navistar facility in Hyderabad and at a number of other sites in the region. Our intelligence has indicated that Navistar has done little to prepare for Y2K, and as such, Fabian will look at first glance as a Y2K problem. By the time its IT departments investigate infrastructure outages, it will be too late, as Fabian is destructive enough to kill everything that it is linked to." Nash brought up a timetable on the screen, which was presented in bullet format.

"At 12:01:00 precisely, Fabian will send a signal to the fire alarm, which will lock all doors within the facility. Navistar uses the Fail

Secure option to lock its doors, meaning when the power fails or the fire alarm is activated, the locks will keep everyone on the outside from entering. However, those on the inside are allowed egress all the time. As no security guards patrol the inside of their buildings in the evenings or night-time hours, nor have they keys, they will be completely shut out and will have no idea there is a problem inside. At 12:02:00, the sprinkler system in the entire facility will activate, except for the main communications room and the generator room. At the same time, a signal will be sent to the main power system to shut down, as well to any backup power system. At 12:03:00, the servers inside that room will be attacked by Fabian directly and destroyed beyond repair."

Nash paused and looked up at the time in New Delhi, aware that the times that he was talking about were fast approaching.

"At 12:04:00, the Halon fire suppressant system will activate in the communications room. The device is antique, and it is likely that it will not function, but if it does, then the chemicals will render the space inaccessible for up to twelve hours. At the same time, the sprinkler system will finally activate in the generator room, completing the attack."

Nash paused to look around the room. Everyone was silent but paying close attention.

He continued, "As the sprinkler system's shutoff valve is on the inside of the building, the security guards will be unable to shut the water off, unless they can locate the main supply valve from the city. Even if the guards do see the problem with the water, they will not be able to use telephones to communicate, as the telephone main distribution frame is located in the communications room, but this too will be damaged by the Halon system. One of the guards will likely take some initiative and get on his motorcycle to get to a phone. We estimate it will take an hour to get some response from a member of the Navistar staff, and by the time a facility manager turns up in the early hours, it will be too late."

Nash paused once again; still no questions. He looked over at Munson. He had a curious look about him, almost aloof and elsewhere, but

Nash resumed his briefing.

"Although Navistar is our primary focus, other versions of Fabian have been deployed at other companies throughout India and Pakistan. The events that I have described are similar in nature to Navistar; however, most are not as severe, and we still want to maintain the blanket of Y2K causing all these problems. There are two sites in Bangalore that will get the full Fabian dose, fifteen others will get a downgraded attack in other parts of India. In Islamabad, one site, Global Prism Technologies will fall prey to Fabian completely, while another eleven will have a minimized approach. As previously mentioned, we will see the results of Navistar and Global Prism in real time, and I am assured by our IT department folks we will see things play out as I will describe on the screen shortly." Nash used his electronic pointer to highlight a particular point of interest. "Here you will see the list of all the sites we are monitoring with their IP addresses. As you can see right now, each of them is green and as such connected to the outside world. I am assured that as soon as Fabian attacks, these green indicators will turn to red and show disconnected. Although these indicators will highlight an offline mode to the outside world, we will not see any Intranet activity from these sites. But if we see that all sites are offline, then that is a good indication Fabian is working." On completion of this last statement, Nash looked around the room.

"Thank you, Richard," the director chimed. "I know we don't have much time, but I just want to let everyone know that I briefed the president this morning on our activities, and he has refrained from reaching out to our allies to inform them of the operation. While I applaud his stance on the matter, there will be some backlash that we will have to deal with. . . . " The director continued to drone on for a few minutes more about the press, Congress, the Senate, and world opinions, but everyone's attention was on the ticking clock.

At 1329 hours, the room went totally silent. Many in the room had been in these types of scenarios in the past and were experienced in playing the waiting game, but there were others who began to fidget and fret.

Two minutes later, the director stated to no one in particular, "I thought we were going to see some fireworks or something."

As the clock shifted to 1332 hours, nobody wanted to respond to the director's implied question. They too were expecting to see something happening on the screen. The seconds ticked by, and finally found 1333 hours, a bead of sweat ran down the back of Richard Nash, who nervously shifted his weight from one foot to another. Springfold was his brainchild, and it looked as if something was wrong. He moved his mouse a little too frantically to confirm that the screen or computer system hadn't crashed. It was way too early for them to worry about Y2K, but the old traditionalists in the room hated relying on technology and were genuinely worried that something catastrophic was going to happen.

One minute later, there was still no activity on the screen. Nash turned his gaze towards the right-hand side of the display into a small one-way mirror, where two agency IT techs monitored and managed the programs displayed on the big screen. Without being asked a voice squeaked over a speaker, "All systems are functioning correctly, sir," came the almost too-canned response.

Munson closed the folder in front of him and suppressed a smile, enjoying seeing his boss squirm. He watched as Nash conferred with the one-way mirror, but the time was now 13:36, and there was still no activity on the screen. Munson looked around the table and tried his best to avoid eye contact with the director. The first person to make a move was the deputy director for Science and Technology, who turned to his assistant behind him, and after a hushed discussion, the assistant left the room. At 1338 hours, the deputy director for Intelligence copied his colleague from Science and sent his man on an errand.

Munson began to struggle. His mind wandered, and he was beginning to enjoy himself.

Without prompting, the manager for Regional and Transnational Issues got up from his chair and left the room.

Operation Springfold was failing.

At 1340 hours, the director spoke up, "Richard, what's going on?"

His voice was calm and controlled. Although a political transplant and not a product of the agency career pool, he was a seasoned leader.

"Sir," Nash sadly replied, "I think it's too early to say, but we are not getting any information out of India or Pakistan right now. We have assets in the field who can confirm . . ."

As Nash began his explanation, an assistant to the director marched into the room and handed him a note from Moscow Station. When the director began to read, Nash fell silent:

IMMEDIATE DIRECTOR
WNINTEL

1. CASE OFFICER MILLER ARRESTED 1930 HOURS EVENING OF 31 DECEMBER WHILE ON OPERATIONAL RUN TO MEET PER-COLATE. MILLER IS DETAINED BY FSB AND HELD AT LUBYANKA. NO CONSULAR ACCESS AT THIS TIME.

2. NO FILE. END OF MESSAGE.

At 1340 hours, the director spoke up and got out of his chair. "Richard, we need to reconvene in my office. Get someone else to run down Springfold. I want to know what is going on—I need to see results; I need answers. Right now, we need to focus on something else."

Nash stopped what he was doing and grabbed his effects from the dais and then the conference room table. He turned to Munson as he was leaving and commanded, "Looks like a soup sandwich. See what you can do."

Munson dutifully nodded his head and headed for the dais. As he walked, he kept his body in check. He wanted to skip, but instead, he measured his pace. In his mind, he was dancing naked on a beach with a beautiful girl, throwing wads of cash into the sky.

Dana Munson tapped on Nash's office door at 2205 hours, Washington, DC, New Year's Eve, 0835 hours New Delhi, New Year's Day.

"How's it going?"

"Let me ask you, Dana, what's going on downstairs?"

"Same, same. I just bumped into Jimmy G. from Division. He's had his people out most of the night. The lights are still on in India and Pakistan, and says everyone's going about their business as usual. Looks like we floundered."

Nash sat back in his chair and buried his face in his hands and tried to rub the stress away. After a second or two, he placed his hands behind his neck and stared off at the ceiling, looking for answers. Munson was sipping a beverage while sitting on the leather sofa opposite Nash and patiently waiting for him to tell him the reason why the director had pulled him out of the operation.

"Close the door, Dana. We have other problems."

Before Munson sat back down, he was handed the secure cable that had been sent to the director earlier. As soon as Munson finished reading the first piece of correspondence, Nash gave him more to digest.

IMMEDIATE DIRECTOR
WNINTEL
MOSCOW

1. REF CASE OFFICER MILLER ARREST 1930-1935 HOURS EVENING OF 31 DECEMBER WHILE ON OPERATIONAL RUN TO MEET PERCOLATE. MILLER DETECTED NO SURVEILLANCE AT ANY TIME. MILLER DETAINED BY FSB AND INTERROGATED AT LUBYANKA. CONSULAR ACCESS TO MILLER GRANTED AT 0245 AND MILLER RELEASED AT 0400.

2. MILLER ARREST WELL STAGED AS CAMERA AND RECORDING DEVICES ALREADY IN PLACE, INDICATING COMPROMISE OF PERCOLATE. PERCOLATE WAS NOT SEEN AT SITE OF ARREST. MILLER NOTED THAT PEROCOLATE'S CAR WAS PARKED NEARBY AS POSSIBLE SAFETY SIGNAL.

3. MILLER SPOUSE REMAINED AT RENDEZVOUS POINT UNTIL 2300 HOURS. AT 2245 SPOUSE NOTED MANY INDIVIDUALS LOOKING FOR SOMETHING IN HER GENERAL AREA. AT 2255 ELDERLY RUSSIAN MALE ASKED FOR DIRECTIONS TO TRAIN STATION. SPOUSE DEDUCED THAT MALE WAS PROBABLY FSB AND MILLER HAD BEEN ARRESTED. SPOUSE RETURNED HOME AND REMAINED IN PLACE UNTIL MILLER RELEASE.

4. DEBRIEFING OF THE MILLERS IS ONGOING. CABLES TO FOLLOW REGARDING OPERATIONAL DETAILS PLUS INVENTORY OF EQUIPMENT USED, ALL OF WHICH HELD BY FSB.

5. EXPECT EXPULSION NOTICE WITH THE USUAL 48 HOURS OF DEPARTURE. TRAVEL DETAILS TO FOLLOW. END OF MESSAGE.

Nash had his eyes closed and was still leaning back in his chair as Munson pretended he was engrossed in the news in front of him. *YES, YES! Another prick and his bitch wife out of my way,* he gleefully thought, but he continued his po-faced act. "Paul Strong arrested? What the hell's going on, Richard? What's happened to Percolate?"

Nash was brought back to reality and looked over at his junior. Neither Nash nor Munson needed to use the case officer's cover name anymore. "Paul's good people, Dana. He and Mary Kay are some of the best husband-and-wife teams out there. If he got picked up, it's likely Percolate is swinging by his nut sack in Lubyanka and spilled the beans."

"What now?"

"Well, I hope you have your grab bag ready. You're going to make like Steve Martin and John Candy, planes, trains, and automobiles. You're off to Moscow, and that means tonight!"

"Oh, give me a fricking break! You can send some other sap. I need to be on Springfold!" he protested, but deep down, he was only too happy to go. His thoughts went elsewhere again trying to find the right tune for the nude dance on the beach.

"No, we need someone senior to support the station. I need you to be there to debrief Paul and Mary Kay before they get on a plane, and you need to make nice with the ambassador. He's going to have a shit-storm to answer to when he goes to the Russian Foreign Ministry. The director is on his way to see the president to explain to him two things that have gone wrong and why we are all looking like a bunch of dicks pissing in the wind. There's no discussion here; you're getting on a plane."

Munson tried to look as depressed as possible. There was no point in arguing, but he was only too happy to go. He nodded his head in submission. "You know, I got to thinking about Springfold."

Nash threw up his arms in protestation, "Dana, I don't want to hear about it now."

"No, just give me a minute. This won't take long." He wanted to push a point, and finally, Nash submitted but shuffled some papers on his desk hoping that this wasn't going to be too long. "I don't know nearly enough about these viruses and all that computer crap, but isn't it possible that when Fabian was uploaded the correct procedure wasn't followed making it completely obsolete?"

"That may account for one site, but not all of them."

"Yes, that's true, but what we don't know is if at Navistar the virus was uploaded at all. Perhaps it was uploaded incorrectly, and the configuration set off an alarm at some techie's desk that caused everyone connected to Navistar to take action to counter Fabian."

Nash pondered the question for a moment and then squinted his eyes at his junior, "That still doesn't account for Pakistan. What the hell are you suggesting, Dana?"

"Well, it was your man that worked Navistar. Did he follow the correct procedure? He didn't really have much time to get the training he needed. Did he even go inside and do anything? I mean we only have his word on it."

Nash couldn't believe his ears. "Are you for real?"

"No seriously, this guy was just a dumbass driver when you picked him up. He's still a contractor. How do we know that he didn't get caught and is working both sides? Perhaps he folded and squeaked on Springfold and compromised the whole operation."

"And Pakistan?"

"I dunno. Maybe he got one of his team to flip as well and gave the Paks a heads-up. I mean, how much do we trust him? He can't be making that much as a contractor. He is still a foreign national with a green card. Do we really know where his loyalties lie?"

# CHAPTER THIRTEEN

## Indira Gandhi International Airport, New Delhi, India

CHRIS TAGGED BEHIND TWO PALE, TIRED-LOOKING BRITISH BUSINESSMEN as he exited passport control at the bustling and manic international airport in New Delhi. Although Chris had all he needed in his backpack, he still had to maintain the pretense of a business traveler and had to retrieve a throw-away suitcase that carried some spare clothes, books, and toiletries from the baggage area. The suitcase was just a prop in order to shift suspicion from a lone traveler with no check-in baggage to a businessman in town for a few days with every intention of leaving again.

It wasn't the first time he had been to the airport, and he knew he had to take a medicine cabinet full of patience while he waited for the useless suitcase to appear. All the other members of his flight were nervously waiting around the stationary carousel and complaining to nobody in particular about the inactivity of the baggage handlers. There were three or four false starts when the carousel eventually started up, only to die minutes later with no bounty in sight. After almost an hour of waiting, he finally retrieved his luggage and was pleased when he was simply waved through Customs. On exiting the arrivals hall, he was battered with a chorus of sounds that could only be compared with a hundred people shouting over the noise of a dozen trash cans being thrown down a glass staircase. The pleasant feel of air conditioning in the baggage area was being battered by the outdoor heat in the space between the Customs area and the curbside where a thousand and one vehicles of all shapes and sizes were vying for prime parking spaces like water buffaloes surrounding a drinking fountain. It was organized chaos, and only the Indians could make it work, if they felt like it.

Satish, in driver all-white uniform, stood at attention near one of the exit doors holding a sign that read O'Brien. Chris marched over to him, nodded, to which Satish played the part of subservient chauffeur and took the suitcase away from Chris and begged him to follow him to his car. Nothing more was said between the two until they were in the safety of the car and heading southeast towards the city of Gurgaon.

"How have you been, my friend?"

"I'm good, Satish. How are you?"

"As well as could be expected, and I am thankful for that." His head bobbed a little as he spoke.

"Can you give me an update now? Do we have time?"

"Certainly, certainly, we still have some distance to cover. I think we are clean."

Chris did not need to look around or behind him. This was Satish's backyard, and Chris had every confidence Satish knew what he was doing by making sure they were not followed.

"Where are we headed?"

"You are staying at the Hilton Garden Inn in Gurgaon. Tonight you will get a full briefing from Rory Weitz. The two gentlemen you spotted in Hyderabad a few weeks ago have returned and have been really active."

"Who's Weitz?"

"He's the agency case officer from the embassy."

"And we don't have anything on these guys?"

"No, Rory wants you to confirm that these are the same men you saw at Navistar. They have been to many interesting places, most recently at the ammunition depot in Inayatpur. We are passing close by right now. You can't see it, but it is a few kilometers over to the right."

Chris strained his view over to the right as if he had X-ray vision. It wasn't his job to figure out what Stretch and company were doing in New Delhi; his task was to identify and track if necessary. The strategy decisions were above his pay grade, and he would be at the beck and call of Rory Weitz for the duration of his stay in India, however long or short that might be.

"What about Deepak. Have you heard from him?"

"Yes, he has been around, and I have used him from time to time. He's been taking pictures, but I haven't seen them yet."

Chris paused. *That's usually Satish's job. Why did that dipshit take over? Hmm, save that one for later.* "What happened in Hyderabad? Why didn't he show up?"

"He won't tell me. I think it was a family matter, but it is rude to ask about such matters. I think he will tell us when he is ready."

Chris nodded in silence. *That arsehole would give an aspirin a headache.* But something told him that the explanation seemed too convenient. He had never liked "Dopey Deepak," as Chris called him. It was just a gut reaction to Deepak's demeanor and overall bearing on their first encounter that he cautioned himself into trusting him fully.

As Satish expertly navigated his way through the dense traffic, Chris engaged with him once more to discuss the locations of the sites that the two persons of interest were visiting. They were still talking when they reached the driveway of the hotel; Satish had a lot to say, but Chris cut him off.

"Here's your sat-phone, Chris."

"Thanks. I'll go check in, get cleaned up, and then I'll meet you back here tonight. But come before Weitz gets here, okay?"

"Okay, Chris. Good to have you back, my friend. It's always a pleasure to work with you."

"The feeling's mutual, Satish. I'll see you later."

The staff at the hotel were courteous and friendly and whisked Chris through the check-in process painlessly.

As soon as Chris entered the elevator and was out of site of the lobby, the clerk picked up the phone.

The ride to the sixth floor of the hotel was a disorientating experience for Chris as he felt a little light-headed, which he put down to jet-lag and pre-operation stress. On exiting the elevator, he pulled his two-wheel suitcase soundlessly down the plush hallway carpet. He heard a door opening down the hall, which in most hotel circumstances would be normal. But here, the two occupants who exited the room stood and stared directly at Chris and did not say a word. One of them was carrying a two-way radio.

Without freezing in place, Chris quickly turned around and headed for the nearest staircase. He didn't look back as his instincts and survival mode took over. When he reached the emergency exit door, he pulled the suitcase into the landing with it forming a small but effective barricade in case the two "hotel guests" charged after him. He tightened the straps on his backpack and started jogging down the staircase. When he got to the fourth floor, he heard a radio crackle from below him and a man answering the device in what Chris assumed was Hindi. He stopped dead in his tracks; he was now caught between the third and sixth floors with no escape, unless he took a risk and entered another floor not knowing if there were people waiting for him. He began weighing his options but was prompted into action when the suitcase trap was tripped as one of his pursuers crashed down the stairs. From the commotion above, the man with the radio below him spurred himself into action and began ascending the stairs as fast as he could. Chris's military training took over as he recalled battles of days gone by and how it is easier to close on an enemy down a hill rather than fighting an upward battle. He rushed downwards to meet the threat.

As Chris rounded the stairs between the third and fourth floors, radio man was rushing up towards him. When they saw each other, they both stopped and stared. Radio man started squawking into the radio but then continued his ascent. He was now on the first and second steps of the stairway and almost in reaching distance to his prey. Chris didn't hesitate any longer. He grabbed the rail to his left, steadied himself on the wall to the right, front-snapped a kick into the solar plexus of the man in front of him. The blow caught radio man in exactly the right spot and toppled him backwards, but the kick was too good, too powerful. The man landed on the stairway on his neck. Chris began to run past him but stopped midway. The man wasn't moving.

Chris bent over to feel for a pulse. When he did, he felt the broken neck before he found the carotid artery. *Shit, shit, shit!*

Footsteps and loud voices came from above. The radio squawked again. Chris closed the eyelids on the man in front of him and carried on downwards towards his escape. He found the ground floor emergency exit door and bolted through it quicker than a scalded dog but came to a screeching halt. Before him were two uniformed police officers carrying lathis, batons that were normally used for crowd control. Behind the uniformed officers were two or three plainclothes officers listening or talking into radios and searching for action.

Chris made a move to the right, but the policeman closest to him rushed in and swung his three-foot baton and caught him just behind his right knee. The blow didn't connect completely, but it was enough to sting him and knock him off balance. Just as he was recovering, his peripheral vision caught sight of a second baton coming towards his head. Again it was a glancing blow, but he felt a jarring at the side of his head, which made twinkling stars look touchable. The swinging of batons continued, but this time with accuracy, and if it were not for the intervention of the plainclothes officers, he could have sustained a lot of damage. His sense of reprieved safety was only minimal as the plainclothes officers drew in and began to beat Chris while he was on the ground. What seemed an eternity for Chris was only a minute of real time when another police officer, this time wearing enough colored spaghetti on his chest and scrambled egg on his cap to constitute any form of authority, ordered the men to cease and back off.

The plasticuffs bit into Chris's wrists every time the mini-van braked, accelerated, or bounced over even the smallest of potholes in the road. Although he sat on a bench in the rear of the vehicle, the ride was becoming more painful with every mile, as he had no way of controlling his balance with his hands, which were secured firmly behind his back. The rear of the van was large enough to make him fall forward to the floor each time the brakes were applied and when he did fall, he felt two sets of powerful hands pick him up to place him back on his seat, only to repeat the exercise two or three minutes later. The Indian Police could have easily shackled him to a fixture within the vehicle to counter his discomfort, but their aim was to inflict pain on their captive and disorient him enough that his head would spin and he wouldn't know which way they were heading—left, right, or wherever.

To add to Chris's misery, a hood was placed on his head preventing him from seeing anything at all. But it was not the blindness that upset him; it was the stench from the cover itself. As soon as they put it on him he knew it was not fresh from the dry cleaners, nor had he seen anyone remove it from a hygienic plastic wrapper. He rightly assumed that the hood had been used over and over again by men who sweated, spat, snotted, bled, and cried all in the same spot. It was more than enough to make him nauseous, which led him to believe, further, that someone had more than likely thrown up in the hood as well.

After countless trips to the floor, he felt a little reprieve as the road smoothed out and the falls were becoming less frequent, which meant to Chris they were on well-maintained roads and probably nearing New Delhi city center itself. Things started to calm down, and Chris tried his best to assess his situation. He thought there were a driver and passenger in the front and then two more people in the back with him. He had no idea of where he was headed or what he was being detained for, but looking back at the incident in the hotel staircase, he realized that he had dropped himself into some serious shit. If he had taken the time to rationalize the situation as he had exited the hotel elevator, he could have played dumb and pretended to be that jet-lagged business-man looking for some much-needed rest. Instead, he had relied on his gut feeling and bolted causing the death of someone, whom he perceived to be a police officer. It didn't matter what justifications he made for his actions or to whom he made them; he had just killed a man.

During the ride, Chris finally got past the smell and thoughts of someone else's puke in the hood on his head. He'd been wearing it long enough that new smells were attacking his senses. He thought he caught a whiff of gasoline from the minivan's engine, but now and again, a waft of some other foul odor found its way to his nostrils. His fears were confirmed when he heard one of his companions in the vehicle open a window. Normally the professional crew remained silent during a capture and transportation, but now it seemed to Chris that three of them were complaining to one of them who had just farted. Whatever was being said, Chris could not understand, but he was getting the gist as more windows opened. As they did, the toxic cop moved from his position and sat next to Chris, only to fart once more. As the fumes began to kill off any insect life forms, Chris felt a strong hand grab the back of his neck. His hood was ripped off his head, and he was forced downwards into the man's crotch to a tumult of laughter from the rest of the team. Chris was allowed a brief reprieve and allowed up for a breath of polluted air, only to be forced down again to sample the man's disgusting aroma. It smelt as if a rat had crawled up his arse and died. All he could think of was Tom Berenger in the movie *Platoon* when he held the mouth of an injured soldier and yelled, "Take the pain! Take it!"

After a few minutes more of horsing around, the noxious cop had finally finished his lethal olfactory attack and an air of seriousness returned. The men in the minivan went silent as they slowed down when they approached a high-walled compound. Chris managed to take in a little of his surroundings, which was a blessing as until this point he had no frame of reference. When the farting cop noticed that his prisoner was having a good look-see, he grabbed Chris's neck a little too forcefully and pushed him down to the floor of the van. Chris now had to rely only on sounds as the van trundled to a halt. He heard the hum of an electric gate being opened and the low rumble of the van as the vehicle crossed the threshold of the compound. The vehicle stopped, and he heard the hum of the electric gate again indicating that the outer gate needed to be closed before they could proceed. A huge wave of fear entered his mind as another gate opened to the front. The vehicle proceed forward and continued for a few seconds, and that was when he knew he wasn't in a police station. Chris was in a prison.

## DAY 21
### Marlborough, United Kingdom

Pam replaced the phone in its cradle and tried to decipher the message that she received when she called into her answering service. For a few seconds, she tried to recall the codes and phrases, and she was pretty close to understanding the content, but she retreated back to her bedroom to consult her diary, which in effect was her code book, while Terry and his mother got ready for his upcoming doctor's visit.

The code was a very simple system of numbers and letters that translated into a message, much like solving an algebraic test. After she finally put the last parts together, she tore the papers she used into a dozen pieces and flushed them down the toilet. She had what she needed for her next mission: Scandic Hotel, Gothenburg, Sweden, two days.

## DAY 21
### Barvikha, Russia

Dana Munson exited the car to a rapturous welcome from Vasili Timoshev, who stood in the cold winter snow patiently waiting for him to arrive. The Russian, a gaunt six feet two inches towered over the smaller, pudgier American and gave him an affectionate hug.

"Dana, Dana! At last, you have come to my home. I can't begin to tell you how happy this makes me. Please, please come inside." As they walked along the tree-lined path, the snow continued to fall relentlessly. Although they were only twenty-five kilometers from Moscow city center, they could have easily been in Siberia, as the wooded enclave situated outside the city of Barvikha silenced any intruding sounds.

"I see that you made it through our crazy traffic."

"Your driver was superb, Vasili." Munson turned around to see how close the driver was walking behind them, and for his benefit, he praised the man. "He did a magnificent job of driving in circles while keeping me totally safe. You will be happy to know I would never be able to find this place again." Dana did try his best to memorize the routes and landmarks, but he was completely lost. He thought he had seen a tail two or three times, but he knew if they were there, they were there for his safety.

The Russian chuckled and countered sarcastically, "I am offended, Dana, that you think I would deceive you on your route here." *If only you knew how much we invested in getting you here, you wouldn't be so patronizing,* he thought. "Let's not waste time on such trivial matters. Please, come, come inside to the warm. I have some friends I would like you to meet."

As Dana and Vasili entered the upscale, two-story house, they shook off the small mountains of snow from their coats and stamped their feet to rid themselves of the accumulation on their shoes. The driver followed close behind carrying Dana's overnight bag. He placed it in the hallway and shut the door as he exited without a word. Vasili took Dana's coat off and hung it on a peg and did the same for his. It was only a two-minute walk from the car to the house, but the cold bit through Dana's gloves and attacked his bones giving him a chill. He was glad for the warmth of the house, and although he entered with trepidation, he was eager to sit in front of a wood-burning fire.

As they entered the living room, three men who were seated all rose simultaneously. Vasili headed over towards the oldest of the three.

"Deputy Director Bielawski, may I introduce Agent P, Dana Munson." Both men shook hands. Bielawski was beaming and began speaking in Russia while still holding Munson's hand. "The director offers his apologies, but he does not speak English. However, he is honored that you are here, and he hopes that our relationship continues to grow and will be fruitful to both of us for a long time to come." Dana's Russian was non-existent, but he nodded with genuine happiness. However, he assumed the statement was well-prepared, and he wondered how often they had used this place, this play. As Vasili introduced the other two men who were deputy this or that, Dana focused his attention on the director. After all, it was this man who would decide his fate. Although this was not the KGB anymore, the tactics they used and the manipulative games they were trained for were ingrained into every SVR officer's being. The philosophy of the Russian spy agency hadn't changed that much from the old ways, and Munson knew that, although he was their man at the CIA, he could be only one bullet away from lying face down in the Moscow River. He needed to be careful.

"Before we begin, Dana, we want to show you our appreciation. Please sit." A laptop was placed in front of him by one of the two lackeys in the room; the other brought a tray of vodka. Once the screen had refreshed itself, it showed Dana's Swiss bank account. Bielawski cleared his throat and launched a ton of platitudes towards Dana and his efforts to bring valuable information from the CIA to his organization. After his dialogue and a chorus of nodding and smiling heads, the director reached over to the enter key on the laptop, and three hundred thousand dollars was transferred to Munson's account.

Bielawski raised his glass, and everyone followed suit. "Nostrovia!" the Russians bellowed together.

Dana raised his glass "Nostrovia!"

The fun fest continued with more drinking, and a few jokes and war stories were passed around by each and all. As if on cue, one of the lackeys took away the vodka bottle and glasses, and then Vasili turned to Dana. "We do not have much time. Unfortunately, we need to get down to work. We have a lot to get through, but we have plenty of food and drink, and tonight you will be comfortable as our guest here. Tomorrow we will get you back to the hotel early enough so that nobody will miss you."

Dana glumly nodded his consent. He knew this was the reason he was here, but he was feeling very content drinking and laughing with these men. He also thought how they weren't too unlike his other colleagues who liked to do much the same over beer and burgers. However, he wondered if this society, this way of life, was as materialistic as the one he grew up in. He wondered what his life would be like if he was here and if it would be better, away from a world of convoluted political correctness. He shook his head; he knew such thoughts were the drink talking. Munson was not that naïve. If there was one place in the world that embodied corruptness, political nepotism, and a fragile democracy, it was here in Russia. He reminded himself to stay away from the politics of the situation and that the only two reasons he was here were for the money and to fuck the CIA.

When Gennady Bielawski rose to leave, all the Russians got up and stood almost to attention. Dana thought, *Here we go again, another Stalinist speech.* He smiled through his pretense of feigned interest and extricated himself from the comfort of the couch. Vasili continued to translate, and it was more of the same drivel that he was dealt when he first entered. He was getting bored with the old man. Dana tried his best to concentrate while smiling, nodding, and thanking him for his kind words. At the very end of the monologue, the director switched to heavily accented English, "Thank you for Operation Springfold Dana."

# CHAPTER FOURTEEN

THE DEBREIFING LASTED MORE THAN FOUR HOURS, and it was plain to the men that were asking the questions that Dana was fading quickly. His answers were short, to the point, but sometimes rude. Everyone knew this would not be an easy task, and time was definitely not on anyone's side, so the questions were specific to ongoing operations like Springfold, Primal Ocean, and the arrest and pending deportation of Paul Strong. In normal circumstances, the debriefing would take months to complete so as to extract as much information as possible, but Dana needed to be back in Moscow by the early hours and get back to work at the embassy before he was truly missed.

Vasili tried to comprehend what the man must be going through to turn on his nation, to be a traitor, to betray his colleagues and friends. The only redeeming aspect Vasili could find with the American was, although he often spoke of hating certain personnel at the CIA, he was adamant that he did not want to harm anyone. Dana wasn't a violent man and saw no benefit from it. As endearing as that was, what perturbed Vasili was Dana kept asking for more money during the debriefing. At first, it was a joke to which everyone laughed, but the subject came up again and again. It wasn't so much that the SVR didn't have the funds to supply the demand; it was more a question of what was happening to the money. It was a tricky situation for both the spy and spy handler, as money usually led to unexplained acquisitions or extravagant spending sprees and usually showed that someone was living beyond his or her means and, therefore, had another, possibly suspicious, source of income.

To counter the problem, Vasili floated a proposal with his boss that would, at least, stymie Dana's greed and potential spending habits. With the affirmation from the top, Vasili had free reign to control the situation. He found an appropriate time to stop the questioning.

"I think we have gone as far as we can go today, gentlemen."

"You got that right," Dana answered. "I'm famished. Is there anything to eat?"

"Of course, Dana, of course." Vasili picked up a phone on a side table and gave a few instructions to the other end. As he did, the two interrogators packed up their recording equipment and notes and made to leave the house.

Dana had felt quite comfortable with his newfound friends and was sorry to see them go, but he was tired, hungry, and in need of a drink. Perhaps a quiet fireside chat after dinner with Vasili was what he needed to wind down. He didn't need more boring of his brain today.

After the two men left, Vasili brought out two fresh glasses and a new bottle of vodka. The two men sat beside the fire and chatted as if they were best friends, and each shared a little his past life. When Dana heard a commotion from the kitchen, he shot a quizzical look to Vasili.

"Catering. We shall eat shortly. You are in for a treat tonight, my friend."

After a short time, a young waiter entered the room and spoke to Vasili to let him know that dinner was ready. As Dana struggled to get out of the comfy chair, he complained, "TV dinner by the fire would work for me."

"Not tonight, Dana. Please come. I would like to introduce you to some of my more social friends.

When both men entered the dining room, Vasili spoke first. "Dana, may I introduce Katja and Tatiana."

Dana was flabbergasted. He knew that Russian women were beautiful, but these two were stunners. Speechless, he sat in an empty chair next to the blue-eyed blond Katja, who stroked his leg and smiled at him as he got comfortable. The party had started.

Dana Munson woke up with the worst headache in his life. He rubbed his face with his hands and tried to erase the pain that was in his head to no avail. After blinking a dozen times, his vision became clearer, and he started to recognize the bed he had fallen into. He tried to sit up but was prevented from doing so by an arm draped across his belly. When he traced the limb, he saw the blond hair of Katja sleeping quietly next to him. He managed to pry her arm away, and as he tried to exit the bed from the other side, he was met with another obstacle, the feet of Tatiana. He lifted the covers to be greeted by her naked ass. "Jesus Christ, what a night!" he said softly with a smile. When he finally made his way out of the bed, he found a dressing gown that he donned, and he crept out of the room and headed to the kitchen.

"Good morning, Dana. Coffee?"

"Damn straight, black and strong."

Vasili poured him a cup "I assume from the look of your face you had an entertaining evening?"

"Vasili, don't be a dick. . . . I don't know what you are talking about. I had a quiet evening and went to bed early . . . by myself."

"Which one was better, huh?"

There was a pause as Dana pondered the question and then began to laugh. "I don't remember."

They both laughed some more as they sat at the kitchen table. "What happened to you, Vasili? I thought you were going to take Titiana, I mean Tatiana."

As he corrected himself, the young waiter came in with fresh bread rolls and placed them on the table. Vasili looked over to the young man and smiled. "I was otherwise engaged, Dana."

Munson followed his glare and embarrassingly put two and two together. "Oh . . . oh! Um, well, great, good for you then."

Vasili smiled both on the inside and out. The closest that he had come to the waiter was from another room, as he recorded the drugged Agent P performing sex acts on not the two Russian models but the young man. Vasili now had the ammunition that he needed to curb Munson's greed.

Prior to the meeting with Dana, Vasili and his boss discussed options for curtailing and controlling their CIA asset. They discussed at length the reasons why all spies and intelligence officers turn against their countries, and they came to the conclusion that there are usually four reasons. The first was money, which Munson wanted in spades and wanted more and more. The second was ideology, which wasn't a problem with the American as he didn't care if he was dealing with pacifists, communists, or terrorists; he just wanted cash. The third justification for betrayal was blackmail or compromise, which the SVR did not have up to that point. Now after last night's partying, they had a way of keeping him line by paying him less and blackmailing him for more information. The fourth option was ego. Although Dana Munson was egotistical, he did not think that he was smarter than the CIA or SVR; he just thought he was smart enough to play high stakes poker with the big boys and win.

"We need to get you cleaned up, Dana. Would you like Tatiana or Katja for a shower?"

"Holy shit, no, no. I'm not that old, Vasili, but my heart won't be able to take it. Besides, I think I did enough last night to keep them asleep for a while longer."

Vasili granted him his manliness with a nod and a wide grin. *Give me a break. You like boys, and you just don't know it yet.*

"I think you're right, Dana. I think I can hear one of them snoring. Why not get showered? Breakfast will be ready for when you return, and then we can get you back to Moscow."

## DAY 22

## Sunninghill and Ascot, United Kingdom

It was a torturous, white-knuckle drive from Marlborough to Ascot for Pam. Although she had a number of lessons from Chris for driving in the UK, she could still not wrap her mind around the perpetual roundabouts that dotted the British landscape like blood splatter from a crime scene. There were thousands and thousands of the damned things, and Pam got an earful of car horns and inappropriate hand gestures from almost everyone around her as she clumsily crossed into the circles of death, to breathe normally only when reaching the other side. When she finally parked her car at the St. Michael and All Angels Church, she shook her head in frustration and reminded herself she would have to do it all again if she was to get out of there and out of harm's way. *That was the hard part. Now for the easy stuff,* she thought.

Night had fallen as she trekked along the bridle path that she and Chris had taken almost eleven days previously. She hoped nothing would or could have changed in that time, and she felt confident she knew exactly where she was going to lie up to survey George St. Clair's residence. By the time she reached the edge of the tree line, she continued to avert her eyes away from the house to ensure that her night vision was tuned into her immediate surroundings. She stood, listened, watched, and waited patiently until she was totally at ease with her environment. Other than the trees swaying in the wind, there were no other sounds around her. In the distance she could hear a car traversing some of the same streets that she had travelled, but there was no activity from the house. Only one light was on upstairs, but downstairs the main-floor lights cast small snippets of illuminance outside to highlight the driveway and garage. As the rest of the property was cloaked in blackness, she chose a route through the shadows to approach the house towards the rear. Her only concern was that St. Clair had upped his security game by employing guards and installing security equipment, but after Chris had put the fear of homosexual exposure on the table in front of the MI5 man, she doubted he went to ask for counter-measures from his bosses. She hadn't seen any motion lighting or cameras on her first visit, so she felt confident she could get close to the house and hopefully find an opening to enter.

It took Pam thirty painstaking minutes to get to the rear of the garage and into an area of total darkness and perceived safety. Moving from the tree line, she walked cautiously, stopping every few feet to check for sounds and motions. She would remain in place for minutes, crouched low to reduce her profile before she continued on. Her self-discipline and need for restraint prevented her from rushing to the objective and making a costly mistake. Even as sure-footed as she was, she did not want to take any unnecessary risks when they weren't needed.

It took her another fifteen minutes to get to the base of the lit kitchen window, which was slightly open. She heard the voices from within,

"Why don't you go up and have a bath, my love? I'll clean up here, and then I'll bring you a cup of cocoa. If you're lucky, I may be convinced to give you a back rub when you are done relaxing."

"Oh, George, you are such a dear. You don't need to do that for me."

"Perhaps I want to. After all, you've been working very hard this week; you deserve to be pampered a little. Now run along, and Georgie will bring you a hot cocoa in a few minutes."

*Well, isn't that sweet,* Pam thought.

Pam waited patiently and heard the clatter of dishes and cutlery being washed and put away. She didn't need to peek into the kitchen window; she had the layout memorized from her first visit to the place. Then she heard the gas stove being used and a pot being filled with water. Still she waited. It was shortly after she heard St. Clair pouring the contents of a pan into a cup and footsteps walking away from the kitchen that she began to make her move. She warily made for the kitchen door and tried turning the knob gently. It gave, and she entered the premises silently and smoothly. Still crouched, she made her way to the living room and stopped. She could hear the mumbling of voices from above. Her eyes began a quick scan of the room and fixated on the sword case on the side table as before. She carefully removed the weapon from its case, dropped it to her side, and slinked off to a darkened corridor near the front door.

It didn't take St. Clair long to return to the kitchen. As Pam crept slowly back towards her quarry, she could hear the scraping of a chair on the tiled floor and a newspaper being unraveled. In her mind, she pictured St. Clair sitting at the kitchen table reading the newspaper.

Now she had to decide how to proceed. If he was facing away from her as she entered the kitchen, she could take him in the back, but if he was facing her, then the element of surprise might be lost. Pam couldn't stay in situ any longer; she had to shit or get off the pot. She took a few silent steps forward into the kitchen. When she briefly peeked around a corner, she saw that St. Clair was facing her, but the newspaper was shielding his view.

Pam got within a few feet of him when St. Clair dropped the newspaper and shot a look of horror as he saw the sword plunge toward him. Pam rammed the weapon home into St. Clair's chest, but as it drove in, she let it go in surprise as the blade wobbled in her hand. It was too weak to cause enough damage to the bones protecting his chest and just stuck there. A pair of scissors would have done more damage. St. Clair tried to say something, but words would not come. He looked down at the blade protruding from his chest and then looked at Pam. Their eyes met. Pam lunged forward, grabbed the sword again, and pulled it hard from St. Clair's chest. She didn't hesitate a second longer and thrust the sword into his neck. This time, the blade passed through muscle and sinew and slipped through his throat with ease. Pam forced the weapon through as far as it would go, left it there, and retreated from St. Clair and stood back to look at her handiwork. His eyes were wide open, and she saw him blink. She moved forward and whispered in his ear, "Nobody fucks with my man!"

She stepped back a few more feet from the table so she could hear any movement from behind and then watched as St. Clair in the throes of death, arms dangling by his sides, gasping, spitting while trying to breathe but couldn't. It didn't take long for him to die. She looked around the kitchen before she left. *Oooh, After-Eights.* She picked up a few of the chocolate mints off the counter and walked out casually munching on the treats as she retraced her route back to her car.

# DAY 23
## New Delhi, India

It took Chris only a short time to figure out that he was wrong about being in a prison. After spending an hour in a cell, alone, naked, and chained to a wall, he realized that the worst jails in hell would be luxurious in comparison to where he was and what he was about to face. Even as he was being dragged to his cell, he heard the screams of a man from somewhere in the building, and that alone should have told him he was in an interrogation center, but he was in denial.

The solitary experience gave Chris a reprieve and a chance to assess his situation. His memory flicked back to his training and what he was supposed to do when taken. He was happy that he had succeeded in the first of four actions that he should have taken when captured—he survived. He was alive, meaning they needed him for something. Figuring that out was another challenge. However appealing survival was, he now had to focus on three remaining elements to being captured—resistance to torture, escape and evasion. There was not much he could do to get himself out of the cell he was in, and the best escape plans came only with time. And time was the enemy that needed his full attention right at this moment. But for all the joining of dots, applying logic to situations, and rationalizing his actions or the actions of others, it came back to the hardest question any man had to ask himself: how long could he hold out to torture before he would either be rescued or escape?

As time moved on at a snail's pace, Chris tried his best to acclimate to the cell. It wasn't easy. The place was rank with the smell of feces and urine. If a toilet could walk, it would have run away from the stench. He wondered how long it would be before they introduced bugs into the cell, but he thought if they did, the army of insects would go on strike for better working conditions. It was a miserable place to be but perfect for deflating the morale of the most ardent of captives. If the real physical torture was in another room, then the psychological battle began here.

Chris began to retrace his steps in his mind and all that had happened before he landed in the dungeon. He tried his best to figure out what was going on and why he was about to get picked up at the hotel. Would he have gotten a better reception if he hadn't eluded the men in the hotel and waffled his way out of a situation? Would things have been different if he hadn't killed radio man? He didn't know, but he kept telling himself that things were going to work out, that he had no worries, that someone would be bailing him out any second.

For a while, thoughts of the Seventh Cavalry racing over the horizon with Nash leading a thousand men filled his mind. His boss had bailed him out once before, so if Chris could hold on, perhaps Nash would do it again. As much as he tried to boost his own spirits, a nagging but painful thought came back to haunt him—the words of George St. Clair. *Mark my words Chris. One day the Americans will turn their back on you, they will not come to your rescue, and if you pursue any type of activity here, neither will we.* Chris closed his eyes tight and fought back a tear as the reality of the situation took a dump on him. *Jesus Christ, what have I done? Am I going to fucking die here?* With nightmare scenarios in his head, he managed to fall asleep into a pool of self-doubt, self-pity, and depression.

Chris was glad in a way he was chained to a wall—it stopped him from pacing and showing his true nervousness. He thought about torture and the horrors that it brought. He thought about the way the agency prepared him and how he would react, but for all the preparation, he still didn't know how he would truly act. Would he shout and scream? Would he cry? Would he take the pain and suffer in silence? Would he piss himself? Would he die? Would he give away the farm? He didn't know.

As much as the agency tried to prepare a person for resistance, it was ultimately a personal choice. During the CIA's enhanced interrogation training program, they used the basics of sleep deprivation, confined dark spaces, facial slaps, and even waterboarding, but what he was expecting was as far from kindergarten torture as he could get. Chris thought these guys probably didn't even know how to spell human rights, let alone follow any guidelines or rulebooks. Besides, what the hell did he have to offer? He knew he wasn't a CIA officer, but did they? Were they going to get him to confess to something that he had no knowledge of? The what-if permutations rattled around in his head, but when he drifted off to sleep again, he woke only to ask himself the same questions. He needed to take his mind off the doom and gloom; he needed some form of outlet.

At first Chris wasted his time by trying to keep track of time. He counted as best he could, but his brain could not keep up with the multitude of numbers floating around his head, and he didn't know any more if he had been in the cell for one hour or one day. He gave up the futile exercise and thought about something positive, Pam. He focused his mind at some minuscule point of happiness with her and tried his best to enhance that feeling by multiplying all the happy memories.

Chris began to find some solace, but his happy place was short-lived, as the door to his cell was unlocked, and two men walked in. One was built like a brick shithouse, and the other was built like a communal brick shithouse. They placed the familiar black hood back on Chris's head and unlocked his shackles, a good sign he thought—they didn't want him to see something, which to him meant he would get out of the hellhole at some point. Both men picked him up under the armpits and began dragging him out of the cell to turn left and down the corridor. He tried his best to count the footsteps of the shithouse brothers, but they were good. They marched quickly, they stopped, they walked slowly, they stopped, they ran, they turned left, they turned right, they spun in a circle, and they walked backwards and did it all again. These tactics were good news for Chris. If they were trying to disorient him, they were doing a great job, well enough for him to feel confident he was going to get out of there alive.

On the last left turning that Chris could remember, he felt he was in a different place. It was confirmed when he was forced into a chair and his hands were bound to the armrests. His heart rate was pumping at forty thousand revs per minute. He was excited and scared at the same time; his blood pressure was boiling like a steam kettle. Except for the sound of shuffling feet and two familiar noises, water and the crackling of a fire, the room was silent. He must have sat there for a full minute before his hood was removed. His eyes were shut, and he began to blink to clear his focus. All he could see was a blank wall about five feet in front of him. As he was about to twist his head around to look at the rest of the room a man appeared in front of him and gave him a hard slap across his face. "Chris, so good to see you again, my friend!"

"Deepak, you fucking wanker!"

His former colleague slapped him again twice more. The Indian did not understand the insult. "What did you call me?" He slapped him again.

Chris wisely remained mute and just stared back at him.

Deepak walked away but came back in a hurry with a bucket of blood that he threw into Chris's face. As Chris tried to blink away the mess, he spat out globs of claret. He thought he was going to puke. While he was reeling from the attack, the shithouse brothers picked up the chair that he was in and turned it around 180 degrees. Chris gagged. In front of him hanging by his arms from a hook in the ceiling was Satish's limp body, blood from gouges on his neck, chest, and stomach draining into the bucket that Deepak had just used.

"Oh fuck!"

"Oh yes, fuck indeed, Chris!"

# CHAPTER FIFTEEN

**DAY 23**

**New Delhi, India**

CHRIS LOOKED AROUND AT THE GARDEN VARIETY OF TORTURE ITEMS in the room in disgust and fear. He was naked and afraid and felt about as vulnerable as a Chihuahua quaking in front of a pack of rabid pit bulls. Although the tools were macabre enough, what he was also worried about were the methods that could be used to extract information. It was one thing to place a hot iron bar on your leg and feel pain and smell burning flesh, but the psychological image of expecting it to happen was just as agonizing as the act itself. He saw a fire pit with branding irons, a water hose, the water board, drills, scalpels, hammers, and other devices that he cared not to think about. He wondered what would be first.

Deepak smiled with glee. "That's right, Chris. Take a good look around you."

"What the fuck do you want from me?" Chris spat.

Before Deepak could answer, the torture room door opened. Chris heard a gut-wrenching scream from another place in the facility, and in walked Farty Pants, followed closely behind by Stretch and one of the two men that he had spotted at the Navistar offices in Hyderabad.

*Outstanding! The guys I'm supposed to ID and track are standing in front of me. Good job, Chris, well done!* Chris said to himself.

"I don't want anything from you, Chris. We all know about you and Viewpoint, but it is these gentleman who want to meet you and get to know you a little better."

Chris was confused. "Who is 'we'?"

"Since you are not going to be with us much longer and none of your American friends are going to rescue you, by the way, I may as well introduce myself. Col. Dinesh Mohan, Indian RAW at your service."

*This is just great, just great. I've pissed off one intelligence agency, and now, I'm going to get my nut hairs trimmed by another. And who the fuck is Stretch?*

"I can see that you are still confused, Chris. Let me enlighten you." Dinesh was in his face, almost in kissing distance. Chris noticed the two strange men in the background whispering to one another. "My Iranian friends here are concerned that the virus you uploaded at Navistar, which failed miserably, by the way, has somehow affected the programs that they are working on. I have assured them that the CIA is not that clever and doesn't even know of the link between our programs and our two governments. I have told them that you are nobody of interest and should just be disposed of. But they insisted on meeting you and would like to see what you know. I have given them enough information, but it seems they have something specific to question you about."

As scared as Chris was, he tried to put on a brave face and began to analyze the information he was just given. Still looking for a possible out to the situation, he willed himself to think quickly. *So if dipshit here is a colonel in RAW, then he is either in external intelligence, counter-terrorism, or security of India's nuclear program.* Chris looked at Stretch and his buddy. *Okay, Stretch maybe military, cop, and/or executive protection. He's the doer, not the thinker, which leaves briefcase boy. He's the one that's important in this equation.* Chris stared at the two Iranians without saying anything; it was up to them to make the next move.

"Colonel, there is no need for this. These are barbaric methods, I am sure we can talk in a more comfortable surrounding?" Briefcase boy's command of English was excellent.

"I will choose the time and place of questioning. Please do not ask me about my methods again." Dinesh replied without looking at the Iranian, but he turned his gaze to focus on Stretch. "You have some questions, let's get on with it."

Briefcase conferred with Stretch in Persian. The taller of the two men did not speak English.

*Okay, got it Stretch doesn't speak English and is using his buddy to translate. Briefcase guy looks sympathetic, almost a little dainty, and put off by Satish's hanging corpse. If Stretch was important, he would be doing a lot more to get the conversation going the way that he wanted.*

The man that Chris called Stretch was in deep turmoil. It wasn't the first time he had been in a torture chamber, but each time he had wished he was elsewhere. Conscripted to join the Iranian Army to fight in the Iran-Iraq war, Hasan Rahami had survived the first Battle of Khorramshahr but was wounded during the retreat and loss of the city. While convalescing at his family's home in Bazar in a southern part of Tehran, he watched as thousands of Iranians were continually slaughtered by Saddam Hussein, and as much as he detested war, he decided that despite his wounds he needed to defend his homeland and thus he returned to the fight.

On returning to the action, it was during the liberation of the Khorramshahr in 1982 that Hasan became involved in the interrogation of Iraqi prisoners and where he learned the trades of torturer and executioner. While he begrudgingly followed orders and killed many men, his psyche took its toll, and he became sickened to what he had become. However disaffected on how he carried out his duties, others took notice of his proficiencies, and towards the end of the conflict, he was recruited by Iran's Revolutionary Guards Special Forces unit, Quds Force.

Much to his inner sorrow, he continued to excel in his activities for Quds and travelled from one end of the fight to the other extracting valuable information by gruesome means. All that slowed him down was an Iraqi artillery shell that dispensed mustard gas and planted shrapnel in his arms, and despite all the precautionary methods to prevent chemical attacks, his wounds became infected. He was evacuated to Tehran for treatment for the second time and never saw the battlefield again. To his dismay after the war, Quds Force kept him on the payroll and on a tight leash and held him in reserve for other activities, which involved seeking out dissention within Iran.

Now, many years later, he was standing in front of another bound prisoner, and the many faces in the room were looking at him to interrogate the poor man covered with blood. The thought sickened him. He hoped his face didn't show it, but he wanted to weep and find a corner to crawl into; he never wanted to see a place like this again, but here he was tortured by his own memories and about to inflict pain on another casualty of circumstance. As he looked at the poor western-er before him, he reflected that his life had become so different shepherding nuclear scientists to overseas conferences and meetings that he never thought the nightmares he had on a regular basis would come back to haunt him in real life. He had thought he was past it and could have a normal life and put the hundreds of dead faces to rest. But now his inner pain was resurrected.

Hasan conferred with the man he was supposed to be there to pro-tect while the Indian colonel berated the man in the chair. When the Indian finished with the prisoner, he turned back to Hasan and said something that the tall man did not understand. Hasan took the initiative and walked over to the fire pit to pick up a branding iron with his left hand. Once he was satisfied it was white hot, he walked over to the captive and looked down on him. Then he looked over to Dinesh. The Indian made another comment, which Chris thought was encouraging Hasan to get on with it even goading the Iranian to do it. The Indian could have been speaking Persian, but Hasan only saw the Indian shout. Hasan didn't hear anything. He felt as if he was in a glass tomb and all he wanted to do was to stop the madness. He had had enough and suddenly snapped away from the prisoner and shoved the hot iron into the chest of the Indian. As it started to burn, Hasan drew his weapon with his right hand and shot Farty Pants in the head.

While Chris was trying to comprehend what was going on in front of him, he heard the distinct sound of an explosion nearby, followed closely by a second, which shook the room he was in. The next thing he knew he was still strapped to the chair but lying on his side with something heavy shrouding him. The lights were out, and there was a heavy ringing in his ears. He thought he heard another crumple of an explosion, but he couldn't be sure. As he lay on the floor, his vision became clearer, and he saw the dead face of Satish above his head. He was trapped under his body. Chris kicked and pushed as hard as he could to free himself from the entanglement. As he was doing so, a set of helpful hands appeared and started to help him get out from the mess. It became clear to him then that it was not an easy task, as the roof of the building had collapsed into the room from an explosion, and there were body parts, rubble, and debris everywhere. When he was finally fished out from beneath Satish, Chris heard the sound of automatic gunfire in the distance. If Chris was confused before, now he was totally upside down with his thoughts. He looked around the half-demolished room and shouted too loudly, "What the hell's going on?"

A man standing with a briefcase held to his chest said, "I don't know. There was an explosion, and the roof came down."

As they were standing there, two men ran into a breach in the wall with automatic weapons. The looked at the naked Chris covered in blood and at the Iranian, paused for a second, realized they were not a threat, and made their way through what was left of the room and headed to the door to the corridor that had fallen off its hinges. Free of his bonds, Chris made his way over to a water hose, turned it on, and began to wash off the blood and grime as best as he could. While he was doing it, he noticed the dead bodies of the shithouse brothers and Stretch. A movement to his right caught his attention. It was Dinesh; he was still alive but pinned down under a pile of rubble. His face was looking upwards through the open air timbers to the night sky.

Chris went over to him and kneeled next to him. He was about to say something but went back to retrieve the still running water hose. "Mate, are you all right?"

"Chris, Chris, please!" he groaned.

"What's the matter, mate? Are you thirsty?"

Dinesh began to shake his head. "I'm trapped. I can't feel my legs."

Chris ignored his problem, then placed a strong hand on the Indian's head, and rammed the rubber hose down his gullet as far as it would go. "Enjoy your last drink, you piece of shit."

"You!" Chris pointed and shouted at the Iranian. "What's your name?"

"Doctor Farhad Mousavi."

"Doctor?"

"Doctor of nuclear science."

"What? Well, Doctor, I hope you know your way out of here. Let's go. Lead the way, now. Move, move, go!"

Chris and the doctor scrambled through the maze of corridors and rooms to find a way out. Now and again they would have to stop as a burst of automatic fire caused them to take shelter. "I need to find my clothes and my things. Do you know where they might be?"

"Yes, we inspected your backpack earlier. It's in the main office."

"Show me."

When they finally found the office that they were looking for, the two armed men that they saw earlier were rifling through filing cabinets and drawers. One of them was about to reach for Chris's backpack, but the Brit grabbed it away from the man. The gunman pointed his weapon at Chris, who offered an empty hand and started to back up. "Mate, this is mine. You don't need it. I'm just going to take it and leave, okay?" The gunman stared at him not understanding what was being said. The brief standoff came to an end when his partner shoved a wad of papers in his face and motioned for them to go. Chris stood his ground and tried to look as sheepish as he could hoping that they would simply go away. The doctor found Chris's clothes and intervened by handing them to him. The gunman lowered his weapon with a sympathetic eye and followed his partner out the door.

The sound of sporadic automatic fire could still be heard around the compound. Chris didn't understand what was going on, but he got dressed and checked to see if the sat-phone was still in his bag. It was, along with his passport and wallet. While he was getting ready, he was trying to piece together what was going on all around him. All he could think of was a jailbreak, but he did not have time to dwell on the subject. If there was a hole in the wall, he was going through it. "Well, thanks, Doc. It's been a blast. I've got to run. Thanks for your help."

"No, no, please," he pleaded. "I need to go with you. Don't leave me here!"

"A few minutes ago I was going to have a new tattoo on my chest, and I have a feeling that it would have been Mickey Mouse and all the other Disney characters, and now you want me to take you out of here. Get a life!" Chris started to make his move, but the doctor grabbed his arm.

"You don't understand. Hasan wasn't going to hurt you. We needed your help."

"What the hell are you talking about?"

"We wanted to come over to the West. I want political asylum."

# DAY 24
## Ostadkulle, Sweden

Rita had been in and out of the hide for three days, each time using her cross-country skis to get to the final firing position with her spotting scope and noting the activities around the area. Satisfied she had all the information she needed at the attack site, she concentrated on escape routes, rendezvous points, and alternate target options. By the time Pam and Crauford arrived in Sweden, Rita's plan was discussed in depth by the team, and with a few tweaks here and there, they were ready to commit to the mission.

The Bosnian had chosen the hide wisely. Nestled far enough back from the edge of the tree line, it provided them with a wide arc of fire while being well concealed from prying eyes at the target house. With the forest as a backdrop, the wide-open, snow-covered field in front of them offered an expansive view and a perfect line of sight to the objective—two red-colored houses. When Rita prepared the range card, she estimated the distances from the tree line to the nearest manmade objects, the houses, a woodshed, the range to the corner of each house, parked vehicles, roads, and the barn. She then broke things down closer for distances to other prominent features such as trees and bushes and other natural vegetation. In pre-arranged jargon that only the sniper and spotter could use and understand, all bases were covered, and if other targets or threats appeared, Pam would know in an instant where other hazards might surface.

The only thing that gave the team concern was the fact the target rarely left the house. In the dead of a Swedish winter, locals in this area of the country usually hunkered down with enough food and firewood to last them for days or weeks on end. The only time they would venture out would be to check on neighbors or feed livestock. Although the target was not a farmer, he was one of those hermits who preferred the comfort of a hot meal and a good wood-burning fire.

Pam rightly argued that shooting through a window would be too ineffective, as they did not know the thickness of the glass she would shoot through and the possibility of getting a clean shot was minimal at best. Crauford came up with a fallback plan that if after two days of daylight observation were unsuccessful, then he would draw the target out of the house. Both Pam and Rita had their reservations.

Now, with both women lying in the snow for the second day, the window of opportunity was getting smaller and smaller. As in all other missions, they rarely stayed at a target site for more than forty-eight hours due to environmental conditions and local activities. It would only be a matter of time that someone would find them, even if it was an innocent passer-by. Although bundled up with enough winter clothing, the cold bit through gloves and ski masks, and if the temperature dropped anymore, the risk of freezing fingers would jeopardize the mission completely. Sniping in winter was not for the faint-hearted.

Pam had been on scope for thirty minutes and passed watch over to Rita, who used her spotting scope to take duty. Pam closed her eyes and rested. Although she remained awake, she was still attuned to her surroundings, so much so that after five minutes of rest, she heard a vehicle in the distance from a mile away. Rita did not say anything, but she heard it too. After a few seconds, she gave Pam a nudge. A vehicle was in sight and heading towards the target house. Pam came back on scope and zeroed in on the driveway at the house. There was a possibility that the vehicle would pass on by. But there was so little in the way of activity each vehicle, each person, every flock of startled birds, each sway of a branch or bush, or any type of movement anywhere demanded looking at. As the vehicle entered Rita's field of view, she whispered, "Red pickup truck . . . Toyota Hilux."

Pam did not respond. She didn't need to.

"One hundred fifty yards to the main house, 130, 100, 80; they are pulling in."

Pam adjusted the range on the AWM bolt-action sniper rifle just a hair. The range to the vehicle was 550 yards, well within the efficiency of the weapon. The yardage was perfect for the rifle and the .338 Lapua Magnum round; anything over 600 yards in low winter temperatures could cause the bullet to drop and miss by six inches. The sound of the pickup's horn got the attention of the occupant of the house.

Rita reported, "Target outside house, walking towards pickup. Fifteen yards, ten, at the vehicle."

Pam remained silent. She too saw the movement and tracked the target across the driveway. She gauged the man's gait and walking speed and stored it to memory.

"Two occupants exiting the vehicle."

Pam moved the rifle slowly to catch the faces of the two men that moved towards the main house. From her vantage point, they did not look a threat. Rita was about to continue her commentary, but Pam moved her left foot over Rita's right and back again, an unspoken communication for her to be quiet.

The two women kept an eye on the driveway and understood what was happening as one of the two visitors began to remove supplies from the rear of the truck bed. Within fifteen minutes, the men had dropped off four large boxes and prepared to leave. The target, bundled up to ward off the cold, remained in the driveway and said his farewells. Pam repeated the leg movement, a sign to continue the narrative and keep an eye on the pickup as it left. "Vehicle on the main road heading south."

As the target began to return to the house, Pam put her crosshairs on a spot that she knew the target would have to walk through to get back to the safety of his house. She applied two and a half pounds of pressure to the trigger of the weapon to send the bullet on its way and kept the trigger depressed until all movement from the rifle had stopped. Then she automatically chambered another round ready to fire, but she knew that if the target's head was no longer in the crosshairs, then he was down.

Rita, calm and controlled, whispered, "Target down."

"Vehicle?"

"Vehicle stopped four hundred yards."

Pam moved the scope downwards to look for signs of life from the target. Except for blood seeping onto the snow, there were none.

Rita upped her tone, but she was still in control. "Vehicle turning around."

"Shit!"

# CHAPTER SIXTEEN

AS PAM HASTILY BEGAN TO PACK UP THE RIFLE, Rita remained in place on the spotting scope watching the red pickup as it headed back to the house. "Red pickup has stopped in the driveway. Two men have gotten out. . . . Wait, a third man has exited the vehicle."

Pam stopped what she was doing and shot a look across the field. She retrieved her rifle and looked down the scope. Neither Pam nor Rita had spotted another person in the back of the extended cab of the pickup truck earlier.

The man who got out last checked on the body before him and then tried his best to judge where the shot had come from. Looking at the dead man's position in the snow, he guessed correctly that the shot had come across the field. He stared intently over the expanse, looking for a sign, a movement of any kind. Although there were none, he concentrated on a spot that he thought would be a place for a sniper to hide. Both Pam and Rita watched the man through their optical equipment and realized that he was pinpoint accurate. Without him knowing it, he was looking directly at them.

Neither Pam nor Rita moved an inch, they watched and waited for the next move. It didn't take long for the man who seemed to be in charge to issue orders to his crew. Rita could see his breath evaporate into the cold air as he gave the two men a command and pointed south. As the two men got back in the truck and took off, the commander went into the house and within a few seconds returned and headed to a parked vehicle in the driveway. Pam lowered the barrel of her gun. She didn't need a scope to see what was happening—they were about to be hunted.

When the last man left the target house in a Volvo station wagon and headed north, Pam decided the need for cover and concealment was over. Now it was time to escape and evade. They rapidly packed everything that had been taken into the hide, but Pam did not disassemble her rifle. She slung it over her pack and grabbed her skis and then joined Rita who was already jogging through the forest and heading back to the trail that they had used to get to the kill area.

After the women had been skiing for ten minutes, Rita was still setting a blistering pace and leading Pam by one hundred meters. This was not by design or some tactical procedure; it was just that Rita was by far the better cross-country skier, and she knew that unless they put some distance between the target house and the hunters then the chances of capture were high. As they came to a fork in the trail, Rita stopped suddenly. Pam closed in quickly behind her. Neither of them spoke, but they both listened. A vehicle was approaching, and it sounded if it was coming at speed from behind them. Rita made a snap decision, she pointed Pam to take the left fork, and she would take the right. Pam was hesitant. She had the only weapons and thought it was a bad idea to split up, but there wasn't any time for a debate. Each accepted the risks, but each knew where to go if things went sideways. They still had seven kilometers of cross-country skiing to go before they would reach the safety of Crauford. They had to split if they were to survive.

Before Rita took off, she gave Pam a warm smile and a wave. Pam gave a pitiful smile and a pathetic wave back but cursed as she took the left fork on the trail, "Fuck, fuck, fuck!"

Pam skied with all her strength. She knew Rita would be hard to catch if there was another skier in the area, but there were two men in a pickup and another in a Volvo chasing them, so the odds of creating true distance were diminished. Pam's only hope was that the vehicle they heard was following her and not Rita. Her fears were compounded when she stopped to listen to the progress of the vehicle. She heard nothing. Either the vehicle had stopped, or it was now so far away that the natural environment was masking the sound of the engine and was still in the chase. She wanted to go back, she wanted to do something, but that something had to be to get to the rendezvous point and then plan the next move. Conflicted, she took the weapon off the backpack and anxiously looked back to where she had come from.

Rita had a great head of steam going. Even with her disability, she managed to overcome the discomfort of wrapping her hands through the leather straps onto the long cross-country ski poles. She contemplated getting off the trail and moving into the dense forest where no vehicle could pursue, but she also wanted Pam to get away, wanted to play the fox and let the chase be on her. She ploughed on through virgin snow, pushing herself harder than she ever had in her competitions or in her murderous training regimes. In her memory, she unraveled the map that she had created for the escape route and knew if she could make it another two kilometers to the frozen lake, she had a chance to get away. She pumped her arms, her shoulders, her legs faster and faster, like a steam train running at top speed. The only pain she allowed was the memory of her family and the way that they had suffered; everything else was inconsequential. Rita continued to drive and cycle through her motions. She knew her life could be on the line, but she had to keep moving; she had to give Pam an edge. Around the next bend she knew would be the lake. She heard the vehicle closing in behind and saw the open expanse of the frozen water. Although she thought it impossible, she pushed harder. Thoughts of giving up never entered her mind. Crauford would be on the other side of the lake; Pam would be on the north end. She had to keep moving; they would be waiting.

Rita knew from her reconnaissance that, although the lake was covered in snow, the ice below was too thin for a vehicle to drive on to, so if she could make it to the edge at least, she would have a chance.

She also had to gamble that if the men in the vehicle carried only small arms she might be able to get away. But if there was a rifle, then that was a different matter. As her breathing and heartbeat began to become labored, they almost muffled out any other sounds around her, which clouded her judgement. The Toyota Hilux crashed into her while it was still trucking along easily at forty kph. As the front bumper took her legs, the vicious studded tires ran straight over the top of her and chewed her up.

The Toyota skidded to a halt just meters ahead to survey the damage and confirm the kill. When the driver and passenger of the vehicle got out, they both removed pistols from their jackets and approached Rita, who was crawling slowly towards them covered in blood and with a knife in her hand. Both men looked down at her with condescension and watched her suffer for a minute. They could tell her legs had been crushed and she was not going anywhere. The passenger fired two shots into her head, replaced his pistol in his jacket, and they got back in the vehicle.

The Toyota Hilux delicately turned around on the track near the lake's edge and made it away from the frozen water in one piece. As the driver straightened the wheel of the truck, he saw the body of Rita in his way. He didn't hesitate and gunned the engine, wheels spinning over her body as he went. Neither of the men in the vehicle said a word, just another day on the job for the two former Serbian soldiers. As their confidence was running high, the driver started to expertly drift the Toyota around the bend but managed to keep the vehicle moving at high speed. They still had another mission to complete, and their boss, Marko, was adamant that both adversaries were to be killed, no matter what. The passenger in the vehicle admonished his partner for being too cocky as he had almost overcooked a drift taking out a few bushes on the side of the track. The younger driver didn't care. Running on an adrenalin high, he had tasted blood, and he wanted more.

As they negotiated another longer bend in the track, Pam shot three rounds in quick succession to take the driver out. The Toyota still travelling at speed rammed a thick fir tree head on, off to the side or the trail. Pam shot four times more into the vehicle shooting into any window she could see. Satisfied that the vehicle and driver were not a threat, she got up from her prone position on an embankment and ran down towards the enemy drawing a Glock pistol from her jacket as she ran. When she arrived, although there was no movement from inside the truck, she shot five rounds into the cabin with the pistol. Content that no one could have survived the onslaught, she yanked open the passenger door and stood back as the passenger fell out in a bleeding mess. She shot him in the head once. She then focused on the driver who was missing his left eye. She leaned in and shot him in the right temple.

Pam didn't have time to ponder. There was still another vehicle out there, and she wasn't sure if the two in the Hilux were in contact with the man in the Volvo. She ran back to her rifle and skis and then headed back down the trail towards the lake to look for her friend.

When Pam did find Rita, the sight rattled her normally stoic boldness. She wasn't prepared to see the crushed body of her best friend lying on the tracks of the vehicle that killed her. What was left of Rita looked like the remains of a hyena kill on the Serengeti; she was unrecognizable as a human being. Pam fell to her knees and cried, heaved and threw up next to the body, and then she cried more. After crying for another few minutes, she realized she had to go. She didn't want to leave Rita's remains in this mess, but she didn't have a choice. Pam had neither the means, capability, nor time to bury her friend. She retrieved her water bottle from her pack and washed her mouth out and tried to figure out what to do. Looking to the sky in an effort to stem the tears, she realized the sun had disappeared. Crauford might not wait much longer. Pam found Rita's knife and stashed it in her jacket. She tried to go through the other contents of her friend's pack but found it too difficult; she was too fraught with emotion. Before she got up to leave, she knelt in prayer and tears, then strapped on her skis, and made her way onto the lake.

# DAY 24
## New Delhi, India

Chris shouted at his companion for the umpteenth time to keep up. When they finally broke free of the interrogation center, Chris had no idea of where he was or which way they had to go. All he knew was that he had to create some distance from the jailbreak as quickly as possible. What helped his situation was the inordinate number of emergency vehicles speeding by that created a distraction for the throngs of people on the street. Nobody noticed the former British infantryman speed marching into battle as if he was on a yomp across the Falkland Islands. While Chris marched, Doctor Farhad Mousavi jogged behind him to keep up, still holding his precious briefcase close to his chest. "Keep up for fucks sake!" Chris barked again.

The doctor's pleas for an explanation of where they were headed were ignored, and all he received in return were scowls and more verbal abuse.

Chris was completely perplexed. Not only was he trying to wrap his head around escaping the torture chamber, but he was also trying to figure out what his next move should be. He'd been free in the country only a matter of hours before he was picked up by the shithouse boys, so there had been no time to confer with his Viewpoint team about escape and evasion plans. The only thing he had going for him was that he had his passport, a little money, and most important of all, communications. But what weighed heavily on his mind was the fact that he had picked up a potential defector while his countryman lay under a pile of bricks. The situation was out of his scope of work, his training, and his comfort zone; it could easily spiral out of control if he did not take the initiative.

As Chris was trooping through the overcrowded streets and alleyways, he probed his memory for a map of New Delhi. One of the skills he prided himself on was his ability to take a map, study it for a few hours, memorize major landmarks and highways, and then commit it to memory. New Delhi, however, was challenging to learn. As a city with a population of over ten million inhabitants, getting around was difficult at best. He knew if he kept away from areas of less density and more affluence, he would be heading towards the center of the country's capital. But if he took a track that led to a more dilapidated and bustling zone, then he knew he would be heading in the wrong direction. What sometimes confused his logic was that street names were virtually non-existent, which could have easily sent him in a circle. However, his reasoning led him to believe that if he saw street signs he would again be heading along the right path—to the center.

When Chris approached an intersection, his spirits lifted—he saw a sign for the University of Delhi. If he could get there, he would be in spitting distance of the Diplomatic Enclave and the potential safety of the US embassy. He hailed a green-and-yellow motorized rickshaw, and as he got in, he gave the driver instructions for the school just as the good doctor clambered clumsily aboard to join him. The doctor wanted to ask him where they were headed, but he was too out of breath to start a conversation. Besides, he could tell that his chaperone's thoughts were elsewhere, as the young man surveyed the area behind and to the front of them.

The respite was too short for the out-of-shape Iranian. He wished he could have had more time to rest, but within a few seconds of coming to a halt at the university campus, Chris paid the driver and was once again off to the races. "Can we please slow down? I don't think anyone is following us."

Chris ignored him.

Up until this point, the doctor had been compliant with the direction they were taking, but now he persisted. "Excuse me, I am talking to you. You could show me some respect and answer me!"

Chris still moved forward without a word. The doctor grabbed his arm to slow him down. Chris stopped in mid-stride and yanked his arm away quickly. He wanted to punch the man. "Listen, you are the one that decided to be here, not me. I don't know what you have in that case or what is in your head, but honestly, I don't give a flying fuck. I am getting myself out of India, and if you want to get on my bus, you had better just shut the fuck up and do as you are told."

The doctor took a step back and slouched his shoulders. His mind to defect was made, but now he questioned his initial plan to follow this man to fulfill his quest.

Chris could see that the Iranian was falling down a hole, and the last thing he wanted was to hold his hand and sing sweet lullabies to assure him it was all going to be okay. "Look, the longer we stand here bickering like two old wives, the longer we look like we don't belong. I am going up that tower," he motioned to the tall red-brick building behind him, "or as close to it as possible, and then turn on my phone and call my office. Hopefully, I will get some instructions on how to get out of this shitty situation. Now, I'm really sorry if you have a blister on your little tiny tootsies because I walk a little too quickly or I have hurt your feelings when I don't answer you straightaway. But believe me when I say everybody and his donkey are probably looking for us right now, and when they catch up with us, I'd be a little more concerned about your life expectancy than sore feet if I were you. So if you want someone to show you some respect, fuck off the other way to find it and don't follow me. Okay?"

Without giving the Iranian time to dwell, Chris spun around looking for an access point to the roof and set off while restraining himself from jogging away from the problem child. The admonished Iranian scampered along after him without a word of protest.

The phone was answered on the third ring by an automated response. "State your name."

"Klondike."

"Please hold."

The light over the city was fading fast as Chris patiently waited as he looked across the sprawling campus below from the tower on the university grounds. He was relieved that the phone worked the first time it was turned on. A good boost of morale. Within a few seconds, a live person came on the line.

"Klondike, please authenticate."

"Mike Alfa One, Mike Alfa Two . . . Casper."

"Standby, Klondike." As Chris waited, he paced around the rooftop and glanced at the doctor who had his shoes off and was rubbing his feet. A few more seconds expired when the man came back on the phone, "Connecting. Stand by, Klondike."

Within a second, another human answered the phone, "CTC."

Chris repeated the Casper code to indicate he was on an insecure line; he wasn't afforded an encrypted phone like others at the agency. "Casper. I need to speak with Goodwin."

"Negative, Klondike. Unavailable. I have Holden."

*Dammit, Munson, I don't want to talk to that prick.*

"Understood. Is Tilden available?" Chris had tried to locate Nash, but now he was on to Gene.

"Negative, Klondike."

Chris recognized the CTC operator's voice. *Jesus, Jenna, give me a break.* Chris grudgingly relented, "Please connect me with Holden."

"Stand by."

More precious seconds ticked by, and Chris pressed the phone to his ear so hard he thought he would have a permanent imprint if he waited any longer.

Dana Munson came on the line. "Speak!"

*Nice to hear from you too asshole.* "I need an extraction plan."

"What about your OPSEC plan? Why can't you follow that?"

"There was no time to prepare. I was compromised."

Munson suppressed a grin when he heard the news. He was in a small glass-walled conference room in the CTC and didn't want anyone to suspect his joy. "What about your local support element?"

"Also compromised. The cell has collapsed completely."

Munson was silent for a few seconds as Jenna Caya entered the room and laid a report of the Delhi jailbreak in front of him. Dana speed-read through the notes. "We've heard of an incident in your area. Was that something to do with you?"

"Yes, I am not injured, but I have no resources to get out of here. I need a plan."

Munson wondered about Deepak. Chris had mentioned that the cell had collapsed, but losing his Indian lackey would be a blow. "What about your number 1 and 2 assets? Can't they help?"

"Negative, both out of the picture permanently."

Munson flew off the handle. He had groomed Deepak for months to get him to where he needed to be; it was a monumental loss for his private network of spies. He got out of his chair forcefully and stamped his feet like a spoiled brat. "What the hell have you done you, idiot! Don't you realize how long we've been working on this program?" He finally stopped and placed both hands on the table and cussed into the speaker phone. "You are so fu—you are so useless. Where the hell did we find crap like you in the first place? What the hell is this program coming to?"

Jenna was still in the room waiting for instructions from Munson. Her jaw dropped at the outburst, but before she could say something, Dana turned his attention to her. "What are you waiting for, you dumb bitch? Go make some coffee or something useful." When Munson turned away from her, she gave him the finger behind his back before she stomped out.

Chris didn't care about being polite on an insecure phone anymore. "Who the fuck took the jam out of your donut? I don't give a shit about what you think of me, but I'm knee deep in wankers here, and I don't need another one on the phone! I need an extraction plan, and I need it now. If it means I need to talk to someone else to get some action then please someone, someone in your office." He was hinting at Jenna or another CTC operator who was surely listening to the conversation. "Please find me, Goodwin."

Munson's swinging mood changed after he heard Chris's veiled proposal. "Okay, okay, calm down. I get it. Let's get back on track. Goodwin will be informed as soon as he is available. Right now we need to focus on getting you out of there. We are going to need some time to put something together. I need you to call back in two hours. Where are you now?"

"Hard for me to say, but I am going to move from here. I don't think I can stay here much longer." Chris desperately wanted to talk to Nash. He didn't trust Munson, but Chris had no choice. If Munson said Nash was unavailable, it could have meant a myriad of things—he could be in a meeting, taking a dump, having his chest hairs waxed, or flying a plane to the North Pole; Chris would never know.

Munson realized that Chris was being smart about not wanting to give his position away. Although the Indian authorities were unlikely to intercept the sat-phone conversation as such devices were illegal in India, it did not mean they would completely ignore an abnormal signal floating amongst ordinary communication traffic.

"Understood. Call back in two hours."

"Will do." Chris glanced at the tired-looking Doctor Mousavi and added, "You also need to consider another new asset in your plan. Two for extraction."

# CHAPTER SEVENTEEN

AS SOON AS CHRIS SWITCHED OFF THE PHONE, he explored each corner of the rooftop to re-orientate himself and buy a little time to come up with a semblance of a plan. Although he agreed with Munson to call back in two hours, protocol dictated that you double the number given and then add thirty minutes to determine the actual time. Spoken real time held only if there was imminent danger and the dogs were biting at your heels. Although he had confidence that the CIA brain-trust would formulate an extraction plan, he knew he had started an electronic trail of breadcrumbs by using the sat-phone, and to use it again from the same location would be stupid. He needed his own immediate plan to get away from the university and to another high point or, at least, an area open enough to allow him to self-triangulate and get a good signal.

From his vantage point, Chris identified the airport that he had arrived in a few days earlier and immediately crossed the site off as insecure, as he was sure if he was being hunted, the airport would be inundated with red-flag warnings against his name. Having the airport now implanted as a major landmark in his internal locator, he turned his back to it and focused on other areas in the vicinity. In the distance, he could just make out a few flags of different colors and remembered that on the southern edge of the Diplomatic Enclave were the Belgian, Turkish, and Italian embassies, which he reluctantly dropped as potential safe sites. Although he knew there were dozens and dozens of embassies in the area, including the American and British, access to them would be tightly controlled and if two men, one still peppered in crusty blood and the other who looked as if he was about to have a cardiac arrest, rocked up to the door, police would swarm on them like flies on shit.

After conceding that two of his out avenues were closed, he visually explored the area directly to his north. He could make out the busy intersection of the Mahatma Gandhi freeway and Route 8, which they had used to get to the university on the rickshaw. To Chris's discontent, he remembered that a restricted military cantonment lay a few miles further past the intersection, which at the present time was awash with military helicopters. He hoped they were in search of jail breakers and not him, but he couldn't take the chance on that assumption, so another escape route was closed. That left only the south.

Night was fully upon him, as well as a thousand and one mosquitos. Chris looked over the vast sea of light that lay before him and tried in vain to establish a point of reference. He knew of the University of Delhi from studying maps, but he could not remember if there was another large structure or facility in the southern part of the city that they could use as a refuge. Although the Delhi city lights were bright enough to be seen from space, all he saw was darkness and mystery. He did not know what he was looking at, and he did not know what to do. He awkwardly looked over to the doctor who was of no help, as he had his eyes shut and was leaning against one of the outer walls. It looked as if he was asleep.

*Shit, bugger it, shit, shit!*

Chris stood in silence, and his thoughts were becoming increasingly negative. *Munson thinks I am an idiot. St. Clair thinks I'm a nobody. Perhaps they're both right. I'm a fucking useless twat! Maybe I don't have four hours. Maybe I am on my own. Maybe Munson is going to fuck me, and we've got ten minutes. How the hell did I let this happen? What the hell was I supposed to do? I didn't mean to kill the guy. Shit happens.*

"Is everything okay, Chris?" The voice was gentle, soothing.

"I'm okay, Doctor, just trying to get my bearings."

"What is going to happen to us? What did your people say?"

Chris tempered his tone. There was no reason to take his frustrations out on the Iranian anymore. "They are working on a plan to get us out of here, but we need to move. We can't stay here."

"Where will we go?"

*Jesus, I don't know, I really don't. For once in my life, I really don't know what to do. We could be moving forward towards danger or moving further away from rescue, I don't know.*

He stared back at the doctor realizing that his outward appearance was probably not all that appealing nor did it demonstrate confidence. But Chris knew he had to put his misgivings to one side. He realized that, although he didn't know the man's story, he must be brave to do what he was doing, and he showed no thoughts of defeat, only optimism. It made Chris think about why he was here in the first place. He was here to help; that's what his job was, and that's all his personal mission was about. Chris was the one that people turned to for help, the one that got things done, the one with the initiative and drive. So now he had to buck up and show he was in charge and could be relied upon to get them out of here. "We're going to head south. C'mon, let's go. Don't worry. I won't run you into the ground this time."

## DAY 25
## CIA Headquarters, Langley, Virginia

Richard Nash was reading the debriefing notes from Paul Strong's arrest and deportation when his desk phone beeped once and Carla Reeve, his secretary, spoke over the intercom.

"Richard, I have Nick Seymour FBI London Office on the phone. He'd like to have a minute."

Nash stared at the phone and furrowed his brow. "Anything specific?"

"He wants to talk about Chris, but he wants to go secure."

"Okay, transfer me across."

When Nash saw the lights of the phone change color, he picked up the second phone on his desk. "Hello, Nick. How are you?"

"I'm fine, thanks. How's life in the fast lane?"

"Rather be eating real fish and chips and having a pint in a pub with you, but life's good otherwise. What can I help you with?"

Nick knew Nash could do without all the formalities; he preferred direct facts and no bullshit. "George St. Clair was murdered at his home three days ago." Nick let the statement hang.

"Well, I'm sorry for Mr. St. Clair's demise, but what has that got to do with Chris?"

"St. Clair was the deputy division head for E Division MI5."

Nash sat a little straighter in his chair. "And what's E Division?"

"Foreign Nationals, basically the division monitors and investigates questionable foreigners who enter the UK based on intelligence from MI6 and other foreign intelligence agencies, mine and yours included."

"Okay, where are you going with this, Nick? What has this to do with me or Chris?"

Nick went on to explain his phone call from Chris when he was confronted at Heathrow as he entered the UK and then the meeting at the motorway service station in Reading. Nash was sucking it all in and trying to digest it when Seymour spun the story in a different direction. "The thing is I don't think Chris did it."

"Then who?"

"Pam."

Nash dropped his head into his hand and began to rub his eyes, trying to wash away the seriousness of the statement."

"Richard, Richard . . . are you still there?"

"Yes. What makes you think it was Pam?"

"Her prints were found on the murder weapon. But get this. Chris and Pam were both at the house for a social visit before the night of the murder. St. Clair's wife gave her the weapon, a ceremonial sword, to look at. Pam picked it up and toyed with it for a while. Pam's were the only prints found on it."

*Social visit, my butt,* Nash thought. "Let me get this straight. Chris got into a pissing match at Heathrow with some MI5 guy and paid him a visit to straighten things out. Then Pam picked up a sword in the house a few days before a murder, and now she is a suspect? That's pretty thin, Nick, even for the FBI. Anyone with a grudge could have done it. Shit, for all I know it could have been his wife." Knowing full well what Pam was capable of, he didn't doubt the FBI man. "What's Scotland Yard doing?"

"They've got some physical evidence, muddy footprints, etc. They have issued a warrant for her arrest . . . and they want to talk to Chris."

"Chris flew to India from the UK. I'll get Carla to give you his flight details, and I'm guessing he was out of the country when this happened, which should be enough to keep them off your back for a bit. But do you really think Pam could have done such a thing? Really, Nick, you know her."

"I don't know. It seems highly unlikely, but the Brits seem to think she was involved with something, and they are being pretty tight-lipped about it."

Nash was happy to hear that Nick didn't know about her special extracurricular activities but not surprised that the Brits were on to something. "Well, she was heavily involved with the war crimes tribunal. Perhaps she was chasing down a lead or something. I'm sure we will find out soon enough. Do we know where she is?" Nash knew full well without having to ask.

"No, I was hoping Chris could shed some light for us. When will he be available for a chat?"

"I don't know, Nick. He's out in the field, but as soon as he surfaces, I will let him know we talked and I'll get him to give you a call."

Nick desperately wanted to tell Nash to warn Chris not to enter the UK anytime soon, but knowing the call was probably monitored, he thought better of it. His only hope was that Chris did not have a return ticket to London.

Almost fifteen minutes after ending the call with Nick Seymour, Carla Reeve entered Richard Nash's office and placed a cable on his desk. She left without saying a word.

IMMEDIATE DDO
WNINTEL
STOCKHOLM

1. PRIMAL OCEAN TEAM MEMBER RITA KILLED IN ACTION.

2. NO OTHER CASUALTIES, TARGET CONFIRMED DECEASED.

3. NO FILE ATTACHED. END OF MESSAGE.

"Carla!" Nash shouted. When she stood in front of his desk once more, he calmed a little and then whisked off some commands. "I need time with the director. Tell him I need to close Primal Ocean. That should get his attention. Walk over there; don't make a call. Work your magic with the other girls and get me in ASAP. Second, find me Gene and Robert Crauford. I don't care where they are in the world. I need them on the phone or in this office yesterday. Third, cancel all my appointments for the day. Then find out for me what's happening with Chris. Call down to CTC and get them to give me a briefing within the hour on what he's doing in India. If I'm with the director, send them up there. And if you see Dana on your travels, get him in here."

As Carla walked away, she reminded him of another engagement. "Don't forget you're supposed to be at the farm tonight."

"Goddammit, thanks, Carla."

# DAY 26
## New Delhi, India

Night-time cloaked Chris and Doctor Mousavi's movements as they ducked in and out of mangled suburbs and ramshackle shantytowns while crisscrossing their way south of the University of Delhi. At one point, they found an open area to the rear of what looked like a shopping mall. There, covered by some trees, they rested and waited for the time to hit the appropriate hour for the next call. Chris ruled out the possibility of sleep, not only to maintain a watch for pursuers but also as a guard against possible snakes, rats, and spiders. He found himself a large stick and placed his back against a tree trunk and watched as the minutes ticked by. The doctor sat by his side. They were both tired, hungry, and thirsty.

"Thank you, Chris," the doctor whispered.

"What for?"

"For helping me to get to the West."

"We're not there yet. There's a long road ahead, but I've been thinking. Why didn't you just approach the American or British embassies?"

"We couldn't. We were constantly under watch. We had no real opportunity."

"So why didn't you ask the Indians for help?"

"They are part of the problem, Chris. We were supposed to go back days ago, but I insisted we find a way to not go back to Iran and not stay in India."

"We? You mean your bodyguard?"

"Yes, Hasan was my friend. I will miss him, but he was prepared to give his life for me. . . to help me get to the West. We were of the same belief about our corrupt and draconian government, and he was sick and hoped to get better care outside of Iran."

Chris wanted some peace and quiet, and he didn't want to brood on any more negatives either. "You don't need to tell me this. In fact, I really don't need to know, but what do you have to offer? It's not as if I can help you very much. I'm not an officer of the CIA. I'm a contractor. But I'm curious. Why you are doing this?"

The doctor realized early on in the escape from the jail that Chris was one of those soldiers that would put himself in harm's way if the cause was just. In some weird way, Mousavi thought Chris was similar to his late bodyguard. Right now, the doctor was feeling lonely and afraid. For the last three years, Hasan had been his nursemaid, and now he was gone. Mousavi was taking steps into the unknown, and he was not sure what would happen next or, if the Indians were to catch up with them, if they would survive. He had no choice but to trust Chris; there was no one else.

"I know who you are, Chris. The first time I saw you at Navistar, you gave me the idea of finding someone from the West to help us. The opportunity fell into our laps when Deepak or Dinesh or whatever his name was told us they were holding someone. I am not an intelligence officer either, but Hasan came up with the idea of trying to free you so you could help us."

Chris nodded. He never had the opportunity to thank the man he called Stretch.

"I am a scientist, Chris. I believe in the creation of the universe and the great unknown that lies before our tiny little world. I believe in empirical data and facts. I love science and all facets of experimentation, exploration, and discovery. What I don't believe in is mutual self-destruction, and we as a human race are on the path to ultimate devastation. Although Iran is an isolated country, it is not backward in any sense. We are quite advanced, despite the embargoes that the United States and the UN have imposed on us throughout the years."

Chris didn't need a lecture but was nonetheless intrigued as to where this was going. He let the doctor continue while silently monitoring the grounds before him and playing inattentively with his stick.

"My role for my government was to work on a new navigation system for a nuclear weapon."

Chris almost shit his pants and needlessly jumped up from his sitting position. "Jesus Christ!" He stood in front of the doctor not knowing what to say next and let him carry on.

"The information that I have," he tapped his briefcase and then his head, "will show the West that, despite public intentions of peace, collaboration, and reconciliation purported by Iran, it is in fact receiving aid from India and Russia to enhance its military nuclear capability."

Chris was almost gobsmacked. "Jesus, Doc, I was expecting some political activist story or some religious persecution thing. What the hell? I mean, shit, this puts a different spin on things." Chris was quick to translate the information that he had just received, "So not only are they looking for me for killing a cop, but you're the one they really want."

The doctor nodded in silence, knowing what capture would entail.

Chris also knew and also remained silent. He paced around, deep in thought, but after a short while, he sat back down next to the tree. "Where do you want to go?"

"I need to go to Berlin first and then Canada."

"Berlin? That's a great city, but why there?"

"I have a friend who works at the Canadian embassy. I think he can help me resettle after this mess is cleared up." Mousavi could see the bewildered look on Chris's face. "I know what you are thinking, Chris. We drove past many of the embassies here in Delhi, but each of them is well guarded, and our movements were closely watched. There was no possibility to get away, and here we are."

"So this friend of yours, is he in a position of authority, someone that can really help? How do you know this guy? Can he be trusted, or will he want to help?" Chris had a dozen questions, none of which he should have been asking. That would be someone else's job. "No, I'm sorry. You shouldn't have to answer that. I'm sure you must have your reasons."

There was a long pause as neither of them spoke. Chris was nervous' the clock was slowly getting closer to the call in time.

The doctor broke the uneasy silence. "I first met him in Esfahan on the Siosepol Bridge. He was trying his best to ask for directions to a restaurant, but nobody could understand his Persian, so I helped him along the way. He told me he was interested in ancient architecture and he was here to visit the city, which had a reputation as the most beautiful in all of Iran. I was proud to show off my knowledge of the area, and I took him to a restaurant that I knew of on the Zayandeh River where we ate *chelow* kebab and *akbar mashti* ice cream. He was searching for something traditional, something unique to Iran, so I gave it to him. We toured the city and talked for hours. I told him I was a doctoral student and I came to find out he worked at the Canadian embassy in Teheran as the cultural attaché."

Chris looked over at Mousavi. From the way he was talking and the glimmer in his eye, Chris could tell the doctor was talking of someone he was close to. He let the doctor continue.

"We vowed to keep in touch, and it was only when I continued my studies at the University of Tehran that we finally made contact and saw each other again. . . . I think I fell in love with him after the first time I saw him. He told me for him it was the second time." He turned to face his companion. "So you see, Chris, I can never return to Iran. Even if I wasn't a scientist, persecution of my kind in that country is too much to take. I don't think the world realizes how bad it is for people like me."

Chris was concerned and felt genuine sympathy towards the man. "What happened to him?"

"He was transferred out. At first, he said it was a typical rotation for staff at the embassy, but he told me later he was trying to protect me from the regime. But what he was doing was sentencing me to a life of loneliness and oppression. We were together two years, and I miss him dearly. I want to see him before I decide what I should do with what I know. I need to find out if there can be a relationship between us again. . . . Do you understand, Chris?"

"Yes, Doctor, I do." Chris couldn't find any more words, he was in a state of shock. He felt sorry for the man and wanted to help him, but he also realized he had an extremely valuable asset in his hands. He thought of Pam as they sat in silence and patiently waited to make the next phone call. *I should have asked her. I should have asked.*

# CHAPTER EIGHTEEN

DANA MUNSON GLIDED CASUALLY NORTHWARD ALONG THE ANACOSTIA RIVER in his kayak on the return leg of an excursion downriver to the Langston Golf Course. He was not a fitness fanatic, nor was he a perfect model of a healthy, middle-aged man, but he liked to try to stay in shape as best as he could, and the only sport that he enjoyed was kayaking. It was a bit of an advantage having his ailing mother live on Tilden Road only a few miles from the Bladensburg Waterfront Park—he usually kept his kayak at the facility and left his gear at the house that he grew up in and stayed for a night to comfort her. For a while he was able to make it a weekly occurrence, but with his position at the agency, he was forced to live closer to his work and further from the only leisure activity he had.

It was still pretty early in the day on the river without much traffic to worry about. Now and again there would be a group of high school kids learning on the water, but today the river was placid with little movement or activity. As he came into view of the dock, he saw only one other person getting ready to head out onto the water. When he approached, he saw it was a young woman preparing a rowing scull. As he bumped alongside the dock, the woman stopped what she was doing and made a move to help Munson shore up.

"Let me help you with that," she happily offered.

"Thank you, but there's no need."

The woman ignored the reply and held on to the front of the kayak as Munson extricated himself onto the dock. "There is a scientist that has gone missing. We believe he is trying to get to the West. This cannot be allowed to happen. You must stop him at all costs. Vasili sends his regards and wished that he could be with you on the water. Perhaps another time."

She tied off the front of the kayak for him, boarded her scull, and rowed quickly off into the distance. Munson went about the business of removing his craft from the water and carrying it back up the gangway to the storage area. He looked around as he went hoping and praying there wasn't a dark-colored Ford Crown Victoria with two men wearing shades in the parking lot. His image of the FBI was immature, but he worried that the encounter was noted by someone and that multiple eyes from multiple directions were on him. The fact Vasili had an asset track him and pass on a message escaped him. It was an unusual occurrence, to say the least, but what worried him was that his SVR handlers were asking more and more of him lately. He considered the encounter as he walked back to his car. *First Springfold, then Primal Ocean, now this. They are asking too much, but I just need a little more, a little more cash, and I can retire for good.* When he eventually got back to his car, he took a minute before he started it to think about his latest accomplishments, *Springfold was a disaster. Thank you, Richard, for the three hundred thousand dollars. Primal Ocean is no more. Pam and Chris are suspects in a murder case. Things are looking up. Now the scientist. I wonder how much he is worth.*

## DAY 26
## New Delhi, India

Chris felt as exposed as a naked soldier climbing out of the trenches in the Somme. He stood at the gates of the Qutub Minar Complex, a popular tourist destination that boasted the tallest brick minaret in the world, as well as medieval monuments that were visited by Indians and world travelers alike. It was still early in the morning, and the only other people around were the street vendors getting ready to ply their trades and a few street cleaners with their straw broomsticks making a futile effort to clean the garbage off the street from the previous day's visitors. To Chris's dismay, he spotted two police vehicles parked in a closed-off area in front of the main gate, as well as a police sub-station that resembled a temporary work trailer more than an official building. He shook his head in disgust. *How the hell could they send me here? This is bullshit. We can't stay here. We have to keep moving.*

As he looked in every direction trying to find a new meeting place, a noise made him spin quickly around to his back as the main gate to the complex was opened by two police officers. Behind them was a metal detector and two more officers approaching with a box full of other equipment used for crowd control. They were getting ready for the anticipated hordes but paid no attention to the two foreigners in the street in front of them. From the amount of litter and the overflowing garbage cans, Chris could tell that whoever chose this location had probably been there before and during a time when there were crowds of people, which under normal circumstances could provide a viable first line of cover. Now at this hour of the morning, as the city was still coming awake, there wasn't a single tourist to be seen, just two disheveled-looking men who looked as if they slept rough the night before. It was a small but important tactical detail that was missed and could have landed them in serious trouble if Chris hadn't been alert. Although they were supposed to meet someone from the embassy there, Chris didn't want to wait around and get questioned by a curious do-gooder cop or tourist guide who was trying to earn a few rupees. But he had a choice to make—be patient and wait for the pickup or move. He didn't wait to think about it too much. There were three roads in front of him—one to the left from where they came by rickshaw, one immediately to his front, and one to his right.

He chose the road to the front and began marching. As he gained some momentum, he spotted a short distance away a shiny white car, which took a parking spot on the side of the road. As Chris got closer, a passenger got out and headed in his direction. Chris immediately checked his left, right, and rear for correlating activities. There were none. No sudden movements, no strangers looking at him, no small crowds, no uniforms. When he looked forward again, he could make out the features of the man who was as pale as a snowman and wore short blond hair. His gait indicated he could be carrying a weapon, but if he was not, he had the look of a military man.

As they both approached each other, the stranger looked Chris in the eye. "Klondike?"

"I am today," he replied.

"Rory Weitz, let's go for a ride."

As they approached the car, Chris slowed down to a stop. "Who's your driver?"

"What?"

"Your driver, who is he? Is he with the office?"

"No, he's a local embassy guy. Is there a problem?"

"Yeah, there's problem. He may know his way around, but does he know how to drive?"

Rory stood in silence for a moment. "Are you shitting me?"

"Let me drive. You just give me directions."

"Chris, you are not in Germany anymore, and don't forget you were once in the driver's seat just like him."

Chris was pissed. It seemed his reputation followed him every-where. He didn't have anything against the driver; it was not personal. Chris just knew the driver wasn't trained to get themselves out of a jam if something came up. Chris had promised Doctor Mousavi that he would do his utmost to get them out of the country, and that meant taking no chances.

An agitated Rory continued, "We've got a lot of ground to cover. Now get in the car and play tourist. If we get stopped for any reason, we are on the way to Agra, the Taj Mahal. Once you are in the car, get some rest. We will not be chatting while the driver is with us. Now there . . . . " "Let me sit up front."

"You can sit on the fucking roof for all I care. Let's go. We're wast-ing enough time spinning our wheels standing here."

The sleep monster was trying its best to get Chris to be submissive, but the former British soldier was having none of it and battled on. Every time his lead-laden eyelids moved south, he took another sip of water that Weitz had so generously provided to combat the fatigue. Along with some fresh bread rolls and a banana, both travelers were feeling a little replenished, but both were in dire need of a warm shower and a comfortable bed. It didn't help that there was total silence in the car, so Chris tried his best to stop yawning and take in his surroundings and identify landmarks along the way and think of what-if scenarios to pass the time. A three-hour drive in most western countries around the world would be monotonous and uneventful, but travelling in India was never boring. The sounds, the smells, the dust, the garbage, the poverty, the sheer numbers of people all required a second and sometimes third look.

Although Chris had needlessly disparaged the embassy driver earlier, he admired the man's skill in avoiding all sorts of hazards, including the venerated cow. Each time the vehicle got up to speed, the driver would come to a screeching halt to give room to the beasts that freely wandered the landscape causing regular near-death experiences. Chris changed his what-if game to that-was-the-closest-one-yet, which applied not only to the livestock on the road but also all other manner of human activity, motorized or pedestrian. With the mass of people in India, there was simply not enough room for everyone.

After about thirty minutes of passing into the state of Uttar Pradesh, the driver veered from Route 2 and made his way onto Route 22A. Chris snapped his head left and right trying to see where they were going. He saw a sign that read Aligarh, but as they were travelling at speed, he could not be sure. He wanted to ask Rory a bunch of things but refrained from doing so as ordered. Instead, his mind was full of images of wild crash scenes and potential what-ifs and close encounters. He knew he needed to switch off and relax, but when he was in a car and was not driving, not in control, he could not nor would not step down.

Chris had lost all track of time and was feeling too drowsy to care if they killed a cow on the road or ran over a goat or a dog. He had no idea where he was but came back to life when they turned left off the main road and followed a sign to the Dhanipur Air Strip. As they got closer, he saw another sign for a flying school and noted there were two small hangars and four or five other buildings in the complex before them. The driver made his way towards the larger of the two hangars and parked the car. Rory exited the car first, and Chris and the doctor followed suit while the driver remained with the car. When the three entered the hangar, they were approached by a pilot who had obviously been waiting for them. He reached out his hand to Rory.

"Hey, good to see you again."

"Feeling's mutual. What's the status?"

"We are just fueling up. Another twenty minutes or so. If you want to take a break, there's a restroom back there. You can wait in the office if you want. I'll come get you when we are ready after pre-flight checks and all that."

"Sounds like a plan. See you in a bit."

Rory motioned for Chris and the doctor to follow. When the three entered the room, which resembled a mechanics workshop more than an office, Rory sat everyone down at a large desk in the center of the room. "Okay, we've got a bit of time. We need to use it wisely. Doctor Mousavi, I am sorry for not introducing myself earlier, Rory Weitz, US embassy New Delhi. I work for the CIA." He outstretched his hand to shake, which they both did.

Chris looked on. His distrust factor moved up on his personal scale. There was something about Weitz he didn't have a warm and fuzzy feeling about.

Weitz continued, "We have a lot to cover and only a short time to do it in." His tone was even, smooth, and calculated. "But let me say on behalf of the director of the CIA and from the president of the United States, thank you for coming forward to expose this sham of a government in Iran and its nuclear intents."

*Someone's been doing his homework*, Chris noted.

Weitz droned on. "We have been very concerned with activities in your country for a number of years, and I am sure you have a lot to say, but there will be an appropriate time and place for that, and we must ensure that we get things correctly documented and verified. I am sure you understand the gravity of this situation and the ramifications of you coming forward, but today is not the day to go into detail about such things. Right now, I hope you understand, but I need to have a discussion with Chris. Could you excuse us for a few minutes, please?" Mousavi left the room happy to be able to stretch his legs. He was unsure of how these things went, but he didn't want to stray too far from Chris's protection should he need it.

When Mousavi was out of earshot, Weitz shot a look at Chris. "Okay, tough guy, you need to tell me everything that happened to you from the time you arrived in the country until the time we met today. Go!"

Chris stared blankly at Weitz. He wanted to say, *The more you rush me, the slower I go*, but didn't. He knew the CIA man was going to be his ticket out of here, so he had to keep on Weitz's good side. Chris began with a detailed response starting with the arrival at the airport with Satish. When Chris got to the part of escaping the interrogation center, he was curious about how it all transpired. "So this jailbreak, who was behind that?"

"Ever heard of the Naxalites?" Weitz asked.

"I think so. Aren't they aligned with communists?"

"Yes, Maoists, Marxists, whatever you want to call them, but they are terrorists. They've been active since the late sixties, but recently they have been a little more aggressive. The Indians call their area of operations the Red Corridor. Now and again they will hit politicians, police stations, or the military. But this time, it was a jailbreak, and some of their leaders escaped. They were pretty well organized. You got lucky, Chris."

Chris nodded and stared off into the distance. "Shit, I thought I was going to end up with my testicles in my mouth."

Weitz looked off into the distance and commiserated. "Sometimes that's all it takes. You need just one lucky break. You were dealt a good hand, Chris. Be grateful for it."

When all the questions were answered and the explanations were expanded upon, it seemed that Weitz had enough information. "Let's get the doctor back in."

When Mousavi took his place at the desk once more, Weitz faced him and tried to suck up to him again. "It seems the two of you have had a pretty rough time. Thank you again for having faith in us. I want you to know that the director has authorized me to open an account for you in Switzerland, and we have already deposited two hundred and fifty thousand dollars under your new name. We will, of course, hide your identity for you, but you will have access to those funds when the time is right."

Chris caught the last phrase. His body was still tired, but his brain was working just fine. *Time is right? What the hell is he talking about?*

"However, before we invest in you too much, we would like you to go back to Iran. I can give you some training and some equipment, and we will find a way to communicate with you when you return." It was the favored tactic of most intelligence agencies; keeping an asset in place. While defections are great for the initial sharing and discussions of information, the well would dry up at some point. After that, the asset becomes a cost center and a budget-line item. A second option would be to use the asset to spy in another country. However, that scenario only worked if the subject was working in another country like India in an official capacity. Therefore, the best option for the CIA with Mousavi was to send him back to Iran and keep the flow of information constant from within that country.

Chris jumped out of his chair. Mousavi clutched his briefcase harder to his chest as if he was about to have a fit.

"What? Are you taking the piss? He can't go back. What the hell are you talking about?"

"Chris, this does not concern you. Sit down," Weitz ordered and continued to tell the Iranian the plan. "Doctor, I have a plane waiting to take us to Oman, and then you can take a commercial flight back to Teheran. I can give you more details once we are in flight."

Mousavi began to stutter, "I-I can't . . . I can't go back. I can't do this. Chris, you said—"

Chris was standing at the table doing a great impression of Popeye as his muscles began to swell. He started to think of ways out of the situation.

"Don't look at him, Doctor," Weitz said. "This will all work out. We will fly together to Oman. I can give you your training on the plane, and then we will get you home."

"Chris, what do you think I should do? I can't go back." Mousavi's eyes were swelling up.

Chris wanted to calm the situation. "Rory, he can't do it. He's not that type. He'll fold as soon as he lands. It'll be a disaster. Don't do this. It's as good as a death sentence."

Weitz stood and kicked back his chair. "I've had enough of your shit. Sit down and shut the fuck up. This is not your call."

"But it is, Rory. I gave him my word that we would take care of this. He's not going back."

There was a knock on the door. The pilot stuck his nose in. "We're all ready if you are."

Weitz who had his back to the door nodded, "Just a few minutes. Be right there."

The pilot disappeared.

"Rory look—"

Weitz held up his finger and reached into a pocket. He produced an envelope, which he passed over to Chris.

"What's this?" Chris asked as he removed the contents.

"The driver will take you back to Delhi and then on to the airport."

Chris couldn't believe his eyes. "Wow, a first-class ticket to London," he said sarcastically, "and I thought you didn't care about me. How nice."

Weitz picked up on the tone. "Look, asshole, I didn't make that decision. Okay? That was not my call. Give me a break. Look at what I have to deal with here."

Weitz was looking for some sympathy but wasn't going to get it from Chris. "I just had a fart, and that's the closest I'm going to get to giving a shit about your problems, Rory. He's not going back!"

"You are lucky that you are not in an Indian prison right now or getting fired. When you do get back, you need to thank Munson for bailing you out."

Chris started walking towards the door and closer to Weitz. "You call this bailing me out? I killed a cop. They will still want me for that! If I turn up at the airport, they will kick the crap out of me!"

"You don't need to go straightaway. We can delay it a bit for a while if you want."

Chris pondered the last offer and chose a lower gear. "You might be right, Rory. If I can lie low for a while, perhaps we can work something out."

Weitz thought Chris had given up the fight, as he tempered his voice and his demeanor changed. When his body slumped in submission, Weitz thought the Brit looked exhausted and began to relax a little. "You'll be safe, Chris. Don't worry."

"Well I do have to admit I could use a bath and some clean clothes, take a decent shit, eat some proper food."

Weitz smiled wryly believing he'd gotten the better of the upstart and let down his guard enough that when Chris threw the plane tickets at him he was taken completely by surprise. He made a reflex move to try to catch the documents, but as he did, Chris came to his right side and felt his neck being cradled in his opponent's right inner elbow. The next thing he felt was Chris's left arm hook over his head and grasping the left arm in a headlock.

Chris moved around quickly to Weitz's rear. He'd captured the man exactly the way he'd intended in a rear naked choke. When Weitz began to protest, Chris started walking backwards. "Don't struggle, mate. I'm not going to hurt you." He continued to take a few more steps backwards. "You are just going to take a short nap, okay? Nothing to worry about. I'm not trying to kill you." As he dragged him the last few feet, Chris raised his right leg and kicked Weitz behind his left knee bending it and forcing him to the ground. As Weitz fell, the choke cut off his blood flow and knocked him out. Chris gently placed him on the floor and checked his pulse. He was relieved that it was still there.

He looked over to Mousavi. "We've got ten to fifteen seconds. Give me that duct tape behind you." As Mousavi rushed off, Chris retrieved some electrical cable hanging from a wall. "Tape his mouth shut quickly. Don't cover his nose."

Chris unwound the cable as quickly as he could and began wrapping it around Weitz's wrists, and as he was moving to secure the legs, Mousavi joined in and helped him get the job done. Just as they were finishing up, Weitz came to and began to struggle.

"Chill out. The more you struggle, the more pain you are going to be in. Relax."

Both Chris and Mousavi stood back to admire their work.

"Thank you, Chris, thank you. But I can't go back. You know why."

Chris grabbed his arm and dragged him out of the office. He stopped before they left the safety of the hangar and pointed in the general direction of the airstrip. "That plane out there has a flight plan to Oman, we are getting on it. Okay? When we get there, we will figure something out, but you will not be going to Iran, and I am not going first class to London. If the pilot starts a conversation, let me handle it, okay?"

As they approached the Beechcraft King Air B100, the pilot exited the plane. Chris smiled. He'd been on one of these planes before. *This is better than British Airways any day of the week.* "Where's our friend?"

"He's not feeling too good. He's going to stick around here for a while. He's got another ticket for another flight, so no worries, mate."

"Oh, okay, let's get rolling then." The pilot didn't really care. He had a flight manifest for two passengers and that's what he had standing in front of him.

"Will you let me know when our feet are wet? I feel better when we're over the ocean and no longer in India. I can get some shuteye then."

"Will do. Buckle up. Make yourself comfortable. You'll find some refreshments on board."

Fifteen minutes into the flight, Chris was snoring happily away to himself. His idea of remaining awake and alert for possible what-if scenarios while they were still over Indian territory was worthless, as the sleep monster hit him with a vengeance.

# CHAPTER NINETEEN

## Alexandria, Virginia

RICHARD NASH PERUSED THE DINNER MENU AT THE CHART HOUSE RESTAURANT ON CAMERON STREET as he waited patiently for Dana Munson to arrive. Carla Reeve had tracked Munson down by calling his mother and leaving a message for him to call the office as soon as he had finished his kayaking adventure. When Nash and Munson finally talked, they agreed to meet in Alexandria for dinner.

Nash sipped on a glass of lemonade as he looked across the Potomac River, and although there wasn't that much river traffic to watch, he nonetheless enjoyed looking at the panoramic views up river towards Ronald Reagan National Airport and to the lower end of Washington, DC. Although he read the menu five times, his mind wandered from food and on to operational matters. He looked at his watch for the third time since he had sat down. As he did, he caught the eye of the waiter and grudgingly ordered a starter of Kim Chee Calamari. He didn't like eating alone, but he didn't have too much time to wait. If Munson didn't show up soon, Nash would start his meal and get back on the road.

Just as Nash was finishing the last of his appetizer, Munson walked in, and without any how-do-you-do, he snatched a waiter and ordered a Jack Daniels. While they were waiting for the drink, they engaged in menu decisions, and promptly ordered fresh fish when the waiter returned.

"I haven't got much time," Nash said. "I need to be in Camp Swampy tonight. There's a night exercise that's being conducted, and we have some new prospects that need a closer look." Nash was referring to the CIA training facility known as Camp Peary in Williamsburg. It was also known as the farm, but those who had spent any time there deferentially called it Swampy.

"Rather you than me. It'll be colder than a witch's tit down there tonight."

"Tell me about it. I've spent more than one sleepless night in the cold waiting for some idiot to trip over himself in the dark. It's not funny anymore. It's about time you got involved in some of the selection process, by the way. I need to keep my butt warm and attached to my desk chair. But that's not why I wanted to meet."

Munson chewed on a bread roll. He almost rolled his eyes, *Oh please! Don't pretend to fall on your sword when you go down there, you ass. You love showing off to new recruits. You could have given it up years ago. If your ego wasn't as big as this room, you'd have passed on the job to someone else long ago.* He was glad he had his mouth full.

"Look," Nash continued, "this whole thing with Primal Ocean is coming down around our ears. The director is mighty pissed off. We haven't been able to get hold of Crauford yet, so I'm assuming he's in transit. I want you to go to Paris, tell him we need to shut the program down permanently, and then I want you to go with him to The Hague and meet with Pam. I need to find out what the hell she did in the UK and then come up with a plan for damage control."

"Do you really think she killed some guy with a sword?"

"Yes!" Nash replied with conviction. "She's not shy about pulling the trigger on someone she doesn't like. Don't forget that we trained her. Remember that report we got from that time she was in Camp Atterbury, Indiana?"

"When she stabbed one of the Navy Seals in the cheek with a fork. Shit, we were lucky to get her out of there when we did. We should have done a better psych evaluation then, but it was years ago. I thought she'd be more stable after that episode. Perhaps we were wrong."

"Needless to say, we've not been invited back to shoot long range with the Seals again."

"Delta are better anyway."

"Well, that's another topic for another day Dana."

The both ate a few bites of their dinner as the waiter reappeared to top off the water and enquire if everything was to their satisfaction. Once he left, the conversation picked up again.

"So what about Chris?"

"What about him?" Nash questioned.

"He doesn't know about his girlfriend and her hobbies. What if he is there when we show up?"

"Chris should be on a plane right now to Oman. I'm going to get him to babysit our Iranian defector all the way to Berlin. By the time all is said and done, you should have finished up. He won't be any the wiser."

*You dumb shit. He's on a plane to London where Scotland Yard will want to examine the inner workings of his asshole.* Munson inadvertently let out a weak smile.

"What?" Nash asked. "Did I say something funny?"

"No, no, it's just that Chris, for all the smarts that he has, doesn't know he's been living with one of the most competent assassins the CIA has ever trained. That may come back to haunt you, Richard. You should have told him a long time ago."

## DAY 26
## Muscat, Oman

Chris had a rude awakening when the wheels of the Beechcraft touched down at the Muscat International Airport. He wasn't sure how long he had been asleep but was reassured when he saw signs around the airport in Arabic. He looked across to Mousavi, who still had his briefcase held close to his chest. He smiled at Chris. As the plane began to taxi, Chris tried to get his affairs in order and tidy himself up. He sloshed some water around in his dry mouth. A slight headache lingered, but after his ordeal in the torture cell, he was none the worse for wear. As he was ruffling his hair he noticed a pungent stink attacking his nostrils and realized that it was his socks. He didn't remember taking his boots off,

"I just wanted to make you a little more comfortable," Mousavi said.

"Yeah, but you didn't need to almost kill the pilots with the stink of my socks. We could have crashed over the Arabian Sea."

Mousavi smile broadened to show a perfect set of white teeth, "It looks as if we made it, Chris. Thank you from the bottom of my heart. Thank you."

"Don't thank me too much yet. I'm not sure what kind of reception we are going to get once that door is opened."

The aircraft eventually came to a halt, and by the time that both props had finished spinning, Chris had his boots on and his seatbelt off. In the short time he had to reflect on his actions since getting on the plane, he had mentally prepared himself for the worse. He painted a grim picture of his circumstance. The only solace he found was that he was out of India and away from the clutches of Indian authorities.

When the pilot opened up the staircase, Chris took a deep breath and walked out into the bright shiny lights of the Muscat International Airport. They were at a commercial hangar on the western end of the airport and far enough away from the main terminal of prying eyes. He saw the outlines of three men whose features were masked by the fluorescent lighting behind them around the hanger where they stood next to a minivan and were waiting for Chris and Mousavi to approach. Chris made sure Mousavi was behind him as he advanced in the direction of his welcoming committee.

A familiar pudgy figure walked towards them. "Hi, Chris, good to see you again. Dr. Mousavi, my name is Gene. I am here to escort you to a hotel where we can chat, get some food, and get cleaned up." Gene was shouting over the noise of a Boeing 747 as it took off on another runway.

Chris was hoping for a bit of warmth from his friend, but he was not getting it. Either Gene was supremely pissed off, or he was playing a game in front of the Iranian. Chris decided to play along.

As soon as everyone got into the minivan, Gene explained that the two men in the front of the vehicle were security officers and would be with the party until the doctor reached the Canadian embassy in Berlin. Chris was relieved to finally have some backup but was now unsure of his role from here on out as things went silent quickly inside the van. The deafening silence was cut by Mousavi. "Will Chris becoming with us to Berlin?"

Gene was in a sultry mood and wasn't ready to go into too much detail about immediate plans. "Yes."

Chris looked at Gene who stared at the road directly in front. He still wasn't getting the feeling that he was welcome in the transport or in the grand scheme of things. *Shit, might as well walk home from here then.*

Mousavi shot Chris a questioning look, but all he got in reply was a short shrug of the shoulders. Since nothing more was said, Mousavi wondered if he had just jumped out of the frying pan and into the fire with his newfound friends. It seemed that every time that he met someone from the CIA, all he felt was cold, hard steel. He tried to tell himself that these were early days, and things would be confusing and disjointed. If he could get to Berlin in one piece, then things would surely go his way. He turned his attention to the traffic around him and the streets and suburbs flashing by. *One step closer, one step.*

The rest of the journey was completed in silence. For once, Chris didn't ask to take the wheel to get them to where they were to go and accepted the look the two security officers conveyed. He knew if Gene was involved then other professionals would be too. Ever vigilant, he took in his whereabouts, and while he had never been to the country before, he began to take snapshots of major landmarks for future use. As they approached the Intercontinental Hotel, Gene turned to Chris and Mousavi. "We are already checked in, and we are going in through the loading dock. Once we get in the elevator, we will head to the fifth floor. Doctor, you will have your own room. These gentlemen will brief you on security matters, but they have an adjoining room to yours, and they are on duty 24/7. Chris has a room on the same floor, but I will be spending some time with him to discuss next steps. Please order as much room service as you like. We have no activities tonight so get some rest. There are also some clean clothes for you in the room. If I could ask you to remain there tonight, that would be very helpful. But if you feel the need to leave, please contact one of us first. We still have some arrangements to make, and we don't have any time frame when we can board a flight to Berlin. There is quite a bit to arrange as I am sure you can appreciate. But as soon as I know, I will tell you straightaway."

Mousavi nodded and accepted the hospitality, but he was concerned for Chris and noted the cold atmosphere between the two men.

"You look like shit!"

"Yeah, well the Salvation Army called and they want their suit back," Chris shot back.

Gene slumped into the two-seater couch in Chris's room and let out a long exasperated sigh. He took off his glasses and then leaned forward as Chris sat in a chair opposite. "You've dropped yourself in some serious shit!"

"Which part?"

"Oh, I dunno. Assaulting a CIA officer maybe? Killing an Indian cop perhaps?"

"There wasn't much I could do about the cop. I was running down a stairway. He was coming up. I was about to get captured. . . . I had to make a snap decision, and if I hadn't made the one I did, I probably wouldn't be here looking at your sorry face."

"Cut the crap, Chris. This is serious. You're lucky that some of the key players in that whole gig were killed in the jailbreak, so the stories are convoluted to say the best. There's going to be heavy fallout if the investigation continues and if they find out there was some malice or intent, but neither the Indian government nor the US for that matter takes too kindly to CIA contractors killing cops."

Chris nodded his head in submission realizing how lucky he was to be in this hotel room and not wallowing in filth in an Indian jail cell.

"What about Weitz?" he asked.

"He's one pissed off cookie monster."

"A ticket to London, Gene, seriously? I mean if I even went any-where near the airport, I would have been picked up and our scientist would be on his way to Teheran by now."

Gene sat up a little straighter, "What are you talking about? We have set this thing in motion. He's going to Berlin."

"Weitz told him he was going back to work in place and he would train him to use communication equipment. I think he was looking for some long-term relationship with him to provide all the nasty stuff that the Iranians were working on. Weitz was supposed to be on this flight, not me, and I couldn't let that happen."

"All three of you were supposed to be on that flight. Where did this idea of London come from?"

"That muppet Munson."

Gene rubbed his eyes and slid back to the comfort of the sofa. He didn't say a word but knew something was wrong. *Munson wanted Chris to face the accusations in London. What the hell? Was he trying to throw him to the lions?*

"I've never liked that guy, Gene. I don't know what his problem is, but I guess I am too beneath him or something. But why London? Why not let me on this plane?"

Gene was under strict orders from Nash not to discuss what Pam allegedly did in the UK. He wanted so badly to share with him what his girlfriend did and how she barely escaped with her life in Sweden, but he couldn't. He had to keep it all business. Nash had the master plan in his head, and Gene was ordered to keep his emotions out and focus on business. "I don't know, Chris. Perhaps he was trying to create some distance between you and Mousavi, or that was the first available flight out of there, the cheapest way. . . . I don't know. He must have had his reasons."

"Yeah, well I'm not going to be sharing my Happy Meal toys with him anytime soon. Prick!"

Gene smiled for the first time. It was good to hear that Chris was still Chris and he wasn't on a downer. He was not sure how long that would last when he found out about Primal Ocean, but they would cross that bridge when it came to it.

"So tell me more about this guy Mousavi. I know you told Weitz a bunch, but do you have a good gut feeling about this guy?"

"Not 100 percent, but he seems nice enough. I guess I have a little reservation because he has a lot to offer, and he is literally holding everything close to his chest. I don't know what he has in that case of his, but I don't think he has a mean bone in his body, and he's definitely not the type of guy you can rely on in his own country to be an asset. You know his orientation plays a large role in this defection, not that there's anything wrong with it."

"You're right Chris. There's no need to go there, but it is a factor we need to take into consideration. His friend in Berlin was pretty surprised when we told him what was going on. But you've spent the night with him. . . ."

"Asshole."

Gene smirked at his own comedy. "But has he said anything worthwhile?"

"Well I can't verify his bona fides, but what he did share was that he was recruited to work for his government while he was a student at the Sharif University of Teheran. He spouted off a number of agencies and acronyms that he was engaged with over the years, but that part went over my head, so I didn't pay too much attention. But what he did say, and yes this is the bit I paid attention to, was that Navistar was creating guidance systems for Iranian missiles that have nuclear capabilities. In return, the Indians were going to receive certain amounts of short- and medium-range rockets from Iran that could target certain parts of Pakistan. Now here's the interesting part. . . . The Indians and Iranians were both getting nuclear technology from Russia. I don't know if that means militarily or otherwise, but Iran wanted a first-strike option against NATO targets in Europe. . . ."

Gene was looking at Chris as if he had three heads but couldn't find the words.

"I'm guessing the Russians didn't really have a problem with that scenario and are happy to provide the Iranians and Indians with enough material to start a couple of nuclear wars."

"This was not in the brief that I read, Chris. Are you sure he said all that?"

"Yes, now I obviously can't verify anything he's said and he hasn't shown me what's inside his case. But he seems to think he has the stuff we need, and all he wants is to be reunited with his Canadian buddy, and then he will spill the beans."

"I need to go and call this in, Chris. I'm going to head off to the embassy and call Nash. Get cleaned up. You stink. Get some food and rest, and we'll talk in the morning about a game plan."

"You're not going to spend the night, Gene?"

"Asshole."

# CHAPTER TWENTY

## DAY 28
## Rue Pierre Nicole, Paris, France

ROBERT CRAUFORD OPENED HIS APARTMENT FRONT DOOR TO A SCRUFFY DANA MUNSON. Robert Crauford opened his front door apartment to a scruffy Dana Munson. Crauford was cross; he didn't know why the CIA man was here. "Come on in."

Munson shuffled inside. He was worn and torn after the long overnight flights from DC and New York and then the manic and congested metro ride through the city to the Sixth Arrondissement.

Once the door was firmly shut and locked behind them, Crauford said, "I'm surprised to see you here. What's the occasion?"

"Do you have coffee or something? My mouth feels like a gorilla just took a dump in it."

*You mean to hide your whiskey breath?* Crauford thought. "Sure, let me see what I can rustle up. Take your coat off; make yourself at home."

When Crauford made his way to the kitchen, Munson quickly searched for signs of other life in the apartment. There were none. Still with his coat on, he crashed on the sofa, legs extended, shoes on the furniture, and arms crossed over his chest.

Crauford came into the living room to see Munson with his eyes closed. "Are you okay?"

"Yeah, sure, been a pretty hectic few days. Been flying all over the goddamn place."

"Coffee's brewing, Dana. But why are you here? It's not as if I get you agency guys stopping by for a social. What's up?"

Dana straightened himself up and looked at Crauford. "How's Pam?"

"She'll be all right. She's one tough cookie."

"Rita was a good asset. We'll miss her."

Crauford remained silent, but his body went tense. *That's all she was to you, an asset, no sorry for your loss, no sympathy?* Exasperated, Crauford asked again, "What do you want, Dana? Why are you here?"

"I've been mulling this over the entire trip out here, and I have got to say I may have landed myself in trouble back home."

Crauford was intrigued wondering what he was in for.

"I went to the director with this, but I agreed with your report about stopping all Primal Ocean activities after the loss of Rita. At first, he was on board with the idea, and he sent that directive out to the agency and to you to stand down. But Nash kicked things off in a different direction and said that you and Pam were too valuable to put on the shelf, and he was adamant that you remain operational. He said there were dozens more targets, and if you guys needed someone else for the team, he could find someone." Munson could see the confusion on Crauford's face but didn't let him intervene. "I threw a bunch of fucks around and basically told him where to go, that I didn't want to work with him again, told him he was an asshole. You get the picture." He was gesticulating with his hands and putting on a great show. "But he has the director's ear, and I was overruled."

Crauford was beside himself. His anger boiled. "What are you trying to tell me, Dana? We are back in the game? That's ludicrous."

"I know, I know. I guess they stuck me on a plane to cool off, and I have been banished from the kingdom until things quiet down. As I was heading out the door, there was something said about insubordination or not being a team player or some other bullshit; I didn't stick around to find out."

"Holy shit! This is madness. It's way too risky, and we don't have the manpower anymore."

"You don't need to tell me. Is the coffee ready?"

Crauford trotted off to the kitchen, anticipating more information while Munson took off his coat and made himself a little more at ease. When he returned with a tray with two cups and a croissant, Munson happily helped himself and then continued. "I'll have you know I was pretty much against this whole thing from the start. My recommendation was to use the military for these types of missions, but Nash seemed to rely on you—no offence—and your military experience to get things done. Now I won't disagree that we have been successful in getting things taken care of, and it has helped that being an ex-general still has some pull and your professorship offers a great cover. But with a small team such as this, when one part of the equation is missing, the rest cannot achieve success."

Crauford nodded in agreement.

"But here's my dilemma, Robert. There is a high-value target in Berlin that needs to be taken care of, and it's come down from the director himself. I have the details with me in my case. He said this will be the last operation for you, and although Nash wants more, the director told me not to worry and he would rein Nash in. I didn't believe him so I told him that if this was not the last time, I would go to Congress and blow this thing wide apart."

"Dana, you've got to be kidding me. We can't do this with just the two of us."

"It's come from the director, Robert. There's not much more I can say or do. This mission needs to go forward. . . . I can go over the details with you. I think it can be done. But I tell you what, I am handing in my resignation when we are done. I don't think I have a career with the agency as long as Nash is there. This stinks, and I don't want any part of it anymore."

Crauford was dismayed to hear that Nash was stoking the fire and pushing this operation, especially after Rita was killed. He thought that Nash was an honorable man that could be trusted and was intelligent enough to listen to reason and lay things to rest when the time was right. Crauford's report should have been enough to end Primal Ocean, but he was not in the CIA. As a contractor, his job was to follow instructions and not question the strategy. He may not have been a soldier for years, but he still knew how to take an order.

"Show me what you've got, Dana."

After almost spending three and a half hours with Crauford going over the plans to make the hit in Berlin, Munson excused himself and left the professor work out the final details for when he met with Pam. As soon as he left the apartment, he made his way to the Port Royal train station where he caught the next available train to the Gare du Nord station. As he disembarked at the larger train hub, he battled through the throngs of commuters, students, and tourists to find a telephone kiosk. Just as he was making a beeline towards a phone, he bumped into a man whose eyes were blackened and nose was covered by a large Band-Aid. Munson immediately checked for his wallet, which was still there, "Jerk!" Munson barked, and the man offered an apology, which came out in a Middle Eastern accent. Munson thought that the guy must have gotten a nose job the last time he'd bumped into someone. *Slime ball.*

On reaching the public phone, Dana wiped down the handset with a Kleenex that he retrieved from his pocket and dialed a number from memory. It rang three times, and then he hung up. He waited thirty seconds and then dialed again and hung up on the second ring. He waited a full minute before dialing again. On the fourth ring, a voice answered, "Da?"

## DAY 28
## CIA Headquarters, Langley, Virginia

Richard Nash was cleaning up his desk as quickly as he could so he could leave in time to take his wife out for their anniversary dinner. The stack of papers piled on his desk contravened a strict clean-desk policy he knew he could never abide by, as his projects and papers were as muddled as the aftermath of a tornado. He was lucky to have Carla Reeve as his secretary, and it was as if she waved a magic wand each time he was not there to bring order to the chaos. As he was stuffing yet another burn bag, Carla popped her head around the corner to survey the damage and pass on a message.

"I have Gene and Chris on the secure phone from Muscat. Do you want to take the call?"

"Yes, hopefully, this won't take too long. Shout and scream at me if I start to waffle too much. If I want to stay married, I need to get out of here soon."

When Carla returned to her desk, she patched the call through.

"Gene?"

"Yes, I have Chris here with me."

"Good, good. Chris I hope you're rested, young man. I need you to throw yourself into the breach once more."

The loyal soldier responded without haste, "That's what I am here for, Mr. Nash."

"Good, now I need you to sprint ahead to Berlin ASAP. As much as I trust the Germans and our office in Berlin, nobody knows the area better than you. The BKA are working up plans right now for our transport from the airport to the Canadian embassy, which is fine, but I need you to go there, look at what they have, and come up with alternate routes, vehicles . . . all that stuff that you do best. I don't want to take any risks with Mousavi, and I need your expertise on the ground. Gene will follow on a later flight, and he will stay with him the whole time until he walks into the Canadians. Okay, Gene?"

"Yep, got it."

Chris was relieved to hear that the German equivalent of the FBI, the Bundeskriminalamt, or BKA as it was commonly known, was involved and providing security and transportation. He was unsure how serious they were going to take their cargo, but that was Nash's problem.

Nash continued with his directives, and he was on a roll. "Chris, I will get someone to meet you at the airport from the office with a car and a package. Gene, I assume the Beechcraft is still in Muscat?"

"Yes, it is, fueled up, ready to go."

"Good, get Chris on it, get him to wherever he needs to be to find the quickest commercial flight to Berlin. If he needs to go to Dubai,

Saudi, or wherever, I don't care. Understood?"

Gene was always one for few words when it came to orders. "Got it!"

"Once we have Chris in place, I need you, Mousavi, and your two security guys to get to Berlin. What's the latest with that plan?"

Gene, always the great logistics man, replied as if he was reading from a playbook, "The Omanis have a daily military flight to Bahrain. We can be on it anytime, and if I ask nicely, they can hold it for us for a few hours. Once we are there, we can jump on one of our air force flights to Ramstein. I have arranged for an escort from the air force police to get us to Frankfurt airport, and then we will go commercial to Berlin."

"Good." Nash was pleased things were coming together. "These next twenty-four to forty-eight hours are going to tax us all, so I need you two to keep me in the loop at all times."

Carla's face appeared around the door. She looked at her watch and looked at Nash.

He nodded in recognition. "Ok, listen, I have to go. I will be running this thing from CTC as soon as Chris lands in Germany, so that's the best way to get hold of me. Questions?"

There was a pause from the end of the line.

"Silence is golden, I like that. Good. I think we are all on the same page. Let's stay in touch."

"Will do" came the brief reply from Gene.

As soon as the phone line was disconnected, Chris turned to Gene. "He likes to get into the weeds, doesn't he?"

"You got that right. Some people think he is over the top. I don't. I like the guy. Not many people know this, but he wanted to play quarterback when he was at Notre Dame, but because of a back condition he couldn't. I guess he's playing this game in his own way now, which he shouldn't have to do, but he does."

"I'd rather have someone in charge who knows what he is doing any day and not some dickhead like Munson," Chris replied.

"Don't get me started."

# DAY 28
## SVR Headquarters Yasenevo, Moscow, Russia

Gennady Bielawski stood with his hands behind his back as he gazed across the wooded tree line from his office on the seventh floor in the main *Y*-shaped building of SVR headquarters. There was nothing much to see as he looked northwards in the general direction of Moscow, but that was the intent of the designers who had built the campus. Not only couldn't employees of the intelligence agency enjoy a panoramic vista of the surrounding area, but also passers-by on Route 38, curious looky-loos, other intelligence agencies, or just the plain crazy couldn't see much of SVR either. Much like the CIA headquarters in Langley, the purpose and design of such facilities was to keep the noses out and the worker bees working.

As Bielawski stood at the window, he bounced up and down in place to exercise his weary calf muscles. His doctor had been on to him for some time to eat less and become more active. Retirement was just around the corner, and for a man who spent most of his time behind a desk, it would probably spell a short journey to a cemetery if he didn't take care of himself. He was also ordered to de-stress himself, which under current circumstances was getting harder and harder to do.

Vasili Timoshev sipped black tea in a high-back leather chair and watched as his senior process the information they had just received from Munson.

"I really wonder what motivates the man," Bielawski said to Vasili.

"I know money plays a big part, but the information we have been getting from him lately has accelerated at an enormous speed, don't you think?"

"Yes, I do. I don't know what his long-term plans are, but I believe if we keep paying him, he is going to keep sending us information."

Gennady turned around to face his junior officer. "But don't you think he is taking too many risks?"

"He's validating risk to reward, Gennady. He wants one million dollars for this latest piece, but I don't think that's right; he's extorting us."

"I have approved only half a million, Vasili. If he wants more, if he persists, then we will expose him with the party tape. Either he will shut up and continue to work with us, or he will fold under the pressure."

"And if he folds?"

"We will send someone to shut him up. We don't need any political backlash or free press going to town on us, although some clowns in the Kremlin would love to take credit for the work that we do. We will have to be quick. You need to stay close, Vasili. Meet with him, talk to him. Understand his current mental state before we are forced to make a decision."

Vasili nodded in acceptance. He then broached the subject of the defector. "So what about this scientist?"

Gennady walked over to the samovar, poured a cup of tea for himself, and then joined Vasili in a nearby chair. "Yes, now that is a problem. I've been on the phone with dozens of people about that, and he is a serious risk. But it's interesting that Dana wants to use Primal Ocean to carry out the hit. Smart, I'll give him that. My read on that would be he is trying to absolve us of any involvement, trying to protect his paymaster perhaps."

"That's an interesting theory, Gennady, but the other problem we have is these shit farmers from Serbia. They've smelt blood in Sweden, and now they want more."

"They just don't know when to give up, do they? That psycho Arkan is another problem that needs to go away one day. Not today, but sometime soon, I think. Meanwhile, what can we do to appease them?"

Vasili placed his cup on the coffee table in front of him and eyed the fruit bowl on a side table. He was getting hungry. "Well, I told them to look to Budapest and Istanbul for where the Americans are sure to show up, but then Berlin as a slight possibility. That way if they do hear about Primal Ocean being active in Berlin, they can't say we didn't tell them. . . . We have to be careful, though; what we don't want is for them to show up and spoil the show. If there is going to be a sniper, we want it to be a clean shot. If the Serbs send someone fine; there's not much we can do about it, but it's all going to be down to timing. If they get there before the shot is made, then we have a problem."

Gennady smirked at the word "timing." He was about to say something when the phone on his desk chirped once.

"Sir, I have Zoya Girbov for you."

"Thank you. Send her in, please."

Both men stood at the same time. Vasili buttoned his coat jacket and straightened his tie in anticipation. He was surprised and intrigued to hear she was coming to see his boss.

"Zoya, good to see you again. You remember Vasili Timoshev? Please sit. Would you like tea?"

She nodded to Vasili but did not shake his outstretched hand. Instead, she clutched her handbag. "No, thank you, Gennady." She sat herself down in the chair that Vasili had vacated.

Gennady turned to Vasili. "Thank you. I will be in touch."

Vasili left the room wondering if his boss had something up his sleeve. He didn't think too much of the former KGB assassin as he knew the she and Gennady, two antiques of the establishment, were close friends, nevertheless. . . . He brushed the concern off and reflected that Girbov looked sick, infirm, and a little sad, perhaps the bearer of bad news. *It can only be a social visit . . . right?*

"So good to see you. How . . ." Gennady wanted to ask how she was, but he knew her time was limited, and although she looked a little frail, she did not give the impression that she was suffering. He changed the subject. Gennady knew Zoya liked being brief, so he got straight to the point. "I've been thinking about your last request, and I have something for you. Would like you to go to Berlin for us?"

Zoya offered a slim smile. Her face brightened, and she straightened her posture.

"I can give you the particulars of the operation later, but you are to be primary on this operation. There will be a secondary team in play; however, they are to be your backup. I hope you understand my precautions, Zoya."

She remained still and silent but was thinking she would be happy to go, and he was right in having alternatives.

"The other team will be in a standoff position."

Zoya understood this meant a sniper team.

"But I need you to get in close and ensure the target is eliminated. I have spoken with our technical services division, and they have something for you to use for the operation. Are you okay with this arrangement?"

"When do we begin?" she asked.

## DAY 29
## CIA Headquarters, Langley, Virginia

"Richard, I have Jenna Caya for you."

"Okay, send her in."

"Hi, Jen. How are you?"

"Mr. Nash, my name is Jenna. Only my family calls me Jen."

Her feisty reputation was infamous in the confines of CTC, regardless of rank. Nash felt as if he had been put in his place by the petite young girl. *She'll go far, that one.* "Oh, I'm sorry, no offence. What can I do for you, Jenna?"

She stood with a large folder in her hands. "We have Pacer traffic."

"What? Now? Shoot. I don't have time for this. Is it worth reading?"

Jenna stood mute. She could not and would not answer the question. It was her job to decode the information and pass it on to the responsible officer.

Nash accepted the bundle of documents from her and signed for it on the attached sheet. "I'll take it from here, thank you J-E-N-N-A," he playfully added.

She smiled and left his office.

He opened the folder and began to read:

IMMEDIATE DDO
WNINTEL/PACER
MOSCOW

1. YOUR LATEST ASSET IN DANGER.

2. TEAM DEPLOYED TO INTERCEPT AND ELIMINATE IN BER-
LIN.

3. DETAILS TO FOLLOW

4. NO FILE ATTACHED. END OF MESSAGE.

"Goddammit! Carla! Where's Munson?" Nash screamed.

His secretary walked back into his office. "Still in Paris, or he's on the way back."

"Run that down for me. If he's still in Europe, I may need to send him to Berlin. He's going to hate me but love me for the air miles I'm giving him. Do we know if Chris got out of Oman?"

"No I don't know. Let me work on it. Do you want me to get Gene on the phone as well?"

He was so grateful to his secretary/admin/office wife and others like her at the agency who were some of the forgotten heroes of the service. "Yes, I hope this ball isn't rolling as fast as I think it is. Thanks for reading my mind, Carla."

# CHAPTER TWENTY-ONE

## DAY 29
## Berlin Tegel International Airport, Germany

WHEN MARKO DROPPED OFF HIS THREE COLLEAGUES FOR A FLIGHT TO ISTANBUL, he was thoroughly disappointed. It had been five days since the debacle in Sweden where he had lost two of his men and, more important, a former Serbian commander to the sniper team that he had been tracking for weeks. He garnered some praise for having killed one of the enemy team but got lambasted for not following through and killing the others in the crew. Reprimanded by his superiors, he was told to travel to Berlin and wait until further orders, however. New intelligence sources anticipated that targets in Istanbul and Budapest were of more concern than a junior Serbian politician who resided in Berlin and once knew Slobodan Milosevic. After seeing his countrymen board a plane, Marko was wholly convinced that his days as a trusted Special Forces captain assigned for overseas missions were over. On his watch, he had lost Drago in mysterious circumstances in Strasbourg and then three more men in Sweden. He'd be lucky to be entrusted with a church choir, if and when he finally made it home. His punishment was to sit and wait and twiddle his thumbs until a bus ticket was sent to him for a long, long journey home.

Before seeking out a taxi back to the city, he called headquarters from a phone booth per procedure to inform them of the departure of the three Serbians.

The major who answered the phone was shouting as if he had just done three cartwheels while smoking a cigar, "Are they on the plane? Have they gone? Is the plane door closed?"

*What the hell's this guy's problem?* Marko thought and then hesitantly answered, "Yes, I saw them lining up at the gate to get on."

"Has the plane left, you fucking idiot?"

"I don't know. It must have."

"Go and check. If it hasn't, get the men back. You need them."

"What for?"

"Why are you still on the phone? Are you deaf or just plain stupid? Go and check the plane, NOW!"

Marko had to hold the receiver away from his ear. He was sure everyone in the terminal could hear the man screeching from the other end. After he hung up, he jogged his way back to the check-in gate, which was void of any passengers. He craned his neck each and every way to peek inside the waiting lounge. Again, he couldn't see anyone. He asked the gate agent if the flight had left and was informed that the plane was probably at ten thousand feet by now and there would not be any more flights to Istanbul today.

Unsure of what was going on, he made it back to the phone and once again dialed the number to speak with the obnoxious major. This time, Marko defended himself and informed the major that he was following orders to get the men to Istanbul. Everything was out of his control, and there was no way to bring them back. When the major finally calmed down, he told Marko of new information regarding a location in Potsdamer Platz and a possibility of a sniper in the area. While feeling dejected earlier about being left out in the cold, Marko momentarily rejoiced for another chance at the sniper, but then reality sunk in when he realized he was completely on his own.

As Chris made his way through the busy concourse at Tegel airport, he was almost bowled over by a man with Eastern European features but kept focused on his destination and eventually made his way to Terminal D, which housed the rental car agencies. He was not there to rent a car but meet someone from the CIA station in Berlin. He found the Avis desk and looked around for potential candidates—someone unassuming, plain, and who didn't stand out.

As much as he wanted to pace and get to work, he told himself to be patient and not be the one that stood out. The last thing he wanted was some over-efficient cop to ask him the time of day or if he needed help with directions, all while profiling his persona. Chris found a seat and disciplined himself to relax and put up with the inactivity for a little while longer. To allay his toe tapping, he picked up a discarded newspaper and began to re-familiarize himself with the goings-on in Germany. His interest in the newspaper landed him on page three when he noticed a middle-aged chubby woman standing directly in front of him. She was wearing high heels, a colorful poncho, dark glasses and it looked as if she was wearing a wig. *Oh dear God, Bond, Julie Bond.* He tossed the paper aside and stood up.

"Hello, I have a set of keys for you. There's a package underneath the front seat." She was brief, to the point, the way Chris liked it.

"Porsche or Audi?" He said good-humoredly.

She smiled the way only a mother could to a smelly child she was trying to potty train, continuing her act for anyone in earshot. "I was told you were precious. Be happy you have a car at all." She continued to smile but had an air of aloofness about her that Chris didn't warm to. "I'm sure you don't need directions, being an old embassy driver and all."

*What the hell have I done now? I can't please any of these twats!* Chris leaned in, took the keys, and whispered, "Thanks, bitch. I'll take it from here."

Chris left poncho girl standing by herself in the terminal. He didn't give a shit if she needed a ride; he had a job to do, and Nash wanted him to be fully engaged as soon as he landed. Frustrated with the help, Chris took almost thirty minutes to find the car that he was going to use for the next few days—a bright-yellow, two-door VW Polo. Disgusted, he looked the car over. "Someone is seriously taking the piss," he said out loud to nobody in particular and continued his rant. "Fucking arseholes. I've driven sewing machines with more horsepower than this shit!" He got into the car, looked at his surroundings, and shook his head. Someone was sending him a message or playing a cruel joke. *Yellow . . . yellow, really? That's what you think of me? Now I'm a fucking taxi driver? Bastards!*

Chris leaned over and retrieved the package from under his seat. It felt heavy and lopsided. He started the car and moved off. Whatever was in the package did not need to be shown to every donkey in the parking lot, so he headed out and towards the center of Berlin.

After a fifteen-minute drive, Chris pulled over at the side of the road on Spandauer Damm near Schloss Charlottenburg. He felt good about being back in Berlin again, a place he was most comfortable in and most familiar with. Chris opened up the package, and a Sig Sauer handgun slid out, which he stashed away quickly into his jacket. He became cross. *I'm not going need one of these. The last thing I am going to do here is shoot some poor bastard.* When he emptied the remainder of the package, he found a map, cell phone, and the itinerary that provided the times and routes for Mousavi's transportation needs to get to the Canadian embassy. Along with the document, he found a list of telephone numbers and names of organizations and people he needed to deal with to ensure the safe transit of the defector. There was a note stating that a police command post was set up in the center of Berlin and that he should report there to assist in the coordination efforts as soon as possible.

Chris nodded his approval. He appreciatively acknowledged that at least the Germans were taking things seriously, and knowing how accurate and thorough they were, they would not leave anything to chance. He took a look at all the routes and alternates and was again satisfied; they were the same roads he would have taken.

Nevertheless, he was a stickler for details, and he needed to run the streets himself—to see how things on the ground really were. There was no way to know on paper what sorts of hazards or obstacles could get in the way in real time. His skill in interpreting actions and non-actions of people, objects, and timing were the reasons that Nash had sent him there; Chris had an uncanny ability to see the possibilities and decipher threat vs. non-threat and take the correct action if the former appeared.

As he studied the map, he concluded there were two possible areas of concern—the airport and the final destination, the Canadian embassy. Chris reviewed again the details of the itinerary. The German BKA would get Mousavi off the back of the plane and put him in an armored Mercedes. He'd leave by a gate at the western edge of the airport property that would spit him out near the freight hangars. From there the motorcade of three identical armored cars would crisscross their way into the center of Berlin and ultimately to the Canadian building— a safe strategy.

The more Chris thought about the plan, however, the greater was his unease with the final location where Mousavi would have to get out of the Mercedes and walk almost twenty feet into the safety of the building. It gave him pause. There was a footnote at the bottom of the itinerary stating that the entrance to the underground parking lot at the embassy was under construction and thus no vehicles could enter or exit. As such, the front door was the only option.

Chris knew what he had to do. He checked his watch and calculated how much time he had before Mousavi arrived in Berlin the next morning. He had to run the routes, run the alternates, and scout by foot possible areas of attack nearest to where Mousavi would get out of the car. It was going to be a long sleepless night.

Before he started the car, Chris shook the package one more time to see if any other information was lodged therein, and a small piece of paper dropped out. "What goes around comes around MOFO. Enjoy the ride. RW." Chris smiled. "Weitz! That arsehole."

## DAY 30
### Potsdamer Platz, Berlin, Germany

At first, Pam thought the man was a construction worker. They were both on the sixteenth floor, and he was walking quietly around as if searching for something, but the stranger had not seen her. Pam could not make out his features, although she could tell from his movements and his clothing that he did not belong. She had only just arrived from the climb up the stairs with her gear and was still unsure of what to expect. Crauford had told her there wouldn't be anyone working on the floor today, so she shouldn't expect to see anyone. Nevertheless, she had to be vigilant. She gingerly took off her backpacks and laid them down out of sight behind some construction material. Then she reached into her coat and retrieved a .22 silenced pistol, which she hid behind her back as she sneaked forward to investigate.

Moving silently amongst the planks of wood, drywall, cables, and other materials, Pam remained concealed from the man who was stepping cautiously through the office complex. He was still moving away from her, so she was unable to get a full visual of his facial features but stalked the man as carefully as she could and moved from cover to cover, trying her best to remain silent and not to give away her position. It was only when the man turned to head back towards the stairs she had just climbed that she recognized who it was. The last time she'd seen his face was in the telescopic sight of her rifle in Sweden.

Marko resigned himself to the fact that the sixteenth floor of the building was clear. Either the sniper had not yet arrived, was in another location, or was nowhere near here because the intelligence was bad. For a second, he stood and pondered about what to do. He had to satisfy his own curiosity and check the floors and rooftop above. If he hadn't found anything by that point, he would come back down to the sixteenth, wait a while, and then if still nothing had happened, he would bag it and call it a day.

He made his way to the stairs, passed through the door, and waited on the landing to listen to his surroundings. Looking over the bannister down through the middle of the stairs, he checked for anything worthwhile. He would have been happy for a rat or mouse at this point, but nothing stirred; the stairway felt deserted. Marko looked up the stairs to the next level and began to climb. When he made it to the fourth step, he heard the door open behind him and turned to look. The last thing he saw was the face of a woman and a muzzle flash of a gun.

Pam had cringed when her door had opened with a slight squeak. The man had heard it too. She had seen him turn but had not hesitated to pull the trigger after lining up the sights of the gun with his face. She had been a little surprised to see him moving upwards but had known she had a fifty-fifty chance he would be either going up or down.

The first shot caught Marko in the right ear, the second in his right temple, and the third on the right side of his forehead. Pam chided herself for aiming high, a common problem for engaging a target above a shooter, and readjusted her aim down further. As Marko recoiled from the initial shots, she fired three more times, hitting him in the nose, the right side of his jaw and the right side of his neck.

Marko hit the stairs hard and slid down to the bottom feet first. Pam took two steps back to let the man fall like a rag doll. Without taking her eyes off him, she dropped the magazine and reloaded the gun with a fresh clip. She stood, watched, and waited for any movement elsewhere in the area. Then she looked into the man's open eyes for a sign of life, but the lights were out. Pam placed the gun back in her jacket and stared at the man before her. Until this point, she was all business. Her movements, her tactics, her mental preparedness had steeled her just for such circumstances, but this kill was different.

She looked at the man and only saw the mangled body of Rita lying lonely in the snow. Pam felt remorse for letting her down and not being with her to protect her. She took the blame for her friend's death, even though Crauford reassured Pam it had been Rita's choice to take the fork in the track, her choice to be in Sweden, her choice to avenge her parents' death, her choice to be on the team, her choice to be a volunteer. For the most part, Pam agreed with him, knowing what Primal Ocean stood for and the silent, just vengeance it doled out. To her and Crauford, it was the right cause. But Pam missed her friend, her proxy sister, her confidant, her partner in death's deliverance, and no matter what Crauford said to console Pam, it was her fault that Rita had died.

Killing the man in front of her was a reprieve from the grief she felt for Rita. When Crauford had come to her in The Hague to discuss what Munson wanted, he had been at first skeptical and wanted nothing to do with the affair. Pam had thought otherwise and told him that when she had stood over Rita's dead body in Sweden she had promised her she would find the men responsible and make it her life's mission to seek justice for the victims of genocide and Primal Ocean would continue in her name. She had told Crauford she needed to get back in the saddle, and the contract in Berlin was just the rodeo she needed.

Before Pam walked away from the limp body in front of her, she looked into the dead man's eyes. Hatred boiled up inside her; she was satisfied with the kill but wanted more. She ordered herself to organize her thoughts, refocus on the mission ahead, and head back to work, but before she did, she spat in the dead man's face.

Virgil McCain could not believe what he was seeing. At first, he thought it was a dream or another one of his many drug-induced hallucinations, but it was not. He heard the familiar voice of the man shouting at his cell phone, which confirmed his surprise. It had been five arduous, painful, mind-bending years since he had last seen the man who jogged passed him at the Potsdamer Platz S-Bahn, and he never thought that just days after his early release from a German prison he would see his true enemy ever again. McCain had no idea what Chris Morehouse was doing; he just had to get him.

When McCain finally got off the floor from his sitting position, he threw his backpack with everything he owned over his shoulder, stubbed out his joint, and started a slow run after Chris. He could tell straightaway that Chris had kept in shape, as he hardly missed a step, while he, the former US Green Beret, suffered miserably after years of inactivity and drug abuse. McCain had no idea of where he was headed or what he would or could do when he caught up with him but pent-up anger from being locked up abroad needed an outlet. As he ran, the almost ancient foe in front of him began to resurrect painful memories in McCain. He used to be known as call sign Preacher while working for a company with a number of other disenfranchised soldiers that shipped illegal arms and munitions to the Middle East on behalf of a corrupt US politician. By profession, McCain was a soldier; by circumstance, he was a mercenary.

Virgil McCain's demise came in 1995 when Chris caught up with him at the Berlin Tegel International Airport, chased him, and shoved him into a stack of painter's scaffolding, only to be retrieved by two German Police officers. With two dead bodies further up the concourse, McCain's innocence with the attack by Chris was short-lived as the Brit pointed the finger at him as being a player in the attempted assassination of the US ambassador to Germany. He was tried and sentenced to six years imprisonment in a German facility for conspiracy to commit murder of a US diplomat on German soil.

The only thing that kept McCain intact in his first days of incarceration was the animosity and anger he felt towards his accuser. When he first walked into Justizvollzugsanstalt Plözensee in Berlin, he was treated as the new fish, but as an American in a German prison, he was treated differently—everyone wanted a part of him; everyone wanted his blood. His military skills saved him more than once from determined attackers, but there were times when it was two to one, three to one, and even four to one, and for all his self-defense training, tactics, and aggression, he became outnumbered, weak, and vulnerable.

When things seemed to find its lowest ebb, his life took another downward turn when he was gang raped and left to squirm on a blood-drenched bathroom floor as his screams for help went unheard. It was only weeks later after prolonged medical treatment that his life took an uptick. It seemed that since he would not name his attackers, he had somehow passed a test and became a member of a club. It took him a full year to be accepted into the inner society of the inmate population, and by then he fell under the protection of a group of neo-Nazis who plied him with drugs to ease his psychological pain. In prison, he became hooked on heroin, which was supplied by his protectors; in return, when he was released, his job would be to peddle dope on their behalf to a steady market of foreign tourists in the pubs and nightclubs in Berlin.

Throughout his time inside, his mental health was challenged, and he often thought of suicide, but the desire for retribution drove him on. For McCain, he had only one reason for living—to kill Chris Morehouse.

Chris was listening to silence from the other end of the phone line as CTC was evaluating reports in real-time and he was moving on foot and away from his parked car at the Sony Center at Potsdamer Platz searching for clues for a possible shooter in the area. He hadn't started jogging yet, as the brains at the CIA had not given him a solid direction of where to go next. He'd been bouncing around the Canadian embassy since daybreak checking out possible locations and coming up with his own what-if scenarios. At first he refuted his latest order to check out the Sony Center, as that was too far out of the way from the embassy. Reluctantly he followed the order and rushed over there to check things out, but as he did, he voiced his concern that if there was going to be a sniper, he would likely be in one of two skyscrapers to the southwest of Leipziger Platz or atop one of the buildings directly opposite the Canadian embassy. Chris's protestations fell on deaf ears with the Germans, as they stated they already had teams in place to search the buildings surrounding the embassy and the two remaining buildings offered no real sniper capability as the angles for a shot were too acute. The Germans argued that the threat would likely come at ground level and were prepared to counteract any type of attack.

Nash trusted Chris's instincts and told him to stand fast and hold on the line, so they could check on some real-time reports. Chris was getting impatient. The clock was ticking down, and being on the phone waiting for someone to make a decision gripped his balls. "C'mon, we haven't got all day!" he shouted into the mouthpiece. His exasperated plea worked.

Nash came on the line, "Debis Building, Piano Hochaus, go now!"

"On my way!"

# CHAPTER TWENTY-TWO

DAY 30
## Debis Building, Potsdamer Platz, Berlin, Germany

CHRIS HAD MADE HIS WAY INTO THE SIXTEENTH-FLOOR OFFICE COMPLEX. There was nothing more he could do for the dead man in the stairwell. The floor was still under construction, and building materials were evident everywhere. Dust and debris were spiraling all around the area, which supported his hunch that the shooter must be on this floor as it was void of any solid walls or windows, thus providing a clear shot to the streets below.

"I'm close. Going silent. Will keep the channel open as best I can. Respond."

Chris gingerly made his way through the wooden and aluminum frames and structures that would one day house dozens of office workers. Some of the rooms were near completion with drywall in place, so his line of sight at times was limited. As he slowed his movements in an attempt to control his adrenaline, he realized he was cold. After sprinting up sixteen floors, he had finally stopped sweating, and now his damp clothes were beginning to send a chill through his body. He began fine-tuning his senses. Again, he checked his phone. "Jenna respond." Still silence. Chris looked down at his phone . . . no coverage; he had lost the signal. *Shit, shit, shit,* he thought to himself. *Up shit creek without a paddle again. What's new?*

He contemplated his next actions, trying to reason things out quickly. He didn't know how much time he had left. The only way Chris would know he had failed was if the sniper came out of the hide or if he heard the shot; otherwise it was still game on. He thought about backtracking out to the stairwell to find cell phone coverage to get instructions, but at the same time, he gloomily thought if he went backwards and then he heard a shot, all would have been for naught. He ripped his cell phone earbud out of his ear, moved forward, and thought, *Once more unto the breach, Chris . . . once more.*

He was actually happy he didn't have the CTC in his ear, in his brain—respond this, respond that. He wanted desperately to say, *Leave me alone. I know what I am doing.* But he was in the middle of the big game now, right where he wanted to be.

Chris moved forward with trepidation, concentrating on his every move. He needed to be careful about which way he looked, which way his gun was pointed, which way his body was facing, and how much shadow and silhouette his form was giving. He was sure the shooter was focused on getting the shot off, but the sniper could quite easily have heard him moving through the area already, have called off the shot, and now be in hunter mode with Chris as the target.

He tried his best not to get tunnel vision and to keep his eyes scanning for danger. His senses were telling him that it was cold, cold enough to see his breath, cold enough to dry his sweat. The air was crisp, so he knew that the shooter's shot would be true without much heat deflection to push the round off target. It was a dry day without much wind, and the warmth of the sun kept any ice or frost from forming. Although Chris was on a pinpoint edge and ready to pull his trigger, his fingers were reminding him that without many windows, the sixteenth floor was a cold place to be. He regretted not having his coat with his gloves stashed in the pockets. The shooter, Chris assumed, was bundled up in heavy clothing in anticipation of waiting for the target to appear. Being warmly clad would be an advantage for the shooter who did not need to move around too much but had the disadvantage of being restricted needing to move fast.

Once Chris had a better sense of his bearings, he managed to spot an opening at the apex of the triangular building that looked directly over Potsdamer Platz and across the intersection to Leipziger Platz. He spotted the red-and-white maple leaf flag that fell loosely about the pole at the Canadian embassy, and he rightly surmised there was little or no wind to prevent an accurate shot. Chris quickly calculated that the range was about two hundred meters from where he was standing, which in his mind was a perfect spot for a sniper. At first, he thought the intelligence was off, but that didn't explain the body in the stairwell. Just as he was about to move from his position, Chris spotted the motorcade waiting at a traffic light at the busy intersection below. With his back to the point of the triangle, he took a fifty-fifty chance and moved to his left side hoping he would find the shooter somewhere nearby.

Before, his steps had been calculated and choreographed like a dancer's—one foot forward, rear foot brought up to touch the front before taking another step. Now he had to move quickly. His time for remaining covert was over, the motorcade was almost at its destination, and as soon as the defector got out of the car, he would be history. Chris's guess to move to the left of the building was correct, as most parts of this side of the construction zone were just plastic sheeting trying unsuccessfully to keep the elements out. The framed office spaces were bare but from time to time drywall prevented him from seeing into a room completely. Time was running out for Chris who still had not found his quarry. He made it halfway down the side of the building, and when he looked back to see if he could still see the Canadian embassy, he realized he must have missed the shooter because he could not see the maple leaf flag anymore. He began to double back when he sensed something strange and stopped in his tracks. Until now, he was so focused on finding the assassin he forgot about the steps he had heard in the stairwell earlier. Now he could hear someone in the general area, and it sounded as if he—or she—was throwing up. *Can't be in shape*, Chris thought. As the person continued to retch, Chris heard the sound of a foot or object scraping the concrete floor. The shooter had heard the retching too and might be getting ready to investigate. Chris moved toward the scraping sound and came to a room that was enclosed in plastic. He could make out the shape of a person standing with a rifle pointed downwards towards Leipziger Platz.

Chris's orders were clear: intercept and stop the shooting at all costs. But his intuition and need for caution took over, and for a second, he thought he was a cop. "Drop the weapon!" he shouted, not knowing if the shooter could even understand his language.

The shooter did not move.

Chris repeated his order, "Drop the weapon. I am not giving you another warning."

The shooter did not move an inch.

Chris aimed his gun at the head and was about to pull the trigger.

"Chris, this is not the time. Back off."

His blood turned to concrete, and he almost froze in place. "Pam?"

"Chris, this is not the time or place. You don't know what you are getting into."

Chris ran up to the plastic and removed it from its fastenings on the ceiling to reveal his girlfriend clad in a black parka with her right eye placed firmly on the scope of the rifle. Her right finger was poised to pull the trigger. His courage failed him, and he let his gun fall to his side. A tear ran down his cheek. "What the hell are you doing?"

"Keep out of this Chris."

As they were talking, a helicopter from the Bundesgrenshutz hovered over Potsdamer Platz obscuring the view from the sniper's vantage point.

"Goddammit, Chris!"

With the momentary lapse in Pam's concentration, Chris made a move to kick the rifle away, and Pam backed away.

"Chris, behind you . . .!"

The footsteps were back.

Virgil McCain didn't know what to make of the situation in front of him at first. He heard Chris playing sheriff and ordering someone to drop a weapon and quickly supposed that whoever was on the other end of the order was a bad guy and as such a potential ally to him. As dizzy and sick as he felt, his adrenaline pushed his body forward. The need to kill Chris Morehouse overcame any desire to stop, rest, and recuperate. His head was buzzing, and his vision was blurred, but he pushed on towards Chris. Then he saw that his adversary had lowered a gun that was pointing at a woman. With all he had left, McCain sprinted towards his enemy.

When Chris spun around at Pam's warning, he raised his weapon on instinct, but it was a millisecond too late. The man rushing towards him went for the gun. As a struggle ensued, both men were in a death grip fighting for the weapon. Chris started to backpedal and fall backward. As he did, his finger pulled the trigger, shooting a round into the attacker's rib cage. As Chris continued to fall, he let off another round, which caught the man in his right shoulder. Chris could feel his attacker's weight bearing down on him, and as he felt his back hit the ground, he automatically raised his knees to protect himself and kick his opponent up and over his head in a cartwheel. While the motion of his attacker forced Chris flat on his back, his opponent's grip on the weapon slackened, and Chris let off another two rounds, one hitting the ceiling and the other directly behind him where Pam had been standing.

When the attacker finally let go of the weapon, Chris spun quickly over onto his belly and readied his weapon for another attack, expecting to see the injured man in his sights and Pam standing to one side. Instead, he saw the head of McCain falling out the window arms thrashing to grab something to stop his death fall. He grabbed the only thing close to him—Pam's right leg. Chris dove forward, but he was too late. The last thing he saw of her was her blue eyes pleading for help, her hands outstretched towards him.

The low hovering helicopter from the Bundesgrenshutz distracted everyone around Potsdamer Platz. As it remained in place between two skyscrapers, the motorcade finally came to a halt outside the Canadian embassy. Gene Brooks got out of the middle of the three Mercedes, and

Farhad Mousavi followed close behind. As soon as they exited, they were surrounded by BKA protection officers.

An updraft from between the high buildings forced the suspended helicopter into a wild motion and caused the pilot to take evasive action to escape possible danger. The sudden movement and change in tone of the helicopter made each of the party look skywards. As they did, Zoya Girbov stumbled forward towards the entourage and dropped her bag of groceries in front of Mousavi. As oranges and apples rolled beneath his feet, he bent down to help the old lady while still clutching his prized leather case to his chest. No words were said between the two, but he assisted the old woman pack her bag and helped her on her way. Gene caught sight of the activity and immediately ushered Mousavi away and into the safety of the building. The old lady threaded her way through the bewildered BKA men and continued on her way.

Once inside, Mousavi breathed a long sigh of relief and let himself relax as he anticipated his new release on life. He smiled at Gene, who patted him on his back, genuinely happy for the man. Mousavi stood in the lobby of the embassy as he waited for his long-lost friend to appear. He had made it this far, and now the sky was the limit. For once in his life, he was truly free. He was going to be happy, and now that he was here, nothing was going to stop him from meeting his true love. He placed his briefcase on the floor next to his feet. The new irritation on the back of his hand demanded he scratch it immediately.

As Zoya Girbov headed towards the Potsdamer Platz S-Bahn, she twisted her ruby ring back from the inside of her finger to its usual position and replaced the cap to cover the minute blade that protruded from its case. In doing so, her fingers came into contact with the sharp point and whatever remnants of ricin that remained on the blade entered her system. She had known the risks when she had been presented with the opportunity to assassinate the defector. The only method open to her was a close kill, and neither a knife nor a gun would suffice to ensure the man's death. Having a secondary team in place for a standoff kill was a luxury, she generally turned down the option of an explosive device, so poison was the only alternative left.

As she shuffled away, she thought about her last target. By now, he was probably scratching the back of his hand and thinking it just a minor sting or irritation. For the next four to five hours, nothing would seem untoward, but by the end of the day, the man would feel the effects of a severe cold or even show symptoms of the flu. By early afternoon the next day, he would be in a hospital, and doctors would struggle to diagnose his condition, by which time there would be no turning back. The dose injected by Zoya into his system would work much faster than the four days it had taken to kill Bulgarian dissident Georgi Markov who died in London in 1978 when a lethal dose of the toxin was shot into his leg from an umbrella. It was likely that the Iranian would die in the next twenty-four hours and, until then in his dilapidated state, be of no use to anybody.

Before Zoya boarded the S-Bahn, she put on her gloves, not only to shield herself from the cold but also to prevent traces of the poison from reaching any innocents who came into contact with anything that she touched. It was a kind gesture, but she was no animal; there were enough enemies of the motherland that deserved to die and would die one day at the hands of other assassins. But the guiltless people of Berlin, who had suffered enough, did not need to fall because of her last mission.

As she rode the train in silence, she resisted the urge to scratch her fingers. A few other passengers who rode with her noted her sadness and unease, but every time someone tried to start a conversation, she smiled and spoke Russian to keep the curious away.

When Zoya finally made it to Treptower Park, she knew that she had come to her final resting place. The park housed one of three memorials built in the city for the eighty thousand Soviet soldiers who fell in the Battle of Berlin. She walked around the park for as long as she could to reminisce and think about the struggle that she was involved with and the hardships she had endured during the long siege of the city. It wasn't the first time she had been here since the monument was erected in 1949. She had actually taken her first kill as a KGB assassin in this very park, so it was fitting that she should come here to make her peace and remember her fallen comrades that had perished during the war. Zoya finally rested next to one of two large kneeling statues of Soviet soldiers, and as the concoction of cancer medication and ricin began to take its toll, she leaned up against the monument and closed her eyes.

# CHAPTER TWENTY-THREE

## Potomac, Maryland

RICHARD NASH SAT IN HIS CAR AND GATHERED UP HIS BELONGINGS
AND, as per habit, did not close the door behind him when he parked
his car in his garage. Nash was still fiddling with newspapers on the
passenger seat and cursed a little as the garage door light extinguished
itself. He then reached up to the dome light in his car and turned it on
so he could gather up everything he needed for the night.

The momentary lapse in concentration was all Chris needed to
sneak undetected into the three-car garage and hide behind another of
Nash's vehicles, a convertible Porsche. When Nash finally turned out
the car light and began to exit his car, Chris silently crept forward from
the shadows and waited for the opportune moment. As Nash rounded
the front of his car and headed to the three steps that led into his house,
Chris sprang up behind him, drew a stun gun from his jacket pocket
and rammed it into Nash's upper right hip area and deployed one
hundred thousand volts of electricity into his body for two seconds.

Nash dropped everything he was carrying and fell to his knees like a
lead balloon. Chris ran to the garage door control and closed it before
any goody two-shoes neighbor would come looking to see what the fuss
was all about. He returned to Nash and helped him to his feet.

"Up you get, Mr. Nash, up you get."

Nash was dazed and confused. "Chris, Chris, what are you doing?"

Chris began to drag Nash into the house, which was no easy task as
his adversary was heavy, and they both struggled to make their way.
With the stun gun in his right hand, Chris supported Nash under his
shoulder, and they both clumsily entered a darkened corridor and
continued on into the kitchen. They eventually made it to Nash's

library where Chris dumped Nash in his desk chair. He zapped him one more time with the stun gun but held the device in place on his upper right shoulder for four seconds, which made him convulse and shake and fall once more to the ground. Chris ran back to the kitchen, turned on the lights, and retrieved a large cutting knife from a knife stand on the counter. When he returned, Nash was writhing in pain holding his shoulder, but he did not cry out.

The older man eventually propped himself up on his desk, gasping for breath, and looked at Chris who sat in a chair opposite him. "Chris, you don't know what you are doing."

"Do you want me to zap you again?"

Nash didn't answer but the look in his eyes did.

"I didn't think so." Chris made himself comfortable, the stun gun in his right hand and an eight-inch kitchen knife in the left. He stared at Nash with contempt. "You need to keep your mouth shut until I ask you a question."

"My wife will be back any sec—"

Chris stabbed the gun into Nash's right shoulder and activated for two seconds. "Shut the fuck up!" he screamed into his face. He let the effects of the electroshock take its course, and after a few minutes of whimpering from Nash, things calmed down again. "Do you think I am that stupid, and that's not an invitation for an opinion, by the way. But Jill left two days ago, which brings up another good point. She really is a bad driver, Mr. Nash, although she did get to the airport on time. I could teach her a few things."

Nash remained silent.

Chris looked deep into his eyes as if he was contemplating his next move. "Here's my problem, Mr. Nash." Although he hated Nash right now, he still carried an abstract respect for the man and could not bring himself to call him by his first name. "I am debating whether I should cut your fucking head off and leave it in the freezer for Jill to find or mail it into Langley. I'm not sure." He began tapping the knife on the edge of the armrest.

Nash couldn't tell if Chris was bluffing, but everything to this point indicated steely intent.

"But then again, I don't have a big enough box to fit your fat head, so I suppose that it's freezer for you and fingers and toes for the CIA."

"Now, Chris, hang on a se—"

Chris zapped him again. "When are you going to learn? Jesus, and you're the one with all the brains, really?" He got up from the chair and started to pace around the room and was becoming impatient. Nash's recovery time was getting longer each time. Chris didn't want to push things too far, not yet.

"You sent me to kill my girlfriend, so forgive me if I encourage you to be forthcoming with the truth with my archaic methods."

"Chris—"

Chris waved the gun in front of Nash's face. "Don't tempt me again. I ask; you answer. Nod your head like you understand the concept."

Nash complied.

"Good, why did you send me into that building knowing Pam was the shooter?"

"I didn't send her there, Chris, honestly. She wasn't supposed to be there."

"So you acknowledge the fact that she worked for you?"

"Yes, but she should not have been there. She was told to stand down."

"Horseshit! Put yourself in my position for a minute. I see her body on the street from the sixteenth floor. I run down there only to see Gene talking it up with the cops. I start to go ballistic, and he pulls me aside and tells me to shut my mouth because she was working for the CIA. Now you tell me it wasn't you that sent her there in the first place? You're full of shit!"

"It was Dana Munson, Chris. He set her up."

"Bollocks! What's that idiot stick got to do with this?"

"He's working for the Russians. It's complicated, but we think he was under pressure to get rid of Primal Ocean—"

"Prime what?"

"Primal Ocean, it was a team that Pam was part of. She had been working for us for years. She was an assassin, Chris. She was one of the best."

Chris felt like stabbing Nash in the eye with the knife but refrained and let him continue, which he did for a few minutes by detailing the death of Rita in Sweden and all the other recent operations that he had directed. He then went on to broach the subject of MI5. "Can you think of a reason why she killed St. Clair?"

"What are you talking about?"

"She killed him in his home."

"When?"

"As soon as you got on a plane to India. She went there and rammed a sword into his throat."

"Holy shit! I mean the guy was a prick and deserved to have his nuts kicked in, but. . . . I can't believe it. She was so cool and calm when we went to his house."

"And that was stupid of you, Chris. You had no reason to go there. Scotland Yard went ballistic. MI5 is giving us the cold shoulder, and MI6 is calling us all the names under the sun. This thing has set relations back a bit. We'll recover, but it doesn't look good, and you may need to apologize to Nick Seymour. He's in some deep shit because of you."

"St. Clair was a complete arsehole, Mr. Nash. He treated me like shit, and he threatened my family."

"Let me ask you again. Can you think of anything that might have pushed her to do this? Anything at all? Did he threaten her in any way?"

"No, no, it was all directed at me. I guess after he sent his heavies in to beat the crap out of my brother and me, she took it more personally than I thought. She seemed pretty pissed off about it, and her mood did change when we went to see him." Chris's eyes brightened for a second. "Hang on a minute. . . . He did mention something to her at Heathrow I thought strange. He told her not to undertake activities in the UK while she was there, or words to that effect. She brushed it off, and I didn't think too much of it."

Nash let off a long sigh. He rubbed his shoulder where Chris had made contact with the stun gun and looked off into the distance. "It looks as if the Brits were warning her and Primal Ocean. I don't think you were the target of the MI5 inquisition."

Chris kept quiet while he mulled over what he had just learned. After a moment, he said, "That bastard was going to tell me. I had him cornered behind his garage, and he was about to tell me something about Pam. We got interrupted before he said any more." Chris stared at the wall. "The last time I saw her, she was planning to go after the guy, and me being the stupid twat that I am didn't see it. I even taught her to drive in the UK so she could get there and back. Jesus, how did I not know?"

"Chris don't do that. Don't go down that road. I think she loved you and she killed him for you. She could have easily let things be and report back that the guy was sticking his nose where it didn't belong, and we would have taken care of it. But you were her family, Chris. You were everything to her. She always talked about you, always cared for you. She was waiting for you, you know?"

"What? Waiting for what?"

"She was waiting for a proposal, Chris."

"Oh God, what have I done?"

Nash felt genuine sympathy for the young man. He needed a soft touch. "She badgered me so often about you working on Primal Ocean with her, but my hands were tied. You are a contractor working on a Green Card there's no way it would have been approved. Besides, I needed you on Viewpoint. You basically run that program, and I can't say enough about the positive feedback we have received because of your dedication and expertise on the job. The director is aware of every mission that you are sent on, and I can't begin to say how happy he is."

Chris didn't care if the Queen of England was about to give him a knighthood. He felt truly betrayed by Pam and by Nash, two he had respected and trusted so much. She had kept her secret from him for all this time, and he felt so dumb about not seeing through her lies. He had trusted her, he had told her almost everything, and he had wanted to settle down and have a family with her one day. It was bad enough to lose her in the physical sense, but now he thought he never truly had her at all. She had been living a lie that she couldn't share or trust in him. He searched his mind to figure out what was wrong with him and why people betrayed each other and why women could not commit to him fully. He knew he wouldn't find the answers here with Nash, another person he no longer could trust, another ally lost in the combat of life.

Chris thought back to Rita's death and became sad. He knew how close Pam was to her. It was another needless loss. . . . He needed to get Nash off stroking him, and he changed the subject. "So the guy I found with red peppers all over his face was a Serb on the way to take care of Pam?"

"Yes, we were surprised at that, but we think Munson put that together as well."

"So why did Pam move ahead without your knowledge or approval?"

"Munson went to Paris to talk to Bob Crauford and gave him some bullshit story about Mousavi needing to go. Bob set up the logistics of the operation, and she deployed."

Chris started to come down from his search for revenge. He could see the pictures forming in front of him as the puzzles were completing themselves. Although he stared at the knife, he tried to focus on something else to change his mood,

"At least we have Mousavi out of all this. He should be spilling his guts any day soon."

"Chris, do you mind putting the knife down . . . and your little toy?"

Chris, like a little five-year-old, grudgingly complied and set his weapons on the desk.

Nash continued, "Mousavi never made it. He died of ricin poisoning. It seems the Russians had an operative in the area. They took him out as he was entering the Canadian embassy."

"Holy shit! Really?" Chris blurted. "What about all that stuff he had in his prized leather case?"

"Hmph," Nash snorted. "Love letters."

"What?"

"All love letters. There was nothing of value to us at all. We have our crypto guys trying to figure out if they were coded messages, but as of now, they were all love letters that he had exchanged with his Canadian chum." Nash let things sink in. "So now we only have you as a witness to what Mousavi claimed, that the Russians, Iranians, and Indians were all in bed together."

"So basically nothing."

"Correct, we don't have squat!"

"So where is that shit Munson now?"

Nash paused, "We don't know, Chris."

Chris looked at his crude weaponry, "So where does that leave you and me?"

# CHAPTER TWENTY-FOUR

## The Shak Beach Cafe, Placencia, Belize

CHRIS MOREHOUSE LOOKED EVERY PART THE TOURIST WITH HIS PASTY-WHITE SKIN AND BURNED FOREHEAD as he sat in the beach café sipping a pineapple-and-mango concoction, which he thought was the best invention since sliced bread. It was one of those drinks that you never quite knew all the ingredients for but enticed you to have another just to keep on playing the guessing game. It was all part of the tourist trap that this little corner of Belize had to offer. The main draw, however, was not its rustic meals or exotic drinks but the diving and fishing activities, especially when for the full moon in March when whale shark migration was underway in the Gladden Spit.

Robert Crauford returned to the table where Chris was sitting with another two glasses of the magical elixir. "Good, aren't they?"

Chris did not turn around to address him but kept his gaze focused on the jetty directly in front of them. "Dog's bollocks if you ask me."

Crauford sat and made himself comfortable, smiling slightly at the Brit's colloquial use of the English language. He dropped his shades over his eyes and also began the waiting game as he stared across the bay searching for the right boat to appear.

After a full hour of singing mundane tunes in his head, Chris shifted his glass across the table to get Crauford's attention.

"Yep, I see it," the former general whispered.

The thirty-foot LC5 mini-landing craft was now tying up at the jetty. The craft bobbed slightly at the dock as a young man tied off the boat fore and then aft. As soon as he completed the task, a young woman appeared from the cabin and exited the boat. She had a bag over her shoulder and carried another. The young man picked up a third bag, and they both made their way up the jetty and onto terra firma where they threw their baggage into a pickup truck that was parked near the café where Chris and Crauford sat. Chris couldn't help but notice the woman, beautiful enough to be a model, but he wasn't there to lech. Within a few minutes, the couple had left without ever indicating that either party had seen each other.

As planned, Crauford remained seated while Chris took a short recce of the immediate area to ensure the pickup was not returning. He made his way up Placencia Road until he reached a small coffee house, hung around for a short while, and then doubled back towards the jetty.

When Crauford caught sight of Chris heading to the boat, he paid the bill at the bar and left to join him.

Within an hour of driving directly west from Placencia, Crauford slowed the boat as they approached their destination, Hatchet Key. Until this point, Chris had done a fantastic job of navigating their way through the dozens of small islands and atolls that peppered the shallow waters, but now they had to circle the island at least once to get a correct bearing on their position. Satisfied they knew exactly where they were, Crauford slowly motored to the northern side of the island. The island housed a dozen buildings that belonged to a resort consortium, which provided tourist services for anyone who wished to fish, sail, snorkel, or deep-sea dive, and most of its buildings were situated in the southern part of the island. On the northern side, however, were four large bungalows that could be rented for guests who were simply looking for a quiet getaway. Crauford held the LC5 in position as they tried to identify the correct two-story bungalow on the beach. A red beach towel was hanging off a balcony on one of them, the sign they were both looking for. Crauford looked at his watch and made some quick calculations. He nodded to Chris, and they moved forward towards land.

Crauford expertly maneuvered the LC5 onto the beach and lowered the forward ramp onto the sand. Instead of tying up, he kept the motor idling as Chris went ashore, unseen by tourists residing at the resort who were all engaged in outdoor activities away from the island for the day. For the workers on the small piece of real estate, the LC5 was no stranger as such craft were used for all sorts of undertakings, from food and garbage deliveries to smuggling of contraband and people. Locals simply ignored the private goings-on of those who used such craft in these waters.

"Dana, Dana." Chris slapped Munson in the face to draw him out of his stupor.

"Leave me alone, leave me alone," he pleaded.

"C'mon, Dana. Up you get. We're going for a walk." Chris pulled Munson off his bed. He was glad to see the man was still clothed.

"Katja, Katja, my love."

Munson was still delirious. The plan to give Munson a dose of flunitrazepam had worked, and the timing couldn't have been better as Munson was now coming out of his drug-induced sleep. Chris assumed that Katja was the stunning blonde he had seen at Placencia. He didn't know who she really was, but she had played her part well, for which he was grateful.

"Let's go, Dana. We've got to go. Katja's waiting for you."

"Katja? . . . Where is she?"

"She's waiting down on the beach. Let's go." Chris helped him to his feet and supported him as he stumbled towards the door.

"Who are you? I know you. Where's Katja?" Munson mumbled as he held his hand to his head and struggled and bumped into tables and chairs as they both maneuvered through the bungalow. The sun shone down on his face and blinded him as they made it outside. He kept repeating his quest to find Katja.

For the most part, Chris ignored Munson. He didn't want to have a loud conversation with him and attract any undue attention. Chris murmured, "This way. She's over here, Dana. She's got a surprise for you."

Chris finally got a confused Munson onto the boat. Crauford didn't waste any time. As soon as they were aboard, he raised the ramp, slowly edged off the beach, and then turned out towards the deep blue sea. As soon as the ramp was raised, Chris violently shoved Munson to the deck. While he was totally disorientated, Chris speedily tied Munson's hands and then his feet. Once complete, he fixed a strip of duct tape to his mouth. Only when the tape was applied did Munson became fully aware of who was standing in front of him. His eyes popped like a fish out of water gasping for air. Chris didn't offer any words. He headed into the cabin and stood next to Crauford to study the maritime chart.

After bouncing along the Caribbean at fifty mph for almost one and a half hours, Chris found the spot he was looking for. He was at the midpoint between Hatchet Key and the island of Roatan. Although the sea was relatively flat, the landing craft rode silently with the waves with the engine turned off. They were now above the far western edge of the Cayman Trough, one of the deepest maritime trenches in the world. Chris grabbed Munson and shifted him from the deck to the port side rail and sat him down on the edge of the boat.

Crauford appeared at his side holding an envelope.

"I didn't want to waste time doing this but, orders are orders. I suppose. This . . .," Chris took the envelope from Crauford and waved it in Munson's face, "is a small present from Richard Nash." Chris ripped open the small pack and pulled out a number of photos. Chris laughed out loud at the first image and then showed it to Munson. It was the traitor naked on a bed holding the large penis of a young man. The color from Munson's face drained from him as more images of him engaged in gay sex were stuck in his face. He shook his head in denial, but Chris laughed again. Crauford chuckled in the background.

"I guess that wasn't such a waste of time after all. . . . So, Dana . . . here we are out on an adventure at sea on a beautiful day. Isn't life grand?" Chris's tone was even, controlled, but ominous. He took his time before he spoke again. "I have a bunch of questions I need to ask you, so I'm going to remove the tape, but do us all a favor and do not shout and scream. We are out in the middle of butt fuck nowhere, oops, excuse the pun. But nobody can see or hear us out here, so please just keep the drama to yourself and answer my questions. Don't ask me why, but some people think there's a way out of this for you, so I guess I have to go through the motions. Now just behave, okay?"

Munson nodded and watched Crauford retreat to the wheelhouse. "Stand up a second. I want to make you a little more comfortable." When Munson stood, Chris retrieved a D-clip and a chain from behind Munson and attached it to his bound legs. He ripped the tape off Munson in one swoop causing the man to wince.

"Wait, wait, please, please don't do this. . . . Bob, BOB! Don't let him do this, please." He started to beg and mumble about something to Chris, and tears began to form in his eyes.

Chris couldn't have cared if Munson was telling him who killed Kennedy or the location of sunken treasure worth millions. He was too focused on preparing the man for redemption. "Remember when I said I wanted to ask you something?" Chris asked.

Munson silently nodded, tears streamed down his red face,

"Well I lied!" Chris gave Munson a shove forcing him backwards over the rail. As he began to topple over, Chris grabbed his legs to complete the operation of throwing him overboard. Chris stood back as the chain that he had connected to Munson legs spewed out. Just before it came to the end, he picked up a heavy boat anchor and tossed it over the side as Munson's head bobbed up gasping for air. He was only a few feet from the boat. Chris stood at the rail and looked into the water and the struggling man. A second later Munson was gone. Without any fanfare, Chris turned to Crauford and gave him the signal to leave, mission complete.

## Blue Bahia Bar & Grill, Sandy Bay, Roatan, Honduras

Chris found Richard Nash sitting at a table with his back to the beach and looking at him directly as he entered the beach-side restaurant. Nash wasn't alone. Chris couldn't make out who the man was, as he had his back to him as he walked in, but as Chris got closer, the man stood, shook Nash's hand, and walked away. As they passed each other, they looked each other in the eye, brushed shoulders with each other, but exchanged no words.

Chris sat down heavily in the chair that had just been vacated.

"So, are you happy?"

"Happy is a relative word, Mr. Nash. Am I happy that some shit for brains is sitting on the bottom of the Carib? Yeah, I guess I've had some job satisfaction today."

"But you're not happy with the overall outcome, or what is it?"

"You mean apart from the fact that my girlfriend is dead, no thanks to you, I suppose my level of overall job satisfaction blows chunks. I'm still not sure what I am supposed to be doing here, or where to go next."

Nash let things go silent. He sipped on a margarita, "Do you want a drink, Chris?"

"Excuse me for being so blunt, Mr. Nash, but fuck you!"

Nash looked hard at his protégé. It was obvious the young man needed to vent. Nash wasn't offended at the insult, but he wanted Chris to calm down, control his temper, but at the same time let off steam. Gauging Chris's body language, Nash could tell that something was heading his way.

"I was so tempted to slash your throat when I had the chance. I let you squirm your way out of it, but don't think for one minute I have forgotten what you put me through. There's no need to drag that shit up again. In fact, I'd prefer you never bring up Pam's name again. To you, she was an asset; to me she, was my tiny little world." Chris leaned closer and made sure nobody was in earshot. "I get that you are a cold-hearted bastard and you can't comprehend little things and little people, but just let it be known, you had better not fuck with me ever again. I can and will do you some serious harm." Still fuming, he turned his gaze over towards the beach and the water beyond. He knew he had to control himself. Taking a long breath, he waited for Nash to respond.

Nash nodded and let Chris have his feeling of superiority for just a few seconds. Playing with the umbrella in his drink, Nash then stopped and said, "You know, you've got a big mouth Chris."

*Now where have I heard that bullshit line before?* Chris thought but let

Nash continue before he would counter.

"I don't doubt that you can take care of yourself physically, but you have a penchant for not knowing when to control your temper and when to just shut up."

Chris took the hint to keep quiet but was worried that he'd pushed Nash too far.

"Do you honestly think I've forgotten about your visit to my home? . . . Do you really think I am going to let that slide?" Nash suddenly reached over and grabbed Chris by the wrist, "Look at me you shit!"

Chris almost jumped out of his chair.

"I took pity on you with Pam, and don't you ever tell me what I can and cannot say. I gave you the revenge that you were looking for, despite what you did to me. Now you need to sort your shit out and stop feeling sorry for yourself!" The two men began a staring contest without either saying a word. Nash slowly released his grip and toned down his voice but continued to drive his point home. "You need to be grateful that you didn't end up in a dark cell that night, and I don't mean in a cuddly local police department either. There are a thousand guys just like you I could have called on to take care of Munson, and you would not have been any the wiser. You would have spent the rest of your life looking for that dick, and now it's over. But if you *ever* touch me like that again, you will be swapping spit with Munson on the bottom of the ocean. Are we clear?"

"Yes."

"Good."

After a few minutes of silence a waiter appeared, and Chris asked for some water.

Nash thought that would be the most social his young friend was going to be today, and he let it go. After the drink arrived, Nash looked at Chris again, who was staring at the ocean once more. He seemed empty, void of anything worthwhile, depressed, and lonely. Nash didn't want Chris to wallow in self-pity and had to get him back. "That man you just saw, did you recognize him?"

"Yes, but I can't remember where."

Nash wanted to give him a hint, take his mind off Pam and the tense conversation they just had. "His code name is Pacer, thanks to you."

"Huh? Don't try to placate me, Mr. Nash. What the hell do I have to do with him?"

"His name is Vasili Timoshev. He works for the SVR. He has been an asset of ours ever sin—"

"Since 1994, US Ambassadors Fourth of July party," Chris interrupted. "He was dressed as a Russian army officer."

"Exactly! Remember when we had a conversation about him in the car, and I basically told you to mind your own business?"

Chris nodded and grimaced at the memory of being chewed out.

"I took your advice, Chris, and followed your intuition. It turns out he was the deputy chief of station for the SVR in Germany. He wasn't an army officer, but he was trying to reach out to us."

"That's all well and good, Mr. Nash, and I'm happy for the CIA, but it doesn't mean much to me."

"It should, Chris. Pacer gave us Munson. He supplied the intel for the job you just carried out. He's been a great asset to us, and I think we are going to continue our relationship with him for a long time to come."

"You and your assets, spies, and games. It's all bollocks."

"Yes, it is a game, Chris. The question is do you want to be a pawn or make moves for yourself? Are you a strategist, a general, a doer, a killer, a deceiver?"

Chris felt as if he'd been down this road before.

Nash continued, "The game of espionage will continue with or without you or me. One day when we are no longer of this Earth, some other chump will be doing exactly what we are doing now, plotting, scheming, killing, and dying. It's the way of the world we have chosen to accept." Nash took a long drink so his statement could sink in a little and then continued, "Now do I want to retire to a log cabin on some lake in Washington State and grow apples for the rest of my life? Nope. Do I want to continue making a difference in my country's safety and security, a better place for us all and for the generations that follow? You betcha!" Nash leaned forward drawing Chris closer into the conversation. "And you are the same as me, Chris. Don't deny it, but you want the same. I don't see you digging a ditch or selling car insurance or even bouncing kids on your lap. You are still a soldier. Whether you like it or not, you are in this game, and I've been in it long enough to know that when it gets into your blood there is no substitute for it, and I can see that you, my young friend . . . have the same stuff running through your veins, and more important, you have the balls to take this on and play your part."

"So what the fuck do you want from me? By rights, like you said, I should be in jail for almost frying your arse and plotting to carve you up. But I can't trust you or anyone associated with you. My life is in the shithouse, and I have just committed murder. I don't have your magic 'get out of jail' card, and right now I feel I should be on the run and as far away from you as possible. You have the umbrella of the CIA over your shoulders. I've got squat, so don't preach to me about being a soldier. You have no idea what I am going through!"

"That's where you are wrong, Chris. I do understand, and I have something for you, what I know you want. I am ready to protect you."

"What now?"

"When we return to the States, I can have a judge swear you in. Your application for US citizenship has come through. When we've done all that we want you to, come on board full time with my office."

"So I'm supposed to do backflips now?"

Nash didn't reply but let Chris stew on the latest offer on the table.

Chris was conflicted. What Nash was proposing sounded enticing. But the loss of Pam was still fresh, and although he felt a slice of satisfaction from Munson's death, he was unsure if he wanted to throw his lot in with the CIA and a full-time career of doing Nash's bidding.

Nash was tempted to leave and let him simmer a little longer but decided to prod instead. "Do you remember the barn test at the farm?"

"Yes. What of it?"

"You were told to go to the barn to get instructions. When you entered, it was pitch black, and you were told by a voice to close the door and then turn to your left. You then had to climb a ladder up four stories. When you got to the top, you were told to reach out for a bar behind you and then once you were on it, you were supposed to let go."

"So what? I got out of it okay."

"Yes, you did, and so did everyone else. It was more than an exercise to see if you would follow orders; it was a test to see what type of person you were. If you followed the order to let go, you would have dropped only a few feet to another platform; you would have been safe. If you chose this option, you would be considered for everyday low-level officer activity as you follow orders well. The second option, which you did not choose either, was to climb back down the ladder to safety, showing that you had good judgement and your career path would have driven you to a more analytical role, a desk job. But you, my young friend, chose the third option. Instead of dropping or climbing down, you chose to find your own way out. You swung on that bar and kicked around and stretched every which way until you found the second ladder, which you climbed down to another platform, and you patiently waited for more instructions." Nash paused for effect. When he saw he had Chris hooked, he carried on. "You chose an option that only a very small percentage of candidates take. You looked for other solutions to find a way out. You did not give up, and you put trust in yourself. It is these types of character traits that we look for in our commanders, our leaders. This is where I see you going, Chris. You may not think it now, but you have the potential to rise through our ranks. You are in the trenches now, and I think you can still do some more work there. But one day, my friend, one day. . . ."

Chris had nothing to say. He had arrived at the meeting with a bucket full of hate and remorse. A part of him still wanted to take his frustrations out on Nash, but Chris couldn't. He believed in what Nash stood for, and Chris at his core was similar. He wanted to help someone, somewhere, he wanted justice in some form or another, he wanted to make a difference, and Nash was offering him a chance to do exactly that.

"So what about it, Chris? Do you want to come on board?"

## END

33206985R00148

Made in the USA
San Bernardino, CA
27 April 2016